"Go away," Colleen told Bobby. "I don't want another big brother."

Bobby shook his head. "Wes asked me to—"

Damn Wes. "He probably asked you to sift through my dresser drawers, too," she countered, lowering her voice. "Although I'm not sure what you're going to tell him when you find my collection of black leather bustiers."

Bobby looked at her, something unrecognizable on his face.

And as Colleen looked back at him, for a moment she lost herself in the darkness of his eyes. He looked away, clearly embarrassed, and she realized suddenly that her brother wasn't here.

Wes wasn't here.

Bobby was in town *without Wes.* And without Wes, if she played it right, the rules of this game they'd been playing for the past decade could change.

Radically.

Dear Reader,

Welcome to another month of hot—in every sense of the word—reading, books just made to match the weather. I hardly even have to mention Suzanne Brockmann and her TALL, DARK & DANGEROUS miniseries, because you all know that this author and these books are utterly irresistible. *Taylor's Temptation* features the latest of her to-die-for Navy SEALs, so rush right down to your bookstore and pick up your own copy, because this book is going to be flying off shelves everywhere.

To add to the excitement this month, we're introducing a new six-book continuity called FIRSTBORN SONS. Award-winning writer Paula Detmer Riggs kicks things off with *Born a Hero*. Learn how these six heroes share a legacy of protecting the weak and standing up for what's right—and watch as all six find women who belong in their arms and their lives.

Don't miss the rest of our wonderful books, either: *The Seduction of Goody Two-Shoes,* by award-winning Kathleen Creighton; *Out of Nowhere,* by one of our launch authors, Beverly Bird; *Protector with a Past*, by Harper Allen; and *Twice Upon a Time,* by Jennifer Wagner.

Finally, check out the back pages for information on our "Silhouette Makes You A Star" contest. Someone's going to win—why not you?

Enjoy!

Leslie J. Wainger
Executive Senior Editor

Please address questions and book requests to:
Silhouette Reader Service
U.S.: 3010 Walden Ave., P.O. Box 1325, Buffalo, NY 14269
Canadian: P.O. Box 609, Fort Erie, Ont. L2A 5X3

SUZANNE
BROCKMANN
Taylor's
Temptation

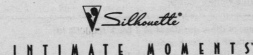

Silhouette®

INTIMATE MOMENTS™

Published by Silhouette Books

America's Publisher of Contemporary Romance

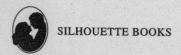

 SILHOUETTE BOOKS

ISBN 0-373-27157-3

TAYLOR'S TEMPTATION

Copyright © 2001 by Suzanne Brockmann

All rights reserved. Except for use in any review, the reproduction or utilization of this work in whole or in part in any form by any electronic, mechanical or other means, now known or hereafter invented, including xerography, photocopying and recording, or in any information storage or retrieval system, is forbidden without the written permission of the editorial office, Silhouette Books, 300 East 42nd Street, New York, NY 10017 U.S.A.

All characters in this book have no existence outside the imagination of the author and have no relation whatsoever to anyone bearing the same name or names. They are not even distantly inspired by any individual known or unknown to the author, and all incidents are pure invention.

This edition published by arrangement with Harlequin Books S.A.

® and TM are trademarks of Harlequin Books S.A., used under license. Trademarks indicated with ® are registered in the United States Patent and Trademark Office, the Canadian Trade Marks Office and in other countries.

Visit Silhouette at www.eHarlequin.com

Printed in U.S.A.

Books by Suzanne Brockmann

Silhouette Intimate Moments

*Tall, Dark & Dangerous

SUZANNE BROCKMANN

lives just west of Boston in a house always filled with her friends—actors and musicians and storytellers and artists and teachers. When not writing award-winning romances about U.S. Navy SEALs, she sings in an a cappella group called Serious Fun with her husband, she sings in a band called The Dick Mac Wedding Garage Band with her daughter (shades of the Partridge Family!), manages the professional acting careers of her two teenagers, volunteers at the Appalachian Benefit Coffeehouse and always answers letters from readers. E-mail her at SuzanneBrockmann@aol.com or send an SASE to P.O. Box 5092, Wayland, MA 01778.

In loving memory of Melinda Helfer, *Romantic Times* reviewer—a friend of mine, and a friend of all romance.

The first time I met Melinda was at an RWA book signing years ago—right after *Prince Joe* and *Forever Blue* had come out. She rushed up to me, dropped to the floor in front of my table and proceeded to kowtow! She told me she *loved* those two books, and couldn't wait for the next installment in the TALL, DARK & DANGEROUS series to be released. She was funny, enthusiastic and amazingly intelligent—a fierce and passionate fan of all romance, and a good friend.

Melinda, this one's for you. (But then again, I think you probably knew that all my TDD books were written for you!) You will be missed.

Acknowledgments:

Special thanks to Mary Stella
of the New Jersey Romance Writers,
friend and fellow writer, for her help
in creating a suitable match for Bobby Taylor.

Prologue

"It was amazing." Rio Rosetti shook his head, still unable to wrap his mind around last night's explosive events. "It was absolutely amazing."

Mike and Thomas sat across from him at the mess hall, their ham and eggs forgotten as they waited for him to continue.

Although neither of them let it show, Rio knew they were both envious as hell that he'd been smack in the middle of all the action, pulling his weight alongside the two legendary chiefs of Alpha Squad, Bobby Taylor and Wes Skelly.

"Hey, Little E., get your gear and strap on your blue-suede swim fins," Chief Skelly had said to Rio just six hours ago. Had it really only been six hours? "Me and Uncle Bobby are gonna show you how it's done."

Twin sons of different mothers. That's what Bobby and Wes were often called. Of *very* different mothers. The two men looked nothing alike. Chief Taylor was huge. In fact, the man was a total animal. Rio wasn't sure, because the air got kind of hazy way up by the top of Bobby Taylor's head, but he thought the chief stood at least six and a half feet tall, maybe even more. And he was nearly as wide. He had shoulders like a football player's protective padding, and, also like a football player, the man was remarkably fast. It was pretty freaky, actually, that a guy that big could achieve the kind of speed he did.

His size wasn't the only thing that set him apart from Wes Skelly, who was normal-size—about Rio's height at five-eleven with a similar wiry build.

Bobby was at least part Native American. His heritage showed in his handsome face and in the rich color of his skin. He tanned a real nice shade of brown when he was out in the sun—a far nicer shade than Rio's own slightly olive-tinged complexion. The chief also had long, black, straight hair that he wore pulled severely from his face in a single braid down his back, giving him a faintly mystical, mysterious air.

Wes, on the other hand, was of Irish-American descent, with a slightly reddish tint to his light brown hair and lep-rechaun-like mischief gleaming in his blue eyes.

No doubt about it, Wes Skelly came into a room and bounced off the walls. He was always moving—like a human pinball. And if he wasn't moving, he was talking. He was funny and rude and loud and not entirely tactful in his impatience.

Bobby, however, was the king of laid-back cool. He was the kind of guy who could sit perfectly still, without fidgeting, just watching and listening, sometimes for hours, before he gave voice to any opinions or comments.

But as different as they seemed in looks and demeanor, Bobby and Wes shared a single brain. They knew each other so well they were completely in tune with the other's thoughts.

Which was probably why Bobby didn't do too much

talking. He didn't need to. Wes read his mind and spoke—incessantly—for him.

Although when the giant chief actually *did* speak, men listened. Even the officers listened.

Rio listened, too. He'd learned early on in SEAL training, long before he got tapped to join SEAL Team Ten's legendary Alpha Squad, to pay particular attention to Chief Bobby Taylor's opinions and comments.

Bobby had been doing a stint as a BUD/S instructor in Coronado, and he'd taken Rio, along with Mike Lee and Thomas King, under his extremely large wing. Which wasn't to say he coddled them. No way. In fact, by marking them as the head of a class filled with smart, confident, determined men, he'd demanded more from them. He'd driven them harder than the others, accepted no excuses, asked nothing less than their personal best—each and every time.

They'd done all they could to deliver, and—no doubt due to Bobby's quiet influence with Captain Joe Catalanotto—won themselves coveted spots in the best SEAL team in the Navy.

Rewind to six hours ago, to last night's operation. SEAL Team Ten's Alpha Squad had been called in to assist a FInCOM/DEA task force.

A particularly nasty South American drug lord had parked his luxury yacht a very short, very cocky distance outside of U.S. waters. The Finks and the DEA agents couldn't or maybe just didn't want to for some reason—Rio wasn't sure which and it didn't really matter to him—snatch the bad dude up until he crossed that invisible line into U.S. territory.

And that was where the SEALs were to come in.

Lieutenant Lucky O'Donlon was in charge of the op—mostly because he'd come up with a particularly devious plan that had tickled Captain Joe Cat's dark sense of humor.

The lieutenant had decided that a small team of SEALs would swim out to the yacht—named *Swiss Chocolate,* a stupid-ass name for a boat—board it covertly, gain access to the bridge and do a little creative work on their computerized navigational system.

As in making the yacht's captain think they were heading south when they were really heading northwest.

Bad dude would give the order to head back toward South America, and instead they'd zoom toward Miami—into the open arms of the Federal task force.

It was just too good.

Bobby and Wes had been selected by Lieutenant O'Donlon to gain covert access to the bridge of the yacht. And Rio was going along for the ride.

"I knew damn well they didn't need me there," he told Thomas and Mike now. "In fact, I was aware I was slowing them down." Bobby and Wes didn't need to talk, didn't need to make hand signals. They barely even looked at each other—they just read each other's minds. It was so freaky. Rio had seen them do similar stuff on a training op, but somehow out in the real world it seemed even more weird.

"So what happened, Rosetti?" Thomas King asked. The tall African-American ensign was impatient—not that he'd ever let it show on his face. Thomas was an excellent poker player. Rio knew that firsthand, having left the table with empty pockets on more than one occasion.

Most of the time Thomas's face was unreadable, his expression completely neutral, eyelids half-closed. The combination of that almost-bland expression and his scars—one bisecting his eyebrow and the other branding one of his high cheekbones—gave him a dangerous edge that Rio wished his own far-too-average face had.

But it was Thomas's eyes that made most people cross the street when they saw him coming. So dark-brown as to seem black, his eyes glittered with a deep intelligence—the man was Phi Beta Kappa *and* a member of the Mensa club. His eyes also betrayed the fact that despite his slouched demeanor, Thomas King was permanently at Defcon Five—ready to launch a deadly attack without hesitation if the need arose.

He was Thomas. Not Tommy. Not even Tom. *Thomas.* Not one member of Team Ten ever called him anything else.

Thomas had won the team's respect. Unlike Rio, who somehow, despite his hope for a nickname like Panther or Hawk, had been given the handle Elvis. Or even worse, Little Elvis or Little E.

Holy Chrysler. As if Elvis wasn't embarrassing enough.

"We took a rubber duck out toward the *Swiss Chocolate*," Rio told Thomas and Mike. "Swam the rest of the way in." The swift ride in the little inflatable boat through the darkness of the ocean had made his heart pound. Knowing they were going to board a heavily guarded yacht and gain access to her bridge without anyone seeing them had a lot to do with it. But he was also worried.

What if he blew it?

Bobby apparently could read Rio's mind almost as easily as he read Wes Skelly's, because he'd touched Rio's shoulder—just a brief squeeze of reassurance—before they'd crept out of the water and onto the yacht.

"The damn thing was lit up like a Christmas tree and crawling with guards," Rio continued. "They all dressed alike and carried these cute little Uzi's. It was almost like their boss got off on pretending he had his own little army. But they weren't any kind of army. Not even close. They were really just street kids in expensive uniforms. They didn't know how to stand watch, didn't know what to look for. I swear to God, you guys, we moved right past them. They didn't have a clue we were there—not with all the noise they were making and the lights shining in their eyes. It was so easy it was a joke.''

"If it were a joke," Mike Lee asked, "then what's Chief Taylor doing in the hospital?''

Rio shook his head. "No, that part wasn't a joke.'' Someone on board the yacht had decided to move the party up from down below and go for a midnight swim. Spotlights had switched on, shining down into the ocean, and all hell had broken loose. "But up until the time we were heading back into the water, it was a piece of cake. You know that thing Bobby and Wes can do? The telepathic communication thing?''

Thomas smiled. "Oh, yeah. I've seen them look at each other and—''

"This time they didn't," Rio interrupted his friend. "Look at each other, I mean. You guys, I'm telling you, this was beyond cool—watching them in action like this. There was one guard on the bridge, okay? Other than that, it was deserted and pretty dark. The captain and crew are all below deck, right? Probably getting stoned with the party girls and the guests. So anyway, the chiefs see this guard and they don't break stride. They just take him temporarily out of the picture before he even sees us, before he can even make a sound. Both of them did it—together, like it's some kind of choreographed move they've been practicing for years. I'm telling you, it was a thing of beauty.''

"They've been working with each other for a long time," Mike pointed out.

"They went through BUD/S together," Thomas reminded them. "They've been swim buddies from day one.''

"It was perfection." Rio shook his head in admiration. "Sheer perfection. I stood in the guard's place, in case anyone looked up through the window, then there'd be someone standing there, you know? Meanwhile Skelly disabled the conventional compass. And Bobby broke into the navigational computers in about four seconds.''

That was another freaky thing about Bobby Taylor. He had fingers the size of ballpark franks, but he could manipulate a computer keyboard faster than Rio would have thought humanly possible. He could scan the images that scrolled past on the screen at remarkable speeds, too.

''It took him less than three minutes to do whatever it was he had to do,'' he continued, ''and then we were out of there—off the bridge. Lucky and Spaceman were in the water, giving us the all-clear.'' He shook his head, remembering how close they'd been to slipping silently away into the night. ''And then all these babes in bikinis came running up on deck, heading straight for us. It was the absolute worst luck—if we'd been anywhere else on the vessel, the diversion would've been perfect. We would've been completely invisible. I mean, if you're an inexperienced guard are you going to be watching to see who's crawling around in the shadows or are you going to pay attention to the beach bunnies in the thong bikinis? But someone decided to go for a swim off the starboard side—right where we were hiding. These heavy-duty searchlights came on, probably just so the guys on board could watch the women in the water, but wham, there we were. Lit up. There was no place to hide—and nowhere to go but over the side.''

''Bobby picked me up and threw me overboard,'' Rio admitted. He must not have been moving fast enough—he was still kicking himself for that. ''I didn't see what happened next, but according to Wes, Bobby stepped in front of him and blocked him from the bullets that started flying while they both went into the water. That was when Bobby caught a few—one in his shoulder, another in the top of his thigh. He was the one who was hurt, but he pulled both me and Wes down, under the water—out of sight and out of range.''

Sirens went on. Rio had been able to hear them along with the tearing sound of the guards' assault weapons and the screams from the women, even as he was pulled underwater.

"That was when the *Swiss Chocolate* took off," Rio said. He had to smile. "Right for Miami."

They'd surfaced to watch, and Bobby had laughed along with Wes Skelly. Rio and Wes hadn't even realized he'd been hit. Not until he spoke, in his normal, matter-of-fact manner.

"We better get moving, get back to the boat, ASAP," Bobby had said evenly. "I'm shark bait."

"The chief was bleeding badly," Rio told his friends. "He was hurt worse even than he realized." And the water hadn't been cold enough to staunch the flow of his blood. "We did the best we could to tie off his leg, right there in the water. Lucky and Spaceman went on ahead—as fast as they could—to connect with the rubber duck and bring it back toward us."

Bobby Taylor had been in serious pain, but he'd kept moving, slowly and steadily through the darkness. Apparently he'd been afraid if he didn't keep moving, if he let Wes tow him back to the little rubber boat, he'd black out. And he didn't want to do that. The sharks in these waters *did* pose a serious threat, and if he were unconscious, that could have put Rio and Wes into even more significant danger.

"Wes and I swam alongside Bobby. Wes was talking the entire time—I don't know how he did it without swallowing a gallon of seawater—bitching at Bobby for playing the hero like that, making fun of him for getting shot in the ass—basically, just ragging on him to keep him alert.

"It wasn't until Bobby finally slowed to a crawl, until

he told us he wasn't going to make it—that he needed help—that Wes stopped talking. He took Bobby in a lifeguard hold and hauled ass, focusing all his energy on getting back to the rubber duck in record time.''

Rio sat back in his seat. ''When we finally connected with the boat, Lucky had already radioed for help. It wasn't much longer before a helo came to evac Bobby to the hospital.

''He's going to be okay,'' he told both Thomas and Mike again. That was the first thing he'd said about their beloved chief's injuries, before they'd even sat down to breakfast. ''The leg wound wasn't all that bad, and the bullet that went into his shoulder somehow managed to miss the bone. He'll be off the active-duty list for a few weeks, maybe a month, but after that…'' Rio grinned. ''Chief Bobby Taylor will be back. You can count on that.''

Chapter 1

Navy SEAL Chief Bobby Taylor was in trouble.

Big trouble.

"You gotta help me, man," Wes said. "She's determined to go, she flippin' hung up on me and wouldn't pick up the phone when I called back, and I'm going wheels-up in less than twenty minutes. All I could do was send her e-mail—though fat lotta good that'll do."

"She" was Colleen Mary Skelly, his best friend's little sister. No, not *little* sister. *Younger* sister. Colleen wasn't little, not anymore. She hadn't been little for a long, long time.

A fact that Wes didn't seem quite able to grasp.

"If *I* call her," Bobby pointed out reasonably, "she'll just hang up on me, too."

"I don't want you to call her." Wes shouldered his sea-bag and dropped his bomb. "I want you to go there."

Bobby laughed. Not aloud. He would never laugh in his best friend's face when he went into overprotective brother mode. But inside of his own head, he was rolling on the floor in hysterics.

Outside of his head, he only lifted a quizzical eyebrow. "To Boston." It wasn't really a question.

Wesley Skelly knew that this time he was asking an awful lot, but he squared his shoulders and looked Bobby straight in the eyes. "Yes."

Problem was, Wes didn't know just how much he was asking.

"You want me to take leave and go to Boston," Bobby didn't really enjoy making Wes squirm, but he needed his best friend to see just how absurd this sounded, "because you and Colleen got into another argument." He still didn't turn it into a question. He just let it quietly hang there.

"No, Bobby," Wes said, the urgency in his voice turned up to high. "You don't get it. She's signed on with some kind of bleeding-heart, touchy-feely volunteer organization, and next she and her touchy-feely friends are flying out to flippin' Tulgeria." He said it again, louder, as if it were unprintable, then followed it up by a string of words that truly were.

Bobby could see that Wes was beyond upset. This wasn't just another ridiculous argument. This was serious.

"She's going to provide earthquake relief," Wes continued. "That's lovely. That's wonderful, I told her. Be Mother Teresa. Be Florence Nightingale. Have your goody two-shoes permanently glued to your feet. But stay *way* the hell away from Tulgeria! Tulgeria—the flippin' terrorist capital of the world!"

"Wes—"

"I tried to get leave," Wes told him. "I was just in the captain's office, but with you still down and H. out with food poisoning, I'm mission essential."

"I'm there," Bobby said. "I'm on the next flight to Boston."

Wes was willing to give up Alpha Squad's current assignment—something he was really looking forward to, something involving plenty of C-4 explosives—to go to Boston. That meant that Colleen wasn't just pushing her brother's buttons. That meant she was serious about this. That she really was planning to travel to a part of the world where Bobby himself didn't feel safe. And he wasn't a freshly pretty, generously endowed, long-legged—*very* long-legged—redheaded and extremely female second-year law student.

With a big mouth, a fiery temper and a stubborn streak. No, Colleen's last name wasn't Skelly for nothing.

Bobby swore softly. If she'd made up her mind to go, talking her out of it wasn't going to be easy.

"Thank you for doing this," Wes said, as if Bobby had already succeeded in keeping Colleen off that international flight. "Look, I gotta run. Literally."

Wes owed Bobby for this one. But he already knew it. Bobby didn't bother to say the words aloud.

Wes was almost out the door before he turned back. "Hey, as long as you're going to Boston…"

Ah. Here it came. Colleen was probably dating some new guy and… Bobby was already shaking his head.

"Check out this lawyer I think Colleen's dating, would you?" Wes asked.

"No," Bobby said.

But Wes was already gone.

Colleen Skelly was in trouble.

Big trouble.

It wasn't fair. The sky was far too blue today for this kind of trouble. The June air held a crisp sweetness that only a New England summer could provide.

But the men standing in front of her provided nothing

sweet to the day. And nothing unique to New England, either.

Their kind of hatred, unfortunately, was universal.

She didn't smile at them. She'd tried smiling in the past, and it hadn't helped at all.

"Look," she said, trying to sound as reasonable and calm as she possibly could, given that she was facing down six very big men. Ten pairs of young eyes were watching her, so she kept her temper, kept it cool and clean. "I'm well aware that you don't like—"

"'Don't like' doesn't have anything to do with it," the man at the front of the gang—John Morrison—cut her off. "We don't want your center here, we don't want *you* here." He looked at the kids, who'd stopped washing Mrs. O'Brien's car and stood watching the exchange, wide-eyed and dripping with water and suds. "You, Sean Sullivan. Does your father know you're down here with *her?* With the hippie chick?"

"Keep going, guys," Colleen told the kids, giving them what she hoped was a reassuring smile. *Hippie chick.* Sheesh. "Mrs. O'Brien doesn't have all day. And there's a line, remember. This car wash team has a rep for doing a good job—swiftly and efficiently. Let's not lose any customers over a little distraction."

She turned back to John Morrison and his gang. And they *were* a gang, despite the fact that they were all in their late thirties and early forties and led by a respectable local businessman. Well, on second thought, calling Morrison *respectable* was probably a little too generous.

"Yes, Mr. Sullivan does know where his son is," she told them levelly. "The St. Margaret's Junior High Youth Group is helping raise money for the Tulgeria Earthquake Relief Fund. All of the money from this car wash is going to help people who've lost their homes and nearly all of their possessions. I don't see how even *you* could have a problem with that.''

Morrison bristled.

And Colleen silently berated herself. Despite her efforts, her antagonism and anger toward these Neanderthals had leaked out.

''Why don't you go back to wherever it was you came from?'' he told her harshly. ''Get the hell out of our neighborhood and take your damn bleeding-heart liberal ideas and stick them up your—''

No one was going to use that language around her kids. Not while she was in charge. ''Out,'' she said. ''Get out. Shame on you! Get off this property before I wash your mouth out with soap. And charge you for it.''

Oh, that was a big mistake. Her threat hinted at violence—something she had to be careful to avoid with this group.

Yes, she was nearly six feet tall and somewhat solidly built, but she wasn't a Navy SEAL like her brother and his best friend, Bobby Taylor. Unlike them, she couldn't take on all six of these guys at once, if it came down to that.

The scary thing was that this was a neighborhood in which some men didn't particularly have a problem with hitting a woman, no matter her size. And she suspected that John Morrison was one of those men.

She imagined she saw it in his eyes—a barely tempered urge to backhand her—hard—across the face.

Usually she resented her brother's interference. But right now she found herself wishing he and Bobby were standing right here, beside her.

God knows she'd been yelling for years about her independence, but this wasn't exactly an independent kind of situation.

She stood her ground all alone, wishing she was holding something more effective against attack than a giant-size sponge, and then glad that she wasn't. She was just mad enough to turn the hose on them like a pack of wild dogs, and that would only make this worse.

There were children here, and all she needed was Sean or Harry or Melissa to come leaping to her aid. And they would. These kids could be fierce.

But then again, so could she. And she would not let these children get hurt. She would do whatever she had to do, including trying again to make friends with these dirt wads.

"I apologize for losing my temper. Shantel," she called to one of the girls, her eyes still on Morrison and his goons. "Run inside and see if Father Timothy's coming out with more of that lemonade soon. Tell him to bring six extra paper cups for Mr. Morrison and his friends. I think we could probably all use some cooling off."

Maybe that would work. Kill them with kindness. Drown them with lemonade.

The twelve-year-old ran swiftly for the church door.

"How about it, guys?" Colleen forced herself to smile at the men, praying that this time it would work. "Some lemonade?"

Morrison's expression didn't change, and she knew that this was where he was going to step forward, inform her he didn't want any of their lemonade—expletive deleted— and challenge her to just try washing out his mouth. He'd then imply—ridiculously, and solely because of her pro bono legal work for the HIV Testing and AIDS Education Center that was struggling to establish a foothold in this narrow-minded but desperately needy corner of the city— that she was a lesbian and offer to "cure her" in fifteen unforgettable minutes in the closest back alley.

It would almost be funny. Except for the fact that Morrison was dead serious. He'd made similar disgusting threats to her before.

But now, to her surprise, John Morrison didn't say an-

other word. He just looked long and hard at the group of
eleven- and twelve-year-olds standing behind her, then did
an about face, muttering something unprintable.

It was amazing. Just like that, he and his boys were walking away.

Colleen stared after them, laughing—softly—in disbelief.

She'd done it. She'd stood her ground, and Morrison had
backed down without any interference from the police or
the parish priest. Although at 260 pounds, Father Timothy
was a heart attack waiting to happen. His usefulness in a
fist fight would be extremely limited.

Was it possible Morrison and his clowns were finally
hearing what she was saying? Were they finally starting to
believe that she wasn't going to let herself be intimidated
by their bogus threats and ugly comments?

Behind her the hoses were still silent, and she turned
around. "Okay, you guys, let's get back to—"

Colleen dropped her sponge.

Bobby Taylor. It was Bobby Taylor. Standing right there,
behind her, in the St. Margaret's parking lot. Somehow,
some way, her brother's best friend had materialized there,
as if Colleen's most ferverent wishes had been granted.

He stood in a Hawaiian shirt and cargo shorts, planted
in a superhero pose—legs spread and massive arms crossed
in front of his equally massive chest. His eyes were hard,
and his face stony as he still glared in the direction John
Morrison and his gang had departed. He was wearing a
version of his "war face."

He and Wes had completely cracked Colleen up on more
than one occasion by practicing their "war faces" in the
bathroom mirror during their far-too-infrequent visits home.
She'd always thought it was silly—what did the expression
on their faces matter when they went into a fight?—until
now. Now she saw that that grim look on Bobby's usually
so-agreeably handsome face was startlingly effective. He

looked hard and tough and even mean—as if he'd get quite a bit of enjoyment and satisfaction in tearing John Morrison and his friends limb from limb.

But then he looked at her and smiled, and warmth seeped back into his dark-brown eyes.

He had the world's most beautiful eyes.

"Hey, Colleen," he said in his matter-of-fact, no-worries, easygoing voice. "How's it going?"

He held out his arms to her, and in a flash she was running across the asphalt and hugging him. He smelled faintly of cigarette smoke—no doubt thanks to her brother, Mr. Just-One-More-Cigarette-Before-I-Quit—and coffee. He was warm and huge and solid and one of very few men in the world who could actually make her feel if not quite petite then pretty darn close.

As long as she'd wished him here, she should have wished for more. Like for him to have shown up with a million-dollar lottery win in his pocket. Or—better yet—a diamond ring and a promise of his undying love.

Yes, she'd had a wild crush on this man for close to ten years now. And just once she wanted him to take her into his arms like this and kiss her senseless, instead of giving her a brotherly noogie on the top of her head as he released her.

Over the past few years she'd imagined she'd seen appreciation in his eyes as he'd looked at her. And once or twice she could've sworn she'd actually seen heat—but only when he thought both she and Wes weren't looking. Bobby was attracted to her. Or at the very least she wished he were. But even if he were, there was no way in hell he'd ever act on that attraction—not with Wes watching his every move and breathing down his neck.

Colleen hugged him tightly. She had only two chances each visit to get this close to him—once during hello and once during goodbye—and she always made sure to take full advantage.

But this time he winced. "Easy."

Oh, God, he'd been hurt. She pulled back to look up at him, and she actually had to tilt her head. He was that tall.

"I'm a little sore," he told her, releasing her completely and stepping back, away from her. "Shoulder and leg. Nothing serious. You got me in the dead perfect spot, that's all."

"I'm sorry."

He shrugged. "It's no big deal. I'm taking some down time to get back to speed."

"What happened—or can you not tell me?"

He shook his head, smiling apologetically. He was such a good-looking man. And that little smile… What would he look like with his thick hair loose from the single braid he wore down his back? Although, she realized, he wasn't wearing a braid today. Instead, he wore his hair pulled back into a simple ponytail.

Every time she saw him, she expected him to have his hair cut short again. But each time it was even longer.

The first time they'd met, back when he and Wes were training to become SEALs, he'd had a crew cut.

Colleen gestured to the kids, aware they were all still watching. "Come on, gang, let's keep going here."

"Are you all right?" Bobby stepped closer to her, to avoid the spray from the hose. "What's the deal with those guys?"

"You're why they left," she realized suddenly. And even though mere minutes ago she'd wished desperately for Bobby's and her brother's presence, she felt a flare of anger and frustration. Darn it! She'd wanted Morrison's retreat to be because of her. As nice as it would be, she couldn't walk around with a Navy SEAL by her side every minute of every day.

"What was that about, Colleen?" Bobby pressed.

"Nothing," she said tersely.

He nodded, regarding her steadily. "It didn't feel like 'nothing.'"

"Nothing *you* have to worry about," she countered. "I'm doing some pro bono legal work for the AIDS Education Center, and not everyone is happy about it. That's what litigation's all about. Where's Wes? Parking the car?"

"Actually, he's—"

"I know why you're here. You came to try to talk me out of going to Tulgeria. Wes probably came to forbid me from going. Hah. As if he could." She picked up her sponge and rinsed it in a bucket. "I'm not going to listen to either of you, so you might as well just save your breath, turn around and go back to California. I'm not fifteen anymore, in case you haven't noticed."

"Hey, I've noticed," Bobby said. He smiled. "But Wes needs a little work in that area."

"You know, my living room is completely filled with boxes," Colleen told him. "Donations of supplies and clothing. I don't have any room for you guys. I mean, I guess you can throw sleeping bags on the floor of my bedroom, but I swear to God, if Wes snores, I'm kicking him out into the street."

"No," Bobby said. "That's okay. I made hotel reservations. This week is kind of my vacation, and—"

"Where *is* Wes?" Colleen asked, shading her eyes and looking down the busy city street. "Parking the car in Kuwait?"

"Actually." Bobby cleared his throat. "Yeah."

She looked at him.

"Wes is out on an op," he told her. "It's not quite Kuwait, but…"

"He asked *you* to come to Boston," Colleen realized. "For him. He asked you to play big brother and talk me out of going to Tulgeria, didn't he? I don't believe it. And you *agreed?* You jerk!''

"Colleen, come on. He's my best friend. He's worried about you.''

"And you don't think I worry about him? Or you?'' she countered hotly. "Do *I* come out to California to try to talk you out of risking *your* lives? Do *I* ever say, don't be a SEAL? No! Because I respect you. I respect the choices and decisions you make.''

Father Timothy and Shantel emerged from the church kitchen with a huge thermos of lemonade and a stack of cups.

"Everything all right?'' Father T. asked, eyeing Bobby apprehensively.

Bobby held out his hand. "I'm Bobby Taylor, a friend of Colleen's,'' he introduced himself.

"A friend of my brother, Wes's,'' she corrected him as the two men shook hands. "He's here as a surrogate brother. Father, plug your ears. I'm about to be extremely rude to him.''

Timothy laughed. "I'll see if the other children want lemonade.''

"Go away,'' Colleen told Bobby. "Go home. I don't want another big brother. I don't *need* one. I've got plenty already.''

Bobby shook his head. "Wes asked me to—''

Damn Wes. "He probably also asked you to sift through my dresser drawers, too,'' she countered, lowering her voice. "Although I'm not sure what you're going to tell him when you find my collection of whips and chains, my black leather bustier and matching crotchless panties.''

Bobby looked at her, something unrecognizable on his face.

And as Colleen looked back at him, for a moment she spun out, losing herself in the outer-space darkness of his eyes. She'd never imagined outer space could be so very *warm.*

He looked away, clearly embarrassed, and she realized suddenly that her brother wasn't here.

Wes wasn't here.

Bobby was in town *without Wes.* And without Wes, if she played it right, the rules of this game they'd been playing for the past decade could change.

Radically.

Oh, my goodness.

"Look." She cleared her throat. "You're here, so…let's make the best of this. When's your return flight?"

He smiled ruefully. "I figured I'd need the full week to talk you out of going."

He was here for a whole week. Thank you, Lord. "You're not going to talk me out of anything, but you cling to that thought if it helps you," she told him.

"I will." He laughed. "It's good to see you, Colleen."

"It's good to see you, too. Look, as long as there's only one of you, I can probably make room in my apartment—"

He laughed again. "Thanks, but I don't think that would be a very good idea."

"Why waste good money on a hotel room?" she asked. "After all, you're practically my brother."

"No," Bobby said emphatically. "I'm not."

There was something in his tone that made her bold. Colleen looked at him then in a way she'd never dared let herself look at him before. She let her gaze move down his broad chest, taking in the outline of his muscles, admiring the trim line of his waist and hips. She looked all the way down his long legs and then all the way back up again. She lingered a moment on his beautiful mouth, on his full, gracefully shaped lips, before gazing back into his eyes.

She'd shocked him with that obvious once-over. Well,

good. It was the Skelly family motto: everyone needs a good shocking every now and then.

She gave him a decidedly nonsisterly smile. "Glad we got that established. About time, huh?"

He laughed, clearly nervous. "Um…"

"Grab a sponge," she told him. "We've got some cars to wash."

Chapter 2

Wes would kill him if he found out.

No doubt about it.

If Wes knew even *half* the thoughts that were steam-rolling through Bobby's head about his sister, Colleen, Bobby would be a dead man.

Lord have mercy on his soul, the woman was hot. She was also funny and smart. Smart enough to have figured out the ultimate way to get back at him for showing up here as her brother's mouthpiece.

If she were planning to go anywhere besides Tulgeria, Bobby would have turned around. He would have headed for the airport and caught the next flight out of Boston.

Because Colleen was right. He and Wes had absolutely no business telling her what she should and shouldn't do. She was twenty-three years old—old enough to make her own decisions.

Except both Bobby and Wes had been to Tulgeria, and Colleen hadn't. No doubt she'd heard stories about the warring factions of terrorists that roamed the dirt-poor countryside. But she hadn't heard Bobby and Wes's stories. She didn't know what they'd seen, with their own eyes.

At least not yet.

But she would before the week was out.

And he'd take the opportunity to find out what that run-in with the local chapter of the KKK had been about, too.

Apparently, like her brother, Wes, trouble followed Colleen Skelly around. And no doubt, also like Wes, when it didn't follow her, she went out and flagged it down.

But as for right now, Bobby desperately needed to regroup. He had to go to his hotel and take an icy-cold shower. He had to lock himself in his room and away—far away—from Colleen.

Lord save him, somehow he'd given himself away. Somehow she'd figured out that the last thing that came to mind when he looked at her was brotherly love.

He could hear her laughter, rich and thick, from the far end of the parking lot, where she stood talking to a woman in a beat-up station wagon, who'd come to pick up the last of the junior-size car washers.

The late-afternoon sunlight made Colleen's hair gleam. With the work done, she'd changed into a summer dress and taken down her ponytail, and her hair hung in shimmering red-gold waves around her face.

She was almost unbearably beautiful.

Some people might not agree. And taken individually, most of the features of her face were far from perfect. Her mouth was too wide, her cheeks too full, her nose too small, her face too round, her skin too freckled and prone to sunburn.

Put it all together, though, and the effect was amazing.

And add those heartstoppingly gorgeous eyes...

Colleen's eyes were sometimes blue, sometimes green, and always dancing with light and life. When she smiled—

which was most of the time—her eyes actually twinkled. It was corny but true. Being around Colleen Skelly was like being in the middle of a continuous, joyful, always-in-full-swing party.

And as for her body…

Ouch.

The woman was beyond hot. She wasn't one of those anemic little bony anorexic girls who were plastered all over TV and magazines, looking more like malnourished 12-year-old boys. No, Colleen Skelly was a woman—with a capital *W*. She was the kind of woman that a real man could wrap his arms around and really get a grip on. She actually had hips and breasts—and not only was that the understatement of the century, but it was the thought that would send him to hell, directly to hell. 'Do not pass Go, do not collect two hundred dollars,' do not live another minute longer.

If Wes ever found out that Bobby spent any amount of time at all thinking about Colleen's breasts, well, that would be it. The end. Game over.

But right now Wes—being more than three thousand miles away—wasn't Bobby's problem.

No, Bobby's problem was that somehow *Colleen* had realized that he was spending far too much time thinking about her breasts.

She'd figured out that he was completely and mindlessly in lust with her.

And Wesley wasn't around to save him. Or beat him senseless.

Of course, it was possible that she was just toying with him, just messing with his mind. *Look at what you can't have, you big loser.*

After all, she was dating some lawyer. Wasn't that what Wes had said? And these days, wasn't *dating* just a euphemism for *in a relationship with?* And that was really just a polite way of saying that they were sleeping together, lucky son of a bitch.

Colleen glanced up from her conversation with the station-wagon mom and caught him looking at her butt.

Help.

He'd known that this was going to be a mistake back in California—the second the plea for help had left Wes's lips. Bobby should have admitted it, right there and then. *Don't send me to Boston, man. I've got a crippling jones for your sister. The temptation may be too much for me to handle, and then you'll kill me.*

"I've gotta go," Bobby heard Colleen say as she straightened up. "I've got a million things to do before I leave." She waved to the kids in the back. "Thanks again, guys. You did a terrific job today. I probably won't see you until I get back, so…"

There was an outcry from the back seat, something Bobby couldn't make out, but Colleen laughed.

"Absolutely," she said. "I'll deliver your letters to Analena and the other kids. And I'll bring my camera and take pictures. I promise."

She waved as the station wagon drove away, and then she was walking toward him. As she approached, as she gazed at him, there was a funny little smile on her face.

Bobby was familiar with the full arsenal of devious Skelly smiles, and it was all he could do not to back away from this one.

"I have an errand to run, but after, we could get dinner. Are you hungry?" she asked.

No, he was terrified. He sidled back a bit, but she came right up to him, close enough for him to put his arms around. Close enough to pull her in for a kiss.

He couldn't kiss her. *Don't you dare,* he ordered himself.

He'd wanted to kiss her for years.

"I know this great Chinese place," she continued, twinkling her eyes at him. "Great food, great atmosphere, too. Very dark and cool and mysterious."

Oh, no. No, no. Atmosphere was the dead-last thing he wanted or needed. Standing here on the blazing-hot asphalt in broad daylight was bad enough. He had to clench his fists to keep from reaching for her. No way was he trusting himself around Colleen Skelly someplace dark and cool and mysterious.

She touched him, reaching up to brush something off his sleeve, and he jumped about a mile straight up.

Colleen laughed. "Whoa. What's with you?"

I want to sink back with you on your brightly colored bedspread, undress you with my teeth and lose myself in your laughter, your eyes and the sweet heat of your body.

Not necessarily in that order.

Bobby shrugged, forced a smile. "Sorry."

"So how 'bout it? You want to get Chinese?"

"Oh," he said, stepping back a bit and shifting around to pick up his seabag and swing it over his shoulder, glad he had something with which to occupy his hands. "I don't know. I should probably go try to find my hotel. It's the Sheraton, just outside of Harvard Square?"

"You're sure I can't talk you into spending the night with me?"

It was possible that she had no idea how suggestive it was when she asked a question like that, combined with a smile like that.

On the other hand, she probably knew damn well what she was doing to him. She was, after all, a Skelly.

He laughed. It was either that or cry. *Evasive maneuvers, Mr. Sulu.* "Why don't we just plan to have lunch tomorrow?"

Lunch was good. Lunch was safe. It was businesslike and well lit.

"Hmm. I'm working straight through lunch tomorrow,"

she told him. "I'm going to be driving the truck all day, picking up donations to take to Tulgeria. But I'd love to have breakfast with you."

This time it wasn't so much the words but the way she said it, lowering her voice and smiling slightly.

Bobby could picture her at breakfast—still in bed, her hair sexily mussed, her gorgeous eyes heavy-lidded. Her mouth curving up into a sleepy smile, her breasts soft and full against the almost-transparent cotton of that innocent little nightgown he'd once seen hanging in her bathroom....

Everything about her body language was screaming for him to kiss her. Unless he was seriously mistaken, everything she was saying and doing was one great big, giant green light.

God help him, why did she have to be Wes Skelly's little sister?

Traffic was heavy through the Back Bay and out toward Cambridge.

For once, Colleen didn't mind. This was probably the last time for a while that she'd make this drive up Comm. Ave. and over the BU bridge. It was certainly the last time she'd do it in this car.

She refused to feel remorse, refused even to acknowledge the twinge of regret that tightened her throat every time she thought about signing over the title. She'd done too much pro bono work this past year. It was her fault entirely, and the only way to make ends meet now was to sell her car. It was a shame, but she had to do it.

At least this final ride was a memorable one.

She glanced at Bobby Taylor, sitting there beside her, looking like the perfect accessory for a lipstick-red 1969 Ford Mustang, with his long hair and exotic cheekbones and those melted-chocolate eyes.

Yeah, he was another very solid reason why she didn't mind at all about the traffic.

For the first time she could remember, she had Bobby Taylor alone in her car, and the longer it took to reach Harvard Square, the better. She needed all the time she could to figure out a way to keep him from getting out when they arrived at his hotel.

She'd been pretty obvious so far, and she wondered just how blatant she was going to have to be. She laughed aloud as she imagined herself laying it all on the table, bringing it down to the barest bottom line, asking him if he wanted to get with her, using the rudest, least-elegant language she knew.

"So...what are you going to do tonight?" she asked him instead.

He glanced at her warily, as if he were somehow able to read her mind and knew what she really wanted to ask him.

"Your hair's getting really long," she interrupted him before he could even start to answer. "Do you ever wear it down?"

"Not too often," he told her.

Say it. Just say it. "Not even in bed?"

He hesitated only briefly. "No, I usually sleep with it braided or at least pulled back. Otherwise it takes forever to untangle in the morning."

She hadn't meant while he slept. She knew from the way he wasn't looking at her that he was well aware of what she had meant.

"I guess from your hair that you're still doing the covert stuff, huh?" she asked. "Oops, sorry. Don't answer that." She rolled her eyes. "Not that you would."

Bobby laughed. He had a great laugh, a low-pitched rumble that was always accompanied by the most gorgeous smile and extremely attractive laughter lines around his eyes. "I think it's fine if I say yes," he told her. "And you're right—the long hair makes it kind of obvious, anyway."

"So is Wes out on a training op or is it the real thing this time?" she asked.

"I don't know that myself," he admitted. "Really," he added as she shot him a skeptical glance.

The traffic light was red, and she chewed her lip as she braked to a stop and stared at the taillights of the cars in front of them. "It worries me that he's out there without you."

When she looked at him again, he was watching her. And he actually held her gaze for the first time since they'd gotten into her car. "He's good at what he does, Colleen," he told her gently. She loved the way he said her name.

"I know. It's just... Well, I don't worry so much when he's with you." She forced a smile. "And I don't worry so much about you when you're with him."

Bobby didn't smile. He didn't do much of anything but look into her eyes. No, when he looked at her like that, he wasn't just looking into her eyes. He was looking into her mind, into her soul. Colleen found herself holding her breath, hypnotized, praying that he would like what he saw. Wishing that he would kiss her.

How could he look at her like that—and the way he'd looked at her in the church parking lot, too—and then *not* kiss her?

The car behind her honked, and she realized that the light had changed. The line of traffic had already moved. She fumbled with the stick shift, suddenly afraid she was making a huge fool of herself.

One of Wes's recent e-mails had mentioned that Bobby had finally ended his on-again, off-again relationship with a woman he'd met in Arizona or New Mexico or someplace else equally unlikely, considering the man spent most of his waking hours in the ocean.

Of course, that so-called *recent* e-mail from her brother had arrived nearly two months ago. A lot might've happened in the past two months. Bobby could well have hooked up with someone new. Or gotten back together with what's-her-name. Kyra Something.

"Wes told me you and Kyra called it quits." There was absolutely no point in sitting here wondering. So what if she came across as obvious? She was tired of guessing. Did she have a chance here, or didn't she? Inquiring minds wanted to know.

"Um," Bobby said. "Yeah, well... She, uh, found someone who wasn't gone all the time. She's actually getting married in October."

"Oh, yikes." Colleen made a face at him. "The *M* word." Wes always sounded as if he were on the verge of a panic attack when that word came up.

But Bobby just smiled. "Yeah, I think she called to tell me about it because she was looking for a counteroffer, but I just couldn't do it. We had a lot of fun, but..." He shook his head. "I wasn't about to leave the teams for her, you know, and that's what she wanted." He was quiet for a moment. "She deserved way more than I could give her, anyway."

"And you deserve more than someone who'll ask you to change your whole life for them," Colleen countered.

He looked startled at that, as if he'd never considered such a thing, as if he'd viewed himself as the bad guy in the relationship—the primary reason for its failure.

Kyra Whomever was an idiot.

"How about you?" he asked. "Wes said you were dating some lawyer."

Oh, my God. Was it possible that Bobby was doing a little fishing of his own?

"No," she said, trying to sound casual. "Nope. That's funny, but... Oh, I know what he was thinking. I told him

I went to Connecticut with Charlie Johannsen. Wes must've thought…'' She had to laugh. ''Charlie's longtime companion is an actor. He just got cast in a new musical at Goodspeed-at-Chester.''

''Ah,'' Bobby said. ''Wes will be relieved.''

''Wes never wants me to have any fun,'' she countered. ''How about you?'' She used Bobby's own words. ''Are you seeing someone new?''

''Nope. And Wes isn't, either.''

Okay. She would talk about Wes. She'd gotten the info she'd wanted.

''Is he still carrying the torch for—'' What was her name? ''Laura?''

Bobby shook his head. ''You'll have to ask him about that.''

Yeah, like Wes would talk to her about this. ''Lana,'' she remembered. ''He once wrote me this really long e-mail all about her. I think he was drunk when he wrote it.''

''I'm sure he was.'' Bobby shook his head. ''When you talk to him, Colleen, it's probably better not to mention her.''

''Oh, my God, is she dead?''

''No. Do you mind if we talk about something else?''

He was the one who'd brought up Wes in the first place. ''Not at all.''

Silence.

Colleen waited for him to start a new topic of conversation—anything that wasn't about Wes—but he just sat there, distracted by the sight of the river out the window.

''Do you want to go see a movie later?'' she finally asked. ''Or we could rent a video. I've got an appointment at six-thirty with a guy who wants to buy my car. If everything goes right, I'll be done by seven-thirty, easy.''

That got his attention, just the way she knew it would. "You're selling your car? *This* car?"

When she was fifteen, sixteen, seventeen, this Mustang was all she could talk about. But people's priorities changed. It wasn't going to be easy to sell it, but she refused to let it be the end of her world—a world that was so much wider now, extending all the way to Tulgeria and beyond.

She made herself smile at him. "I am. Law school's expensive."

"Colleen, if you need a loan—"

"I've got a loan. Believe me I've got *many* loans. I've got loans to pay off loans. I've got—"

"It took you five years to rebuild this car. To find authentic parts and—"

"And now someone's going to pay top dollar for a very shiny, very well-maintained vintage Mustang that handles remarkably badly in the snow. I live in Cambridge, Massachusetts. I don't need a car—especially not one that skids if you so much as whisper the word *ice*. My apartment's two minutes from the T, and frankly, I have better things to spend my money on than parking tickets and gasoline."

"Okay," he said. "Okay. I have an idea. I've got some money saved. I'll lend you what you need—interest free—and we can take the next week and drive this car back to your parents' house in Oklahoma, garage it there. Then in a few years when you graduate—"

"Nice try," Colleen told him. "But my travel itinerary has me going to Tulgeria next Thursday. Oklahoma's not exactly in the flight path."

"Think about it this way—if you don't go to Tulgeria, you get to keep your car and have an interest-free loan."

She took advantage of another red light to turn and look at him. "Are you attempting to bribe me?"

He didn't hesitate. "Absolutely."

She had to laugh. "You really want me to stay home? It's gonna cost you. A million dollars, babe. I'll accept nothing less."

He rolled his eyes. "Colleen—"

"Put up or shut up."

"Seriously, Colleen, I've been to Tulgeria and—"

"I'm *dead* serious, Robert. *And* if you want to lecture me about the dangers of Tulgeria, you've got to buy me dinner. But first you've got to come with me while I sell my car—make sure the buyer's really a buyer and not some psycho killer who answers vintage car ads in the *Boston Globe*."

He didn't hesitate. "Of course I'll come with you."

Jackpot. "Great," Colleen said. "We'll go take care of business, then drop your stuff at your hotel before we grab some dinner. Is that a plan?"

He looked at her. "I never really stood a chance here, did I?"

She smiled at him happily. "Nope."

Bobby nodded, then turned to look out the window. He murmured something that Colleen wasn't quite sure she caught, but it sounded an awful lot like, "I'm a dead man."

Chapter 3

Dark, cool and mysterious.

Somehow, despite his best intentions, Bobby had ended up sitting across from Colleen in a restaurant that was decidedly dark, cool and mysterious.

The food *was* great. Colleen had been right about that, too.

Although she didn't seem to be eating too much.

The meeting with the buyer had gone well. The man had accepted her price for the car—no haggling.

It turned out that that meeting had been held in the well-lit office of a reputable escrow agent, complete with security guard. Colleen had known damn well there was absolutely no danger from psycho killers or anyone else.

Still, Bobby had been glad that he was there while the buyer handed over a certified check and she handed over the title and keys to the Mustang.

She'd smiled and even laughed, but it was brittle, and he'd wanted to touch her. But he hadn't. He knew that he couldn't. Even just a hand on her shoulder would have been too intimate. And if she'd leaned back into him, he would have put his arms around her. And if he'd done that there in the office, he would have done it again, later, when they were alone, and there was no telling where that might lead.

No, strike that. Bobby knew damn well it would lead to him kissing her. And that could and would lead to a full meltdown, a complete and utter dissolving of his defenses and resolve.

It made him feel like a total skeeve. What kind of friend could he be to Colleen if he couldn't even offer her the most basic form of comfort as a hand on her shoulder? Was he really so weak that he couldn't control himself around her?

Yes.

The answer was a resounding, unchallenged *yes*.

No doubt about it—he was scum.

After leaving the escrow office, they'd taken the T into Harvard Square. Colleen had kept up a fairly steady stream of conversation. About law school. About her roommate— a woman named Ashley who'd gone back to Scarsdale for the summer to work in her father's law office, but who still sent monthly checks for her share of the rent, who didn't have the nerve to tell her father that, like Colleen, she'd far rather be a public defender and a pro bono civil litigant than a highly paid corporate tax attorney.

Bobby had checked into his hotel and given his bag and a tip to the bellhop. He didn't dare take it up to his room himself—not with Colleen trailing behind, no way. That transaction only took a few minutes, and then they were back out in the warm summer night.

The restaurant was only a short walk into Harvard Square. As he sat down across from Colleen, as he gazed at her pretty face in the dim candlelight, he'd ordered a cola. He was dying for a beer, but there was no way he'd trust himself to have even one. If he was going to survive this, he needed all of his wits about him.

They talked about the menu, about food—a nice safe topic—for a while. And then their order came, and Bobby ate while Colleen pushed the food around on her plate.

She was quiet by then, too. It was unusual to be around a Skelly who wasn't constantly talking.

"Are you okay?" he asked.

She looked up at him, and he realized that there were tears in her eyes. She shook her head. But then she forced a smile. "I'm just being stupid," she said before the smile wavered and disappeared. "I'm sorry."

She pushed herself out of the booth and would have rushed past him, toward the rest rooms at the back of the restaurant, if he hadn't reached out and grabbed her hand. He slid out of the bench seat, too, still holding on to her. It took him only a second to pull more than enough dollars to cover the bill out of his pocket and toss it onto the table.

This place had a rear exit. He'd automatically noted it when they'd first came in—years of practice in preparing an escape route—and he led her to it now, pushing open the door.

They had to go up a few steps, but then they were outside, on a side street. It was just a stone's throw to Brattle Street, but they were still far enough from the circus-like atmosphere of Harvard Square on a summer night to have a sense of distance and seclusion from the crowds.

"I'm sorry," Colleen said again, trying to wipe away her tears before they even fell. "I'm stupid—it's just a stupid car."

Bobby had something very close to an out-of-body experience. He saw himself standing there, in the shadows, next to her. Helplessly, with a sense of total doom, he watched himself reach for her, pull her close and enfold her in his arms.

Oh, dear Lord, she was so soft. And she held him tightly, her arms around his waist, her face buried in his shoulder as she quietly tried not to cry.

Don't do this. Get away from her. You're asking for trouble.

He must've made some kind of awful strangled sound because Colleen lifted her head and looked up at him. "Oh, no, am I hurting you?"

"No," he said. No, she was *killing* him. And count on Colleen to worry about someone else during a moment when most people wouldn't have been thinking of anyone but themselves.

Tears glistened on her cheeks and sparkled in her eyelashes, and the tip of her nose was red. Bozo the Clown, he and Wes had teased her whenever she'd cried back when she was thirteen.

She wasn't thirteen anymore.

Don't kiss her. Don't do it.

Bobby clenched his teeth and thought about Wes. He pictured the look on his best friend's face as he tried to explain. *See, she was right there, man, in my arms, and her mouth looked so soft and beautiful, and her body was so warm and lush and...*

She put her head back against his shoulder with a sigh, and Bobby realized he was running his fingers through the silk of her hair. She had hair like a baby's, soft and fine.

He knew he should make himself stop, but he couldn't. He'd wanted to touch her hair for more than four years now.

Besides, she really seemed to like it.

"You must think I'm a loser," she murmured.

"No."

She laughed softly. "Yeah, well, I am. Crying over a car. How dumb can I be?" She sighed. "It's just... When I was seventeen, I'd imagined I'd have that car forever—

you know, hand it down to my grandchildren? I say it now, and it sounds stupid, but it didn't feel stupid back then.''

The deal she'd just made gave her twenty-four hours to change her mind.

''It's not too late,'' he reminded her. He reminded himself, too. He could gently release her, take one step back, then two. He could—without touching her again—lead her back to the lights and crowd in Harvard Square. And then he'd never even have to mention anything to Wes. Because nothing would have happened.

But he didn't move. He told himself he would be okay, that he could handle this—as long as he didn't look into her eyes.

''No, I'm selling it,'' she told him, pulling back slightly to look up at him, wiping her nose on a tissue she'd taken from her shoulder pack. ''I've made up my mind. I need this money. I loved that car, but I love going to law school, too. I love the work I do, I love being able to make a difference.''

She was looking at him so earnestly he forgot about not looking into her eyes until it was too late. Until the earnest look morphed into something else, something loaded with longing and spiked with desire.

Her gaze dropped to his mouth, and her lips parted slightly, and when she looked once again into his eyes, he knew. She wanted to kiss him nearly as much as he wanted to kiss her.

Don't do this. Don't…

He could feel his heart pounding, hear the roar of his blood surging through his body, drowning out the sounds of the city night, blocking out all reason and harsh reality.

He couldn't not kiss her. How could he keep from kissing her when he needed to kiss her as much as he needed to fill his lungs with air?

But she didn't give him a chance to lean down toward

her. She stood on her tiptoes and brushed her mouth across his in a kiss that was so achingly sweet that he thought for one paralyzingly weak-kneed moment he just might faint.

But she stepped back just a little to look at him again, to smile hesitantly into his eyes before reaching up, her hand cool against the too-hot back of his neck as she pulled his head down to kiss him again.

Her lips were so soft, so cool, so sweetly uncertain, such a contrast to the way his heart was hammering and to the tight, hot sensation in his rib cage—as if his entire chest were about to burst.

He was afraid to move. He was afraid to kiss her back, for fear he'd scare her to death with his hunger for her. He didn't even know how to kiss like this—with such delicate tenderness.

But he liked it. Lord, he liked it an awful lot. He'd had his share of women who'd given him deep, wet, soul kisses, sucking his tongue into their mouths in a decidedly unsubtle imitation of what they wanted to do with him later, in private.

But those kisses hadn't been even a fraction as sexy as what Colleen was doing to him right now.

She kissed his mouth, his chin and then his mouth again, her own lips slightly parted. She barely touched him. In fact, she touched him more with her breath—soft, unsteady puffs of air that caressed him enticingly.

He tried to kiss her the same way, tried to touch her without really touching her, skimming his hands down her back, his palms tingling from the almost-contact. It made him dizzy with anticipation.

Incredible anticipation.

She touched his lips with her tongue—just the very tiniest tip of her tongue—and pleasure crashed through him. It was so intense that for one blindingly unsteady moment he was afraid he might actually have embarrassed himself beyond recovery.

From just a kiss.

But he hadn't. Not yet, anyway. Still, he couldn't take it anymore, not another second longer, and he crushed her to him, filling his hands with the softness of her body, sweeping his tongue into her mouth.

She didn't seem to mind. In fact, her pack fell to the ground, and she kissed him back enthusiastically, welcoming the ferocity of his kisses, winding her arms around his neck, pressing herself even more tightly against him.

It was the heaven he'd dreamed of all these years.

Bobby kissed her, again and again—deep, explosively hungry kisses that she fired right back at him. She opened herself to him, wrapping one of her legs around his, moaning her pleasure as he filled his hand with her breast.

He caught himself glancing up, scanning a nearby narrow alleyway between two buildings, estimating whether it was dark enough for them to slip inside, dark enough for him to unzip his shorts and pull up her skirt, dark enough for him to take her, right there, beneath someone's kitchen window, with her legs around his waist and her back against the roughness of the brick wall.

He'd pulled her halfway into the alley before reality came screaming through.

Wes's sister. This was Wes's *sister*.

He had his tongue in Wes's sister's mouth. One hand was filled with the softness of Wes's sister's derriere as he pressed her hips hard against his arousal. His other hand was up Wes's sister's shirt.

Had he completely lost his mind?

Yes.

Bobby pulled back, breathing hard.

That was almost worse, because now he had to look at her. She was breathing hard, too, her breasts rising and falling rapidly, her nipples taut and clearly outlined beneath her shirt, her face flushed, her lips swollen and moist from his kisses.

But it was her eyes that almost killed him. They were smoky with desire, brimming with fire and unresolved passion.

"Let's go to my apartment," she whispered, her voice even huskier than usual.

Oh, God.

"I can't." His voice cracked, making him sound even more pathetic.

"Oh," she said. "Oh, I'm—" she shook her head "—I'm sorry, I thought... You said you weren't seeing anyone."

"No." He shook his head, tried to catch his breath. "It's not that."

"Then why stop?"

He couldn't respond. What could he possibly say? But shaking his head again wasn't a good enough response for Colleen.

"You really don't want to come back to my place and—"

"I can't. I just can't." He cut her off, unable to bear finding out just which words she would use to describe what they'd do if he did go home with her tonight. Whether she called it making love or something more crudely to the point, however she couched it, it would be a total turn-on.

And he was already *way* too turned on.

She took a step toward him, and he took a step back.

"You're serious," she said. "You really don't want to?"

He couldn't let her think that. "I want to," he told her. "God, I want to. More than you could possibly know. I just... I *can't*."

"What, have you taken some kind of vow of abstinence?"

Somehow he managed to smile at her. "Sort of."

Just like that she understood. He saw the realization dawn in her eyes and flare rapidly into anger. "Wesley," she said. "This is about my brother, isn't it?"

Bobby knew enough not to lie to her. "He's my best friend."

She was furious. "What did he do? Warn you to stay away from me? Did he tell you not to touch me? Did he tell you not to—"

"No. He warned me not even to *think* about it." Wes had said it jokingly, one night on liberty when they'd each had five or six too many beers. Wes hadn't really believed it was a warning he'd needed to give his best friend.

Colleen bristled. "Well, you know what? Wes can't tell *me* what to think, and *I've* been thinking about it. For a long time."

Bobby gazed at her. Suddenly it was hard to breathe again. A long time. "Really?"

She nodded, her anger subdued, as if she were suddenly shy. She looked everywhere but in his eyes. "Yeah. Wasn't that kind of obvious from the way I jumped you?"

"I thought I jumped you."

Colleen looked at him then, hope in her eyes. "Please come home with me. I really want you to—I want to make love to you, Bobby. You're only here for a week—let's not waste a minute."

Oh, God, she'd said it. Bobby couldn't bear to look at her, so he closed his eyes. "Colleen, I promised Wes I'd look out for you. That I'd take care of you."

"Perfect." She bent down to pick up her bag. "Take care of me. Please."

Oh, man. He laughed because, despite his agony, he found her funny as hell. "I'm positive he didn't mean it like that."

"You know, he doesn't need to find out."

Bobby braced himself and met her gaze. "I can't be that kind of friend to him."

She sighed. "Terrific. Now I feel like a total worm." She started toward Brattle Street. "I think, considering all things, we should skip the movie. I'm going home. If you change your mind…"

"I won't."

"…you know where to find me." Bobby followed her about a dozen more steps, and she turned around. "Are you coming with me after all?"

"It's getting late. I'll see you home."

"No," Colleen said. "Thank you, but no."

Bobby knew not to press it. That look in her eyes was one he'd seen far too many times on a completely different Skelly.

"I'm sorry," he said again.

"Me, too," she told him before she walked away.

The sidewalk wasn't as crowded as it had been just a few hours ago, so Bobby let her get a good head start before he started after her.

He followed her all the way home, making certain she was safe without letting her see him again.

And then he stood there, outside her apartment building, watching the lights go on in her apartment, angry and frustrated and dying to be up there with her, and wondering what on earth he was going to do now.

Chapter 4

Colleen had printed out the e-mail late last night, and she now held it tightly in her hand as she approached Bobby.

He was exactly where he'd said he would be when he'd called—sitting on the grassy slope along the Charles River, looking out at the water, sipping coffee through a hot cup with a plastic lid.

He saw her coming and got to his feet. "Thanks for meeting me," he called.

He was so serious—no easygoing smile on his face. Or maybe he was nervous. It was hard to be sure. Unlike Wes, who twitched and bounced off the walls at twice his normal frenetic speed when he was nervous, Bobby showed no outward sign.

He didn't fiddle with his coffee cup. He just held it serenely. He'd gotten them both large cups, but in his hand, large looked small.

Colleen was going to have to hold hers with both hands.

He didn't tap his foot. He didn't nervously clench his teeth. He didn't chew his lip.

He just stood there and breathed as he solemnly watched her approach.

He'd called at 6:30 this morning. She'd just barely fallen asleep after a night spent mostly tossing and turning—and analyzing everything she'd done and said last night, trying to figure out what she'd done wrong.

She'd come to the conclusion that she'd done *every*thing wrong. Starting with crying over a motor vehicle and ending with darn near throwing herself at the man.

This morning Bobby had apologized for calling so early and had told her he hadn't been sure what time she was leaving for work today. He'd remembered that she was driving the truck, remembered their tentative plan to meet for breakfast.

Last night she'd wanted him to *stay* for breakfast.

But he hadn't—because of some stupid idea that by having a relationship with her, he'd be betraying Wes.

Wes, whose life he'd most likely saved, probably countless times. Including, so it seemed, one definite time just a few short weeks ago.

"I can't believe you didn't tell me you'd been *shot.*" Colleen didn't bother saying good morning. She just thrust the copy of Wes's e-mail at him.

He took it and read it quickly. It wasn't very long. Just a short, fast, grammatically creative hello from Wes, who didn't report where he was, who really just wanted to make sure Bobby had arrived in Boston. He mentioned almost in passing that Bobby had recently been shot while out in the real world—the SEALs' nickname for a real mission or operation.

They had been somewhere they weren't supposed to be, Wes reported vaguely, and due to circumstances out of their control, they'd been discovered. Men with assault weapons started shooting, and Bobby had stepped in front of Wes, taking some bullets and saving his scrawny hide.

"Be nice to him," Wes had written to Colleen. "He nearly died. He almost got his butt shot off, and his shoulder's still giving him pain. Treat him kindly. I'll call as soon as I'm back in the States."

"If he can say all that in an e-mail," Colleen told Bobby sternly, "you could have told me at least a *little* about what happened. You could have told me you were shot instead of letting me think you'd hurt yourself in some normal way—like pulling a muscle playing basketball."

He handed her the piece of paper. "I didn't think it was useful information," he admitted. "I mean, what good is telling you that a bunch of bad guys with guns tried to kill your brother a few weeks ago? Does knowing that really help you in any way?"

"Yes, because *not* knowing hurts. You don't need to protect me from the truth," Colleen told him fiercely. "I'm not a little girl anymore." She rolled her eyes. "I thought we cleared *that* up last night."

Last night. When some extremely passionate kisses had nearly led to getting it on right out in the open, in an alley not far from Harvard Square.

"I got coffee and muffins," Bobby said, deftly changing the subject. "Do you have time to sit and talk?"

Colleen watched as he lowered himself back onto the grass. Gingerly. Why hadn't she noticed that last night? She was *so* self-absorbed. "Yes. Great. Let's talk. You can start by telling me how many times you were shot and exactly where."

He glanced at her as she sat down beside him, amusement in his dark eyes. "Trust Wes to be melodramatic. I took a round in the upper leg that bled kind of heavily. It's fine now—no problem." He pulled up the baggy leg of his shorts to reveal a deeply tanned, enormously muscular thigh. There was a fresh pink scar up high on his leg. Where it would really hurt a whole lot to be shot. Where there were major veins—or were they arteries?—which, if opened, could easily cause a man to bleed to death very quickly.

Wes hadn't been melodramatic at all. Colleen couldn't breathe. She couldn't stop staring at that scar. Bobby could have died.

"It's my shoulder that's giving me the trouble," Bobby continued, pulling his shorts leg back down. "I was lucky I didn't break a bone, but it's still pretty sore. I've got limited mobility right now—which is frustrating. I can't lift my arm much higher than this."

He demonstrated, and Colleen realized that his ponytail wasn't a fashion statement after all. He was wearing his hair like that because he wasn't physically able to put it back in his usual neat braid.

"I'm supposed to take it easy," he told her. "You know, not push it for another week."

He handed her a cup of coffee and held open a bag that contained about a half a dozen enormous muffins. She shook her head. Her appetite was gone.

"Can you do me a favor?" she asked. "Next time you or Wes get hurt, even if it's just something really little, will you call me and let me know? Please? Otherwise I'm just going to worry about you all the time."

Bobby shook his head. "Colleen…"

"Don't *Colleen* me," she countered. "Just promise."

He looked at her. Sighed. "I promise. But—"

"No buts."

He started to say something, then stopped, shaking his head instead. No doubt he'd spent enough time around Skellys to know arguing was useless. Instead he took a sip of his coffee and gazed out at the river.

"How many times have you saved Wes's life?" she asked him, suddenly needing to know.

"I don't know. I think I lost count somewhere between

two and three million.'' The laughter lines around his eyes crinkled as he smiled.

"Very funny.''

"It's just not that big a deal,'' he said.

"It is to me,'' she returned. ''And I'm betting it's a pretty big deal to my brother, too.''

"It's really only a big deal to him because I'm winning,'' Bobby admitted.

At first his words didn't make sense. And then they made too much sense. "You guys keep score?'' she asked in disbelief. ''You have some kind of contest going...?''

Amusement danced in his eyes. "Twelve to five and a half. My favor.''

"Five and a *half*?'' she echoed.

"He got a half point for getting me back to the boat in one piece this last time,'' he explained. ''He couldn't get a full point because it was partially his fault I needed his help in the first place.''

He was laughing at her. Oh, he wasn't actually laughing aloud, but Colleen knew that, inside, he was silently chortling away.

"You know,'' she said with a completely straight face, ''it seems only fair that if you save someone's life that many times, you ought to be able to have wild sex with that person's sister, guilt free.''

Bobby choked on his coffee. Served him right.

"So what are you doing tonight?'' Colleen asked, still in that same innocent voice.

He coughed even harder, trying to get the liquid out of his lungs.

"'Be nice to him,''' she read aloud from Wes's e-mail. She held it out for him to see. "See, it says it right there.''

"That's *not* what Wes meant,'' Bobby managed to gasp.

"How do you know?''

"I *know*.''

"Are you okay?" she asked.

His eyes were tearing, and he still seemed to have trouble breathing. "You're killing me."

"Good. I've got to go, so—" She started to stand up.

"Wait." He coughed again, tugging her back down beside him. "Please." He drew in a breath, and although he managed not to cough, he had to clear his throat several times. "I really need to talk to you about what happened last night."

"Don't you mean what *didn't* happen?" She pretended to be fascinated with her coffee cup, with folding up the little flap on the plastic lid so that she could take a sip without it bumping into her nose.

What had happened last night was that she had found out—the hard way—that Bobby Taylor didn't want her. At least not enough to take what she'd offered. At least not as much as she wanted him. It was possible he'd only used his fear of Wes's disapproval as an excuse to keep from going home with her. After all, it had worked, hadn't it? It had worked very well.

This morning she could only pretend not to care. She could be flip and say outrageous things, but the truth was, she was both embarrassed and afraid of what he might want to say to her.

Of course, if ever there were a perfect time for him to confess his undying love, it would be now. She supposed it *was* possible that he would haltingly tell her he'd fallen in love with her years ago, that he'd worshiped her from afar for all this time and now that they'd finally kissed, he couldn't bear to be apart from her any longer.

Bobby cleared his throat again. "Colleen, I, um…I don't want to lose you as a friend."

Or he could say that. He could give her the "let's stay friends" speech. She'd heard it before. It would contain the word *friend* at least seven more times. He would say *mis-*

take and *sorry* both at least twice and *honest* at least once. And he'd tell her that he hoped what happened last night wouldn't change things between them. Her friendship was very important to him.

"I really care about you," he told her. "But I have to be honest. What happened last night was, well, it was a mistake."

Yup. She'd definitely heard it before. She could have written it out for him on a three-by-five-card. Saved him some time.

"I know that I said last night that I couldn't...that we couldn't...because of *Wes* and, well, I need you to know that there's more to it than that."

Yeah, she'd suspected that.

"I can't possibly be what you really want," he said quietly.

Now *that* was different. She'd never heard that before.

"I'm not..." He started to continue, but then he shook his head and got back on track. "You mean too much to me. I can't take advantage of you, I *can't*. I'm ten years older than you, and—Colleen, I knew you when you were thirteen—that's just too weird. It would be crazy, it wouldn't go anywhere. It couldn't. *I* couldn't. We're too different and..." He swore softly, vehemently. "I really am sorry."

He looked about as miserable as she was feeling. Except he probably wasn't embarrassed to death. What had she been thinking, to throw herself at him like that last night?

She closed her eyes, feeling very young and very foolish—as well as ancient beyond her years. How could this be happening again? What was it about her that made men only want to be her friend?

She supposed she should be thankful. This time she got the "let's stay friends" speech *before* she'd gone to bed with the guy. That had been the lowest of a number of low-relationship moments. Or it should have been. Despite the fact that Bobby obviously cared enough not to let it get that far, he didn't care about her the way she wanted him to. And that hurt remarkably badly.

She stood up, brushing off the seat of her shorts. "I know you're probably not done. You still have one more *mistake* and another *sorry* to go, but I'll say 'em for you, okay? I'm sorry, too. The mistake was mine. Thanks for the coffee."

Colleen held her head up as she quickly walked away. And she didn't look back. She'd learned the hard way never to look back after the "let's stay friends" speech. And never to cry, either. After all, smart friends didn't cry when stupid, idiotic, completely clueless friends rejected them.

Tears welled in her eyes, but she forced them back.

God, she was such a fool.

Bobby lay back on the grass and stared up at the sky.

In theory, telling Colleen that they should stay friends instead of rip each other's clothes off had seemed to be the least painful way of neatly dealing with something that was on the verge of turning into an emotional and physical bloodbath.

Physical—because if Wes found out that Bobby had messed with his little sister, he would have been mad enough to reach down Bobby's throat and rip his lungs out.

Bobby had been direct with Colleen. He'd been swift and, if not quite honest, he'd certainly been sincere.

Yet somehow he'd managed to hurt her. He'd seen it in her eyes as she'd turned and walked away.

Damn. Hurting her was the dead last thing he'd wanted to do.

That entire conversation had been impossibly difficult. He'd been on the verge of telling her the truth—that he hadn't slept at all last night, that he'd spent the night alternately congratulating himself for doing the right thing and cursing himself for being an idiot.

Last night she made it clear that she wanted him. And Lord knows that the last thing he honestly wanted was to stay mere friends with her. In truth, he wanted to get naked with her—and stay naked for the entire rest of this week.

But he knew he wasn't the kind of man Colleen Skelly needed. She needed someone who would be there for her. Someone who came home every night without fail. Someone who could take care of her the way she deserved to be taken care of.

Someone who wanted more than a week of hot sex.

He didn't want another long-distance relationship. He couldn't take it. He'd just gotten out of one of those, and it wasn't much fun.

And would be even less fun with Colleen Skelly—because after Wes found out that Bobby was playing around with his sister, Wes would come after him with his diving knife.

Well, maybe not, but certainly he and Wes would argue. And *Colleen* and Wes would argue. And that was an awful lot of pain, considering Bobby would spend most of his time three thousand miles away from her, him missing her with every breath he took, her missing him, too.

No, hurting Colleen was bad, but telling her the truth would hurt them both even more in the long run.

Chapter 5

Colleen had just finished picking up a load of blankets collected by a women's church group and was on her way to a half dozen senior centers to pick up their donations when a taxi pulled up. It stopped directly in front of her, blocking her exit from the parking lot with a TV-cop-drama squealing of brakes.

Her first thought was that someone was late to their own wedding. But other than the representative from the ladies' auxiliary who had handed over the bundles of blankets, the building had been silent and empty.

Her second thought was that someone was in a major hurry to repent their sins, probably before they sinned again. She had to laugh at that image, but her laughter faded as the absolute last person she'd expected to see here at the St. Augustus Church climbed out of the cab.

Bobby Taylor.

His hair had partially fallen out of his ponytail, and his face was covered with a sheen of perspiration, as if he'd been running. He ignored both his sweat and his hair as he came around to the passenger side of the truck's cab. She leaned across the bench seat, unlocked the door, and he opened it.

"Thank God," he said as if he really meant it. "I've been following you for an hour now."

More than just his face was sweaty. His shirt was as soaked as if he'd been running a marathon in this heat.

Wes. Her brother was the only reason she could come up with for Bobby to search her out so desperately. Wes had to have been injured. Or—please, God, no—dead.

Colleen flashed hot and then cold. "Oh, no," she said. "What happened? How bad is it?"

Bobby stared at her. "Then you haven't heard? I was ready to yell at you because I thought you knew. I thought you went out to make these pickups, anyway."

"Just tell me he's not dead," she begged him. She'd lived through one dead brother—it was an experience she never wanted to repeat. "I can take anything as long as he's not dead."

His expression became one of even more perplexity as he climbed into the air-conditioned cab and closed the door. "He?" he asked. "It was a woman who was attacked. She's in ICU, in a coma, at Mass General."

A woman? At Mass General Hospital…? Now it was Colleen's turn to stare at him stupidly. "You didn't track me down because Wes is hurt?"

"Wes?" Bobby shook his head as he leaned forward to turn the air conditioner fan to high. "No, I'm sure he's fine. The mission was probably only a training op. He wouldn't have been able to send e-mail if it were the real thing."

"Then what's going on?" Colleen's relief was mixed with irritation. He had a lot of nerve, coming after her like this and scaring her to death.

"Andrea Barker," he explained. "One of the chief administrators of the AIDS Education Center. She was found badly beaten—barely breathing—outside of her home in Newton. I saw it in the paper."

Colleen nodded. "Yeah," she said. "Yeah, I heard about that this morning. That's really awful. I don't know her that well—we talked on the phone only once. I've mostly met with her assistant when dealing with the center."

"So you *did* know she's in the hospital." Something very much like anger flashed in his eyes, and his usually pleasantly relaxed mouth was back to a hard, grim line.

Bobby Taylor was mad at her. It was something Colleen had never experienced before. She hadn't thought he was capable of getting mad—he was so laid-back. Even more mind-blowing was the fact that she truly had no clue what she'd done to get him so upset.

"The article went into some depth about the problem they've—*you've*— You're part of them, providing legal services at no cost, right? The problem *you've* been having establishing a center in this one particular neighborhood in Boston. The same neighborhood where you just happened to be threatened yesterday while having a car wash...?"

And Colleen understood. She laughed in disbelief. "You really think the attack on Andrea Barker had something to do with her work for the education center?"

Bobby didn't shout at her the way Wesley did when he got mad. He spoke quietly, evenly, his voice dangerously soft. Combined with the spark of anger in his eyes, it was far more effective than any temper tantrum Wes had ever thrown. "And you don't?"

"No. Come on, Bobby. Don't be so paranoid. Look, I heard that the police theory is she startled a burglar coming out of her house."

"I heard a partial list of her injuries," Bobby countered, still in that same quietly intense voice. She had to wonder, what would ever set him off, make him raise his voice? What—if anything—would make this man lose his cool and detonate? If it ever happened, boy, look out. It would probably be quite an impressive show.

"They weren't the kind of injuries a woman would get from a burglar," he continued, "whose primary goal would have been to knock her down so he could run away as quickly as possible. No, I'm sorry, Colleen. I know you want to believe otherwise, but this woman was beaten deliberately, and if I know it, then the police know it, too. The burglar story is probably just something they threw out to the press, to make the real perpetrator think he's home-free."

"You don't know that for sure."

"Yes," he said. "You're right. I don't know it absolutely. But I'm 99 percent sure. Sure enough to be afraid that, as the legal representative to the AIDS Education Center, you could be the next target. Sure enough to know that the last thing you should be doing today is driving a truck around all by yourself."

He clenched his teeth, the muscles jumping in his jaw as he glared at her. That spark of anger made his eyes cold, as if she were talking to a stranger.

Well, maybe she was.

"Oh, Right," Colleen let her voice get louder with her growing anger. What did he care what happened to her? She was just an idiot who'd embarrassed both of them last night. She was just his *friend*. No, not even. The real truth was that she was just some pain-in-the-butt sister of a friend. "I'm supposed to lock myself in my apartment because there *might* be people who don't like what I do? Sorry, that's not going to happen."

"I spoke to some people," Bobby told her. "They seem to think this John Morrison who threatened you yesterday could be a real danger."

"Some people?" she asked. "Which people? If you talked to Mindy in the center's main office—well, she's afraid of her own shadow. And Charlie Johannsen is no—"

"I dare you," Bobby said, "to look me in the eye and tell me that you're not just a little bit afraid of this man."

She looked at him. Looked away. "Okay. So maybe I am a *little*—"

"And yet you came out here, anyway. By yourself."

She laughed in his face. "Yeah, and like *you* never do anything that you're a little afraid of. Like jumping out of airplanes. Or swimming in shark-infested waters. That's a particularly tough one for you, isn't it, Bobby? Wes told me you have a thing about sharks. Yet you do it. You jump into the water without hesitation. You face down your fear and get on with your life. Don't be a hypocrite, Taylor, and expect me to do anything less."

He was trying hard to be patient. "I'm trained to do those things."

"Yeah, well, I'm a woman," she countered. "I've been trained, too. I've had more than ten years of experience dealing with everything from subtle, male innuendo to overt threats. By virtue of being female, I'm a little bit afraid almost every single time I walk down a city street—and I'm twice as afraid at night."

He shook his head. "There's a big difference between that and a specific threat from a man like John Morrison."

"Is there?" Colleen asked. "Is there really? Because I don't see it that way. You know, there have been times when I walk past a group of men sitting out on the front steps of their apartment building, and one of them says, 'Hey, baby. Want to...'" She said it. It was impossibly crude, and Bobby actually flinched. "'Get over here now,' they say. 'Don't make me chase you to get what I *know* you want to give me.'"

She paused for emphasis. Bobby looked appropriately

subdued. "After someone," she said more quietly now, "some *stranger* says something like that to you—and if you want a real dare, then I dare you to find a woman my age who *hasn't* had a similar experience—you get a little—just a little—nervous just going out of your apartment. And when you approach a man heading toward you on the sidewalk, you feel a little flicker of apprehension or maybe even fear. Is he going to say something rude? Is he going take it a step further and follow you? Or is he just going to look at you and maybe whistle, and let you see from his eyes that he's thinking about you in ways that you don't want him to be thinking about you?

"And each time that happens," Colleen told him, "it's no less specific—or potentially unreal—than John Morrison's threats."

Bobby was silent, just sitting there, looking out the window.

"I'm so sorry," he finally said. "What kind of world do we live in?" He laughed, but it wasn't laughter that had anything to do with humor. It was a burst of frustrated air. "The really embarrassing part is that I've been that guy. Not the one who actually says those things, I'd never do that. But I'm the one who looks and even whistles. I never really thought something like that might frighten a woman. I mean, that was *never* my intention."

"Think next time," she told him.

"Someone really said that to you?" He gave her a sidelong glance. "In those words?"

She nodded, meeting his gaze. "Pretty rude, huh?"

"I wish I'd been there," he told her. "I would've put him in the hospital."

He said it so matter-of-factly, but she knew it wasn't just an idle threat. "If you had been there," she pointed out, "he wouldn't have said it."

"Maybe Wes is right." Bobby smiled at her ruefully.

"Maybe you *should* have a twenty-four-hour armed escort, watching your every move."

"Oh, no," Colleen groaned. "Don't *you* start with that, too. Look, I've got a can of pepper spray in my purse and a whistle on my key ring. I know you don't think so, but I'm about as safe as I can be. I've been keeping the truck doors locked, I've called ahead to set up appointment times, I've—"

"You forgot me," Bobby interrupted. "You should have called me, Colleen. I would have gladly come along with you right from the start."

Oh, perfect. She knew without even asking that he was not going to leave, that he was here in the cab of this truck until she made the last of her pickups, dropped off both the donations and the truck, and took the T back to Cambridge.

"Has it occurred to you that I might not be overly eager to spend the day with you?" she asked him.

She could see his surprise. He'd never dreamed she would be so blunt and to the point. Still, he recovered nicely. And he surprised her back by being equally straight-forward.

"It's already too late for our friendship, isn't it?" he said. "I really blew it last night."

No way was she going to let him take the blame. "I was the one who kissed you first."

"Yeah, but I was the one who didn't stop you right then and there," Bobby countered.

She jammed the truck into gear, silently cursing herself for being stupid enough to have even just a little hope left to be crushed. Yet there it was, flapping about like a de-flated balloon on the gritty floor of the truck, right next to her shredded pride and pulverized heart.

"I'm sorry," he said. "I should have been able to control myself, but I couldn't. I'm…"

Colleen looked at him. She didn't mean to. She didn't

want to. God forbid he see the total misery that his words brought her reflected in her eyes. But there was something in his voice that made her unable to keep from turning her head.

He was looking at her. He was just sitting there, *looking* at her, and it was the exact same way he'd looked at her last night, right before he'd pulled her close and kissed the hell out of her. There was hunger in his eyes. Heat and need and *desire*.

He looked away quickly, as if he didn't want her to see those things. Colleen looked away, too, her mind and heart both racing.

He was lying. He'd lied this morning, too. He didn't want them to stay just friends any more than *she* did.

He hadn't given her the ''let's stay friends'' speech because he had an aversion to women like her, women who actually had hips and thighs and weighed more than ninety pounds, wet. He hadn't made that speech because he found her unattractive, because she didn't turn him on.

On the contrary...

With a sudden clarity that should have been accompanied by angelic voices and a brilliant light, Colleen knew.

She *knew*. Bobby had said there was more to it, but there wasn't. This was about Wes.

It was Wesley who had gotten in the way of her and Bobby Taylor, as surely as if he were sitting right there between them, stinking of stale cigarette smoke, in the cab of this truck.

But she wasn't going to call Bobby on that—no way. She was going to play—and win—this game, secure that she knew the cards he was holding in his hand.

Bobby wasn't going to know what hit him.

She glanced at him again as she pulled out of the parking lot. ''So you really think Andrea's attack had something to do with her being an AIDS activist?'' she asked.

He glanced at her, too, and this time he managed to keep his eyes mostly expressionless. But it was back there—a little flame of desire. Now that she knew what to look for, she couldn't help but see it. "I think until she comes out of that coma and tells the police what happened, we should err on the side of caution."

Colleen made herself shiver. "It's just so creepy—the thought of her being attacked right outside of her own home."

"You don't have to worry about that. I'll go home with you after we're done here."

Jackpot. She had to bite the insides of her cheeks to keep from smiling. She somehow managed to twist her mouth around into a face of displeasure. "Oh," she said. "I don't know if that's necessary—"

"I'll check your place out, see what we can do to heighten the security," he told her. "Worst-case scenario, I'll camp out in the living room tonight. I know you probably don't want me to, but..."

No, indeed, she did *not* want him camped out in her living room tonight.

She wanted him in her bedroom.

"Wait," Colleen said, when Bobby would've opened the truck door and climbed down, after she parked outside the next senior center on her list. She was fishing around in her backpack, and she came up brandishing a hairbrush. "The wild-Indian hairstyle needs a little work."

He had to laugh. "That's so completely un-PC."

"What, telling you that your hair is a mess?"

"Very funny," he said.

"That's me," she said. "Six laughs a minute, guaranteed. Turn around, I'll braid it for you."

How had that happened? Ten minutes ago they'd been fighting. Bobby had been convinced that their friendship was badly strained if not completely over, yet now things were back to where they'd been when he'd first arrived yesterday.

Colleen was no longer completely tense, no longer looking wounded. She was relaxed and cheerful. He would even dare to call her happy.

Bobby didn't know how that had happened, but he wasn't about to complain.

"You don't have to braid it," he said. "A ponytail's good enough. And all I really need help with is tying it back. I can brush it myself."

He reached for the brush, but she pulled it back, away from him.

"I'll braid it," she said.

"If you really want to." He let her win. What harm could it do? Ever since he'd gotten injured, he'd had to ask for help with his hair. This morning he'd gone into a beauty salon not far from his hotel, tempted to cut it all off.

Back in California, he'd gotten help with his hair each day. Wes stopped by and braided it for him. Or Mia Francisco—the lieutenant commander's wife. Even the captain—Joe Cat—had helped him out once or twice.

He shifted slightly in the seat so Colleen had access to the back of his head, reaching up with his good arm to take out the elastic.

She ran both the brush and her fingers gently through his hair. And Bobby knew immediately that there was a major difference between Colleen braiding his hair and Wes braiding his hair. They were both Skellys, sure, but that was where all similarities ended.

"You have such beautiful hair," Colleen murmured, and he felt himself start to sweat.

This was a bad idea. A very, very bad idea. What could he possibly have been thinking? He closed his eyes as she brushed his hair back, gathering it at his neck with her other hand. And then she was done brushing, and she just used her hands. Her fingers felt cool against his forehead as she made sure she got the last stray locks off his face.

She was going to braid his hair, and he was going to sit here, acutely aware of each little, last, barely-touching-him movement of her fingers. He was going to sit here, wanting her, thinking of how soft she'd felt in his arms just last night, how ready and willing and eager she'd been. She wouldn't have stopped him from pushing up her skirt and burying himself inside of her and—

Sweat trickled down his back.

What harm was there in letting her braid his hair?

None—provided no one at the Parkvale Senior Center had enough of their eyesight left to notice the uncomfortably tight fit of his pants.

Provided Colleen didn't notice it, either. If she did, she would realize that he'd lied to her. It wouldn't take her long to figure out the truth. And then he'd be a dead man.

Bobby tried thinking about death, about rats, about plague, about pestilence. He tried thinking about sharks— all those teeth, those mean little eyes coming right at him. He thought about the day—and that day *was* coming, since he was no longer in his twenties—when he'd have to leave the SEAL teams, when he'd be too old to keep up with the newer recruits.

None of it worked to distract him.

Colleen's gentle touch cut through it all. It was far more real than any of his worst-imagined nightmares.

Yet it was remarkably easy to picture her touching him like that all over—not just on his head and his hair and the back of his neck, but *all* over. Oh, man...

"If I were a guy," Colleen murmured, "and I had hair like this, I'd wear it down. All the time. And I would have women falling at my feet. Lining up outside my bedroom door. All the time."

Bobby choked. "What?"

"Most women can't keep their hands off guys with long hair," she explained. "Particularly good-looking guys like you who are completely ripped. Hey, did you pack your uniform?"

She thought he was good-looking and *ripped*. Bobby had to smile. He liked that she thought of him that way, even though he wasn't sure it was completely true. He was a little too big, too solid to get the kind of muscle definition that someone like Lucky O'Donlon had.

Now, there was a man who was truly ripped. Of course, Lucky wasn't here right now as a comparison, which was just as well. Even though he was married, women were still drawn to him like flies to honey.

"Hello," Colleen said. "Did you fall asleep?"

"No," Bobby said. "Sorry." She'd asked him something. "Um…"

"Your uniform?"

"Oh," he said. "No. No, I'm not supposed to wear a uniform while my hair's long—unless there's some kind of formal affair that I can't get out of attending."

"No this one's not formal," she told him. "It's casual—a bon voyage party at the local VFW the night before we leave. But there will be VIPs there—senators and the mayor and… I just thought it would be cool for them to meet a real Navy SEAL."

"Ah," he said. She was almost done braiding his hair, and he was simultaneously relieved and disappointed. "You want me to be a circus attraction."

She laughed. "Absolutely. I want you to stand around and look mysterious and dangerous. You'd be the hit of the party." She reached over his shoulder, her arm warm against his slightly damp, air-conditioner-chilled T-shirt. "I need the elastic."

He tried to hand it to her, and they both fumbled. It

dropped into his lap. He grabbed it quickly—God forbid she reach for it there—and held it out on his open palm for her to take.

Somehow she managed to touch nearly every inch of his palm as she took the elastic.

"You know what you're asking, don't you?" he said. "I'll spend the evening fending off all kinds of personal questions. Is it true SEALs know how to rip out an opponent's throat with their bare hands? How many men have you killed? Have you ever killed anyone in hand-to-hand combat? Did you like it? Is it true SEALs are rough in bed?" He let out a burst of exasperated air. "As soon as people find out I'm a SEAL, they change, Colleen. They look at me differently. The men size me up, and the women..." He shook his head.

She laughed as she sat back, finally done. "Yeah, right, Taylor. You tell me that you and my brother haven't taken advantage of the way women react when they find out you're a SEAL."

"No," he said. "You're right. I *have* taken advantage— too many times. It's just...these days I don't get much enjoyment out of it. It's not real. You know, I didn't tell Kyra I was a SEAL until we were together for two months."

"Did she treat you differently when she found out?" Colleen asked. Her eyes were more green than blue today, so luminous and beautiful.

"Yeah, she did," he had to admit. "It was subtle, but it was there." And she'd slept with him that very same night. Coincidence? Maybe. But unlikely.

"I'm sorry," she said. "Forget I asked. You don't even have to come to this thing. It's just...I have to go, and since you're doing this twenty-four-hour bodyguard thing, I thought—"

"I'll call Harvard, have him send my uniform."

"No," she said. "You can go incognito. With your hair

down. Wearing leather pants. I'll tell everyone you're a supermodel from Paris. See what kind of questions you get asked then.''

Bobby laughed as Colleen climbed down from the cab of the truck. ''Hey,'' he said, sliding across the seat and keeping her from closing the door by sticking out his foot. ''I'm glad we're still friends.''

''You know, I've been thinking about this friend thing,'' she said, standing there, hands on her hips, looking up at him. ''I think we should be the kind of friends who have wild sex three or four times a day.''

She shot him a smile and turned toward the seniors center.

Bobby sat there, staring after her, watching the sunlight on her hair and the gentle swaying of her hips as she walked away.

She was kidding.

Wasn't she?

God, maybe she wasn't.

''Help,'' he said to no one in particular as he followed her inside.

Chapter 6

Bobby caught Colleen by the arm and pulled her back, almost on top of him, almost down the stairs that led to her third-floor apartment.

At first she thought she'd won. At first she thought that all the little glances and smiles, and all the thinly veiled—and some not so thinly veiled at all—comments she'd made all afternoon were finally paying off, that she'd succeeded in driving him crazy. She thought he was pulling her toward him to kiss her, the way he'd kissed her in Harvard Square last night.

Yeah, right, Colleen. Dream on.

Kissing her was the last thing on his mind. "Stay behind me," he ordered, pushing her so that her nose was practically pressed into the broad expanse of his back.

She realized then that her apartment door was ajar.

Someone was in her apartment.

Andrea Barker had come home, too, to find someone breaking into her house.

And had been beaten so badly she was still in a coma.

Colleen grabbed Bobby—it was about as effective as grabbing an aircraft carrier. "Don't go in there!"

"I won't," he said. "At least not before I get you out of here." He was holding on to her then, too, turning toward her and practically lifting her up, about to carry her down the stairs.

For the first time in her life Colleen actually felt fragile and petite and in need of rescue.

She wasn't quite sure she liked it.

She was scared, yes. She didn't want Bobby charging in, a one-man assault team, to find John Morrison and his gang in her living room. At the same time, if John Morrison and his gang *were* in her apartment, she didn't want to run away and lose the opportunity to have them all arrested.

"Put me down," she ordered him. They could go downstairs, call the police from Mr. Gheary's apartment.

To her surprise he did put her down, none too gently pushing her away from him. As she struggled to regain her balance, she realized he was charging up the last few stairs toward her apartment door. Toward a man who was coming out.

Wearing an unbelievably loud plaid shirt.

"Bobby, don't!"

She wasn't the only one shouting.

The owner of that shirt was shouting, too, shrieking, really, in pure terror.

It was Kenneth. Bobby had him against the entryway wall, his face pressed against the faded wallpaper, his armed twisted up behind his back.

"Bobby, *stop!* He's a friend of mine," Colleen shouted, taking the stairs two at a time, just as the door to her apartment opened wide, revealing the equally wide eyes of Ashley and her brother, Clark. She did a double take. Ashley's blue-haired brother, Clark.

"What are you doing here?" she asked Ashley, who was supposed to be spending the entire summer working at her father's law firm in New York.

"I escaped from Scarsdale," Ashley said faintly, staring at Bobby, who still had Kenneth pinned, his feet completely off the ground. "Clark and Kenneth came and broke me out."

That explained the blue hair. Nineteen-year-old Clark knew he'd be seeing his extremely conservative father. Say no more.

"Bobby, meet my roommate, Ashley DeWitt," Colleen said. "Her brother, Clark, and his friend, Kenneth. Guys, this is my brother's friend, Chief Bobby Taylor."

"I'm your friend, too," Bobby reminded her as he gently lowered the kid back to the floor. "Sorry."

The kid was shaken, but he pulled himself together quickly. "That was...somewhat uncomfortable, but the adrenaline rush is quite nice, thanks."

"Kenneth's from England," Colleen told him.

"Yeah," Bobby said, following them all into her apartment. "I caught that from the accent."

Man, Colleen hadn't been kidding. It was worse in here than he'd imagined. The small living room was filled, in some cases from floor to ceiling, with boxes. Colleen was in the process of writing, in big, block letters, what seemed to be a Tulgerian address on each of them. As far as he could tell, she was only about a third of the way done.

"So you're a chief, huh?" Clark said as Bobby closed the door behind him. "What tribe?"

"Oh, God! Clark, he's not *that* kind of chief." Ashley gave Bobby an apologetic smile. She was what he thought of as a New York blonde. Average height and slender, with a figure that was just barely curvy enough to be considered feminine, but certainly not curvy enough to be lush. Everything about her was neat and perfectly in place, nothing too extreme. She was cool and beautiful—kind of the way a stone statue was cool and beautiful. You didn't mind looking, but you wouldn't want to touch.

Compared to Ashley, Colleen was a mess. Her hair was everywhere. Her smile was crooked. Her breasts looked as if they were about to explode out from under her T-shirt every time she moved. She was too much of everything—too tall, too stacked, too blunt, too funny, too into having a good time wherever she went. Laughter spilled out of her constantly. Her eyes were never the same color from one minute to the next, but they were always, *always* welcoming and warm.

Desire knifed through him so sharply he had to clench his fists.

"Forgive my brother," Ashley continued. "He's terminally stupid."

He yanked his gaze away from Colleen, aware he'd been staring at her with his tongue nearly hanging out. God, he couldn't let her catch him looking at her that way. If she knew the truth…

Who was he kidding? She'd probably already guessed the truth. And now she was trying to drive him slowly insane with all those deep looks and the seemingly innocently casual way she touched him damn near constantly in passing. A hand on his arm, on his knee. Fingers cool against his face as she fixed a stray lock of his hair. Brushing against him with her shoulder. Sitting so close that their thighs touched.

And the things she said to him! She thought they should be the kind of friends who had sex three or four times a day. She'd only been teasing. She liked being outrageous—saying things like that and trying to shake him up.

That one had worked.

"I'm a chief petty officer," Bobby explained to the kid

with blue hair, working to keep up with the conversation. That kid's name was Clark. He was Ashley's brother—no doubt about that. He had the same perfectly sculpted nose and chin, slightly differently shaped eyes that were a warmer shade of gray. "I'm in the Navy."

"Whoa, dude," Clark said. "With long hair like that?" He laughed. "Hey, maybe they'll take me, huh?"

"Bobby's a—" Colleen cut herself off, and Bobby knew she was remembering all that he'd told her about the way most people's attitudes changed when they found out he was a SEAL. She looked at him and as their eyes met he felt the small room shrink. It was as if he'd been caught in the beam of a searchlight—he and Colleen. Ashley, Clark and Kenneth vanished in the darkness outside his peripheral vision. All he could see was Colleen and her beautiful, laughing eyes.

They were very blue right now.

"Bobby's a very good friend of mine," she said softly, instead of telling them he was a SEAL.

"I should join the Navy," Clark's voice cut through. "Wouldn't *that* tick the old man off?"

"I had big plans for tonight," Colleen said, still looking into Bobby's eyes. "I was going to cook dinner for Bobby and then seduce him by dancing naked in the kitchen."

There she went again. More teasing. She was laughing at him—probably at the look of shock on his face. But as she turned away, as the world opened up again to include the other three people in the room, Bobby got the feeling that she wasn't completely kidding. She'd had plans for tonight, and those plans *had* included him.

"I should go," he said, wanting to stay at least as much as he wanted to keep breathing. But he couldn't stay. No way.

"No," Ashley said swiftly. "We were just going out."

"No, we weren't," Clark said with disdain. "You are

such a liar. You have a headache—so bad that Kenneth was going to the drugstore to get you some painkillers.'' He turned to Colleen. ''Unless you've got some hidden here. Ash wouldn't let me search your bedroom.''

''Gee, I don't know why,'' Colleen said. ''Could it maybe have something to do with the fact that the last time you searched my room I got home and called the police because I thought I'd been vandalized? Besides, you wouldn't have found any. I don't get headaches. Did you look in the bathroom?''

''I'm feeling much better,'' Ashley interrupted. Bobby had just met her, but even he could tell that she was lying. ''We're going out.''

''But what about that letter you were going to write to Dad?''

''It can wait.'' Ashley motioned toward the door with her head, making big eyes at her brother. ''This is Bobby Taylor. Wes's friend?'' Clark stared at her blankly, as only a younger brother can stare at an older sister. ''The Navy SEAL…?''

''Oh,'' Clark said. ''*Oh.* Right.'' He looked at Bobby. ''You're a SEAL, huh? Cool.''

Colleen's smile was rueful and apologetic. ''Sorry,'' she told Bobby. ''I tried.''

Clark grinned at Kenneth. ''Dude! You were almost killed by a Navy SEAL! You should definitely tell the girls at that party tonight. I bet one of 'em will go home with you.''

''Ashley, you really don't have to go anywhere,'' Colleen said to her friend. ''You look wiped. What happened? What'd your father do now?''

Ashley just shook her head.

''What's a Navy SEAL?'' Kenneth asked. ''And do you suppose if he actually *had* killed me then Jennifer Reilly might want to marry me? I mean, if you think she might go home with me if he *almost* killed me...."

"Oh, no way!" Clark countered. "I wasn't thinking Jenn Reilly, dude! Set your sights lower, man. Think B or C tier. Think Stacy Thurmond or Candy Fremont."

"You rank the women you know into *tiers?*" Colleen was outraged. "Get out of my house, scumball!"

"Whoa," Clark said, backing up and tripping over one of the boxes. "We don't *tell* 'em we rank 'em. We'd never say it to their faces. They don't know. Honest."

"Yes, they do," Colleen countered. "Believe me, they know."

"Who is this *we* to whom you keep referring, scumball?" Kenneth asked Clark.

"What tier am *I* in?" Colleen's voice was dangerously quiet.

"A," Clark told her quickly. "Absolutely. You are so completely, gorgeously, perfectly A."

Colleen cut him down with a single word—a pungent profanity that Bobby realized he'd never heard her use before. Unlike Wes, she didn't pepper her everyday speech with four-letter words. As a matter of fact, he couldn't remember the last time he'd heard her say damn or even hell. It was pretty remarkable actually, considering how prone she was to blurting out whatever was on her mind.

I think we should be the kind of friends who have wild sex three or four times a day. Help.

"Once when I was running down by the river," Colleen told Clark tightly, "I went past these two guys who were grading all the women who ran by. The wind carried their voices to me right at the exact moment they were checking me out. They gave me a C minus—probably about the equivalent of your lower C tier."

Bobby couldn't stay silent another second. "They were fools."

"They were...several words I will not lower myself to use," she said, chin held high, pretending that a C-minus ranking by a pair of strangers didn't bother her one bit. Pretending she was above that. Pretending that she hadn't been hurt.

"You're on my A list," Bobby said. The moment the words left his lips, he realized he'd just made a fatal mistake. Although he'd meant it as the highest compliment, he'd just admitted that he had an A list. And that would make him little better than...what had she called Clark? A scumball.

"That came out really wrong," he told her quickly as her eyes started to narrow.

Clark, the genius, stepped up to the plate. "See? All guys have lists. It's a guy thing," he protested, not old enough to know that all either of them could do now was grovel, apologize and pray for forgiveness. "It doesn't mean anything."

"Bobby, strangle him, strangle his strange, plaid-clothed little friend," Colleen ordered him, "and then strangle yourself."

"What I *meant* to say," Bobby told her, moving close enough to catch her chin with his hand, so she now had to look up into his eyes, "was that I find you as beautiful on the outside as you are on the inside."

The searchlight clicked back on, and the rest of the world faded. Colleen was looking at him, her eyes wide, her lips slightly parted. She was the only other person in the entire universe. No one and nothing else existed. He couldn't even seem to move his hand away from the soft smoothness of her face.

"Strangle me?" Bobby heard Kenneth protest, his voice faint, as if coming from a great distance. "Why strangle *me?* I don't put anyone into tiers, thank you very much."

"Yeah, because you can't see past Jenn Reilly," Clark

countered, also from somewhere way back there, beyond Colleen's eyes and Colleen's lips. "For you, Jenn's got her own gigantic tier—and everyone else is invisible. You and Jenn are *so* not going to happen, man. Even if hell froze over, she would walk right past you and date Frosty the Snowman. And then she would call you later to tell you how it went because you guys are *friends*. Sheesh. Don't you know friendship is the kiss of death between a man and a woman?"

"That was very sweet," Colleen told Bobby softly. "I forgive you."

She took his hand and kissed him, right on the palm, and Bobby felt something major snap in his chest.

Oh, God, he had to get out of here before it was too late. Before he reached for her and...

He turned away, forcing himself to focus on blue hair and a loud plaid. Anything but Colleen and her bone-melting smile.

"Yes, I'm thwarted by the curse of being the *friend*." Kenneth sighed. "I'm double damned because Jennifer thinks I'm gay. I'm her *gay* friend. I've told her that I'm quite not, thanks, but..."

"*Every*one thinks you're gay," Clark countered. "Tell me honestly, bro," he asked Bobby. "When you first saw Kenneth—I mean, Kenneth, come on, man. Only a gay dude would call himself Kenneth instead of Ken or Kenny—when you first saw him, Bobby, didn't you think—" he held out his hands to frame Kenneth, like a movie director *"—gay?"*

Bobby didn't bother to answer. He'd spent far too much time around Wes, who was the same kind of hyped-up, whirlwind talker as this kid, to know that his answer wasn't really needed. Which was just as well, because he wasn't completely convinced that he'd be able to speak.

Every time he looked into Colleen's eyes, his hands

started to sweat, his chest felt squeezed and his throat tightened up. He was in desperate trouble.

"You know, my father thinks you're gay, too," Clark told Kenneth. "I enjoy that about you. You frighten him, dude."

"Well, I'm not gay," Kenneth said through clenched teeth.

Bobby cleared his throat experimentally. A few more times and he'd have his voice back. Provided he didn't look at Colleen again.

"Not that there's anything wrong with being gay," Kenneth added hastily, glancing at Bobby. "We should probably make sure we're not offending a gay Navy SEAL here—an extremely big, extremely tall gay Navy SEAL. Although I still am not quite certain as to exactly what a Navy SEAL might be."

Clark looked at Bobby with new interest. "Whoa. It never even occurred to me. *Are* you gay?"

For the first time in a good long number of minutes, there was complete and total silence. They were all looking at him. *Colleen* was looking at him, frowning slightly, speculation in her eyes.

Oh, great. Now she thought he'd told her he only wanted to be friends because he was—

He looked at her, wavering, unable to decide what to say. Should he just shut up and let her think whatever she thought, hoping that it would make her keep her distance?

Colleen found her voice. "Congratulations, Clark, you've managed to reach new heights of rudeness. Bobby, don't answer him—your sexual orientation is no one's business but your own."

"I'm straight," he admitted.

"I'm sure you are," Colleen said a little too heartily, implying that she suspected otherwise.

He laughed again. "Why would I lie?"

"I believe you," she said. "Absolutely." She winked at him. "Don't ask, don't tell. We'll just pretend Clark didn't ask."

Suddenly this wasn't funny anymore, and he laughed in disbelief. "What, do you want me to do...?" Prove it? He stopped himself from saying those words. Oh, God.

She was giving him another of those killer smiles, complete with that two-thousand-degree incinerating heat in her eyes. Yes, she did want him to prove it. She didn't say it in words, but it was right there, written all over her face. She hadn't believed he was gay for one minute. She'd been baiting him. And he'd walked right into her trap. She waggled her eyebrows at him suggestively, implying that she was only teasing, but he knew better.

Help.

Please, God, let there be voice mail waiting for him, back in his hotel room. Please, God, let Wesley have called, announcing that he was back in the States and on his way to Boston. Please, God...

"Now that we've got *that* mystery solved, the two burning questions of the night that remain are why did you come back to Boston," Colleen said to her roommate, "and why blue?" She turned and looked at Clark's hair critically. "I'm not sure it's you...dude."

"What is a Navy SEAL?" Kenneth reminded her. "Burning question number three. I keep picturing beach balls and Seaworld, and I'm confident that's not quite right."

"SEALs are part of the U.S. military's special forces," Colleen said. "They're part of the Navy, so they spend a lot of time in and around the water—swimming, scuba diving, underwater demolition even. But SEAL stands for sea, air and land. They also jump out of airplanes and crawl across the desert and through the jungle, too. Most of the time no one knows that they're there. They carry great big guns—assault weapons, like commandos—but nearly all of their operations are covert.'' She looked at Clark. ''Which means secret. Clandestine—99.9 percent of the time they insert and extract from their mission location without firing a single bullet.''

She turned back to Bobby. ''Did I miss anything vital? Besides the fact that you SEALs frequently kill people— usually with your bare hands—and that you're known for being exceedingly rough in bed?''

Bobby started to laugh. He couldn't help it. And then Colleen was laughing, too, with the others just staring at them as if they were crazy.

She was so alive, so full of light and joy. And in less than a week she was going to get on an airplane and fly to a dangerous place where she could well be killed. And, Lord, what a loss to the world that would be. The thought was sobering.

''Please don't go,'' he said to her.

Somehow she knew he was talking about the trip to Tulgeria. She stopped laughing, too. ''I have to.''

''No, you don't. Colleen, you have no idea what it's like there.''

''Yes, I do.''

Ashley pulled her brother and Kenneth toward the door. ''Coll, we're going to go out for a—''

''No, you're not.'' Colleen didn't look away from Bobby. ''Kick Thing A and Thing B out onto the street, but if you're getting one of your headaches, you're not going anywhere but to bed.''

''Well then, I'll be in my room,'' Ashley said quietly. ''Come on, children. Let's leave Aunt Colleen alone.''

''*Hasta la vista*, baby.'' Clark nodded to Bobby. ''Dude.''

''Thanks again for not killing me,'' Kenneth said cheerfully.

They went out the door, and Ashley faded quietly down the hallway.

Leaving him alone in the living room with Colleen.

"I should go, too." That would definitely be the smart thing. As opposed to kissing her. Which would definitely be the opposite of the smart thing. But he couldn't seem to get his feet to move toward the door.

"You should come into the kitchen," she countered. "Where there are chairs that aren't covered with boxes. We can actually sit down."

She took his hand and tugged him into the kitchen. Somehow his feet had no problem moving in that direction.

"Okay," she said, sitting at the kitchen table. "Spill. What happened in Tulgeria?"

Bobby rubbed his forehead. "I wish it was that easy," he said. "I wish it was one thing. I wish I was wrong, but I've been there a half dozen times, at least, and each time was more awful than the last. It's bad and getting worse, Colleen. Parts of the country are a war zone. The government's lost control everywhere but in the major cities, and even there they're on shaky ground. Terrorist groups are everywhere. There are Christian groups, Muslim groups. They work hard to kill each other, and if that wasn't enough, there's in-fighting among each of the groups. Nobody's safe. I went into a village and—"

Lord, he couldn't tell her—not the details. He didn't want to tell her *any* of it, but he made himself. He looked her straight in the eye and said it. "Everyone was dead. A rival group had come in and... Even the children, Colleen. They'd been methodically slaughtered."

She drew in a breath. "Oh, no!"

"We went in because there were rumors that one of the terrorist groups had gotten hold of some kind of chemical weapon. We were there to meet a team of Army Rangers, escort 'em out to a waiting submarine with samples of whatever they'd found. But they came up empty. These people had nothing. They had hardly any regular ammunition, let alone any kind of chemical threat. They killed each other with swords—these big machete-style things, with these curved, razor-sharp blades.

"No one is safe there." He said it again, hoping she was listening. "No one is safe."

She looked pale, but her gaze didn't waver. "I have to go. You tell me these things, and I have to go more than ever."

"More than half of these terrorists are zealots." He leaned across the table, willing her to hear him, to *really* hear him. "The other half are in it for the black market— for buying and selling anything. Including Americans. *Especially* Americans. Collecting ransom is probably the most lucrative business in Tulgeria today. How much would *your* parents pay to get you back?"

"Bobby, I know you think—"

He cut her off. "Our government has a rule—no negotiating with terrorists. But civilians in the private sector... Well, they can give it a go—pay the ransom and gamble that they'll actually get their loved one back. Truth is, they usually don't. Colleen, please listen to me. *They usually don't get the hostages back.*"

Colleen gazed at him searchingly. "I've heard rumors of mass slaughters of Tulgerian civilians in retaliation by the local government."

Bobby hesitated, then told her the truth. "I've heard those rumors, too."

"Is it true?"

He sighed. "Look, I know you don't want to hear this, but if you go there you might die. *That's* what you should be worrying about right now. Not—"

"*Is* it true?"

God, she was magnificent. Leaning across the table toward him, palms down on the faded formica top, shoulders set for a fight, her eyes blazing, her hair on fire.

"I can guarantee you that the U.S. has special forces teams investigating that right this very moment," he told her. "NATO warned Tulgeria about such acts of genocide in the past. If they're up to their old tricks and if we find out about it—and if they are, we will, I guarantee it—then the U.S. ambassador and his staff will be pulled out of Tulibek immediately. The U.S. will cut all relations with the Tulgerian government. The embassy will be gone— potentially overnight. If that happens while you're there…"

Bobby took a steadying breath. "Colleen, if you go, you'll be in danger every minute of that entire week."

"I want to show you something," she said. "Don't go anywhere. I'll be right back."

Chapter 7

The photographs were in her bedroom. Colleen grabbed the envelope from her dresser, stopping to knock softly on Ashley's door on her way back to the kitchen.

"Come in."

The room was barely lit, with the shades all pulled down. Ash was at her computer, and despite the dim lighting, Colleen could see that her eyes were red and swollen. She'd been crying.

"How's the headache?" Colleen asked.

"Pretty bad."

"Try to sleep."

Ashley shook her head. "I can't. I have to write this."

"Write what?"

"A brief. To my father. That's the only way he'll ever pay attention to me—if I write him a legal brief. Isn't that pathetic?"

Colleen sighed. It *was* pathetic. Everything about Ashley's relationship with her father was pathetic. She'd actually gotten caller-ID boxes for all of their telephones, so they'd know not to answer when Mr. DeWitt called. Colleen loved it when her own father called.

"Why don't you do it later?" she said to her friend. "After the headache's gone."

Ashley's headaches were notoriously awful. She'd been to the doctor, and although they weren't migraines, they were similar in many ways. Brought on by tension and stress, the doctor had said.

Great ailment for a future lawyer to have.

"I'll help you with it," Colleen continued. "You need to tell me what happened—why you haven't called or e-mailed me since mid-May. I assume it's all connected?" It was. She could see that from the look on Ashley's face. "Just let me get rid of Bobby, okay?"

"Don't you dare!" Indignation gave Ashley a burst of energy. "Colleen, my God! You've had a thing for this guy for *years!* He's gorgeous, by the way. And huge. I mean, you told me he was big, but I had no idea. How tall is he?"

"I don't know exactly. Six-six? Maybe taller."

"His hands are like baseball mitts."

"Yeah," Colleen said. "And you know what they say about guys with big hands."

"They have big gloves," they said in unison. Colleen grinned, and Ashley even managed a weak smile. But it was fleeting.

"I can't believe my rotten timing. Of all the times to come running back to Cambridge and get in the way…" Ashley rested her forehead in her hands, elbows on her desk. "I saw him looking at you, Coll. All you have to do is say the word and he'll spend the night."

"He gave me the friends speech," Colleen told her.

"You're kidding!"

"Let's see—would that be something that I, designated

best friend to the entire world's male population, would kid about? No, I don't think so.''

"I'm sorry.''

"Yeah, well…" Colleen forced a smile. "Personally I think he's lying—that he's got some kind of code-of-honor thing going, you know, because I'm his best friend's sister. I have to convince him that it's okay, that he doesn't have to fall in love and marry me—that I just want us to have some fun.''

Although if he *did* happen to fall in love with her… No, she couldn't let herself think that way. That path was fraught with the perils of disappointment and frustration. All she wanted was to have fun, she reminded herself again, wishing the words hadn't sounded so hollow when she'd said them aloud.

"He's probably wondering what happened to you," Ashley pointed out.

Colleen went out the door, stopping to look at her friend, her hand on the knob. "I'll be back in about thirty minutes to get your full report on Scarsdale and your dear old dad.''

"That's really not necessary—''

"I know you," Colleen said. "You're not going to sleep until we talk, so we're going to talk.''

Bobby heard the door shut, heard Colleen coming back down the hall to the kitchen.

He'd heard the soft murmur of voices as she'd stopped to speak to her roommate.

The soundproofing in this old place was virtually non-existent.

That meant that grabbing her when she came back into the room, and having hot, noisy sex right there, on top of the kitchen table was definitely not an option.

Oh, man, he had to get out of here.

He stood up, but Colleen came into the room, blocking his escape route.

"Sit," she ordered. "Just for a few more minutes. I want to show you something."

She took a photograph out of an envelope and slid it across the table toward him. It was a picture of a small girl, staring solemnly into the camera. She had enormous eyes—probably because she was so skinny. She was all narrow shoulders, with a pointy chin, dressed in ill-fitting clothes, with a ragged cap of dark-brown hair. She looked to be about six or seven years old, with the kind of desperate and almost feral air about her that would have made Bobby watch her from the corner of his eye had he happened upon her in the street. Yeah, he'd watch her, all right, *and* secure his wallet in an inside pocket.

"This was Analena," Colleen told him, "two years ago—before my student Children's Aid group adopted her."

She put another picture on the table. "This was taken just last month."

It was the same girl, only now her hair was longer—thick and glossy. She was smiling—laughing—as she ran across a field, kicking a soccer ball. Her cheeks were pink and healthy looking, and although she was still rail thin, it was because she was growing. She was gangly, gawky. She no longer looked as if she would snap in two. And the feral look was gone. She was a child again.

Colleen laid a letter in front of him—written in a large, loopy child's hand. "Dearest Colleen," he read silently:

I dream last night that I visit you in U.S. of A. It such wonderful dream—I want to no wake up. I hope you okay that I gifted Ivan with futball you gifted me. He try to steal many times, I think, why not he keep?

My English, she is getting better, no? It is gift from

you—from America books and tape player and batteries you send. Blessed gift. More better than futball. Ivan make bad noise, don't think this. Still, I teach Ivan English words. Some day he thank me, thank you, also.

Send more letter soon. Love, Analena.

Colleen pulled other photos from the envelope. They were pictures of other kids.

"Analena and about twenty-five other children live in an orphanage, St. Christof's, deep inside Tulgeria's so-called war zone," she told him, "which also happens to be the part of the country that sustained the most damage from the earthquake. My Children's Aid group has been corresponding—for over two years—with the nuns who run St. Christof's. We've been trying to find a legal loophole so we can get those children out of Tulgeria. These are unwanted children, Bobby. Most are of mixed heritage—and nobody wants them. The terrible irony is that we have lists of families here in the U.S. who want them desperately—who are dying to adopt. But the government won't let them go. They won't pay to feed them, yet they won't give them up."

The pictures showed the bleakness of the orphanage. Boarded-up windows, peeling paint, bombed-out walls. These children were living in a shell of a former house. In all of the pictures, the nuns—some clad in old-fashioned habits, some dressed in American jeans and sneakers— were always smiling, but Bobby could see the lines of strain and pain around their eyes and mouths.

"When this earthquake happened," Colleen continued, still in that same soft, even voice, "we jumped at the chance to actually go in there." She looked Bobby squarely in the eyes. "Bringing relief aid and supplies to the quake victims is just our cover. We're really going in to try to get those children moved out of the war zone, to a safer location. Best-case scenario would be to bring them back to the States with us, but we know the chances of that happening are slim to none.''

Bobby looked at her. "I can go," he said. "Colleen, I'll do this for you. I'll go instead of you."

Yes, that would work. He could get some of the other men in Alpha Squad to come along. Rio Rosetti, Thomas King and Mike Lee were all young and foolish. They'd jump at the chance to spend a week's vacation in the number-one most dangerous hot spot in the world. And Spaceman—Lieutenant Jim Slade. He was unmarried, too. He'd help if Bobby asked.

But no way would Bobby ask any of his married friends to spend any of their too-infrequent leave time away from their families, risking their lives.

"This could work," he told her, but she was already shaking her head.

"Bobby, I'm going." She said it firmly, absolutely, calmly. As if this was a fact that wasn't going to change no matter what he said or did. "I'm the liaison with the Tulgerian minister of Public Health. I believe he's our one hope of getting those children moved out of immediate danger. He knows me, he trusts me—I'm going."

"If you're going, I'm going, too," he told her just as absolutely.

She shook her head. "No, you're not."

He sighed. "Look, I know you probably think I'm just interfering, but—"

Colleen smiled. "No, you don't understand. I'd love it if you could come along. Honest. It would be great. But be practical, Bobby. We're leaving in less than a week. It's taken us nearly three weeks to get permission to enter the country and bring aid—despite the fact that people there are wandering around hungry, their homes destroyed by this earthquake. You'll have to go through the same diplomatic channels and—''

''No, I won't.''

She made a face at him. ''Yeah, right. What, are you going to call some admiral and snap your fingers and…?''

''I won't snap my fingers at Admiral Robinson,'' Bobby told her. ''That would be rude.''

She stared at him. ''You're serious. You're really going to call an *admiral?*''

He nodded as he glanced at his watch. It was a little too late to call tonight. The admiral and his wife, Zoe, had twins. Max and Sam.

The twins were pure energy in human form—as Bobby well knew. He baby-sat them once when the admiral and his wife were out in California, when their regular sitter had canceled at the last minute. Max and Sam were miniature versions of their father. They both had his striking-blue eyes and world-famous smile.

Jake would've just finished reading them a story and putting them to bed. Bobby knew he would then go in search of his wife, maybe make them both a cup of herbal tea and rub her shoulders or feet.…

''I'll call him tomorrow morning,'' Bobby said.

Colleen smiled. She didn't believe he was tight enough with an admiral to be able to give the man a call. ''Well, it would be nice if you could go, but I'm not going to hold my breath.'' She gathered up the pictures and put them back in the envelope.

''How many people are going?'' he asked. ''You know, in your group?''

''About twelve.''

Twelve unprepared, untrained civilians running around loose.… Bobby didn't swear—at least not aloud.

''Most of them will actually be distributing supplies to the quake victims. They'll be hooking up with the Red

Cross volunteers who are already in place in the country,'' she continued. ''Of the twelve, there are five of us who'll be concentrating on getting those children moved.''

Five was a much better, much more compact number. Five people could be whisked out of sight and removed from danger far more easily than twelve.

''Who's meeting you at the airport?'' he asked.

''We've rented a bus and made arrangements to be picked up by the driver,'' she told him.

A bus. Oh, *man*. ''How many guards?''

Colleen shook her head. ''One. The driver insisted. We're still arguing over that. We don't want any guns. Our connection to the Red Cross—''

''Colleen, you'll need armed guards,'' he told her. ''Way more than just one man hired by the driver. Three or four at the least. Even just for the short trip between the airport and your hotel. And you'll need twice as many if you're going up north.''

''But—''

''The Red Cross means nothing in Tulgeria. In fact, it's often used as a bull's-eye for terrorists. Don't put the emblem on the bus, don't wear it on your clothes.''

She was looking at him as if he were speaking Greek. ''Are you serious?''

''Dead serious. And instead of a single bus, we should get you three or four Humvees. Something smaller and faster, that'll be less of a target.''

''The bus is so that we can move the children if we get the opportunity,'' she told him.

Oh, damn. Yeah, they would definitely need a bus for that. ''Okay,'' he said. ''I'm going to do what I can to get Admiral Robinson involved—to make this an official operation for one of his Gray Group teams. But if it's official, there's a chance I won't be able to go. I'm still not 100 percent—''

"I'm not sure that's such a good idea," Colleen said. "If we go in there looking like some kind of commando team…"

"Whoever goes in with you, they'll be covert. There'll be three or four guys hanging around with assault weapons for show as if they were hired guards. But everyone else on the team will blend in with your group. I promise."

She looked at him. "You promise. Except you're not going to be there."

"I may not be there," he said. "But I'm sure as hell going to try."

Colleen smiled. "You know, every time someone says that they'll *try,* I think of that scene in *The Empire Strikes Back* with Luke Skywalker and Yoda. You know, the one where Yoda says, 'Try not. Do or do not.'"

"Yeah, I know that scene," Bobby told her. "And I'm sorry, but—"

She reached across the table and touched his hand. "No, don't apologize. I didn't mean to sound as if I were accusing you of anything. See, the truth is I've fought so many losing battles for so many years that I really appreciate someone who tries. In fact, a try is all I ever ask for anymore. It may not work out, but at least you know you gave it a shot, right?"

She wasn't talking about him coming to Tulgeria. She was talking about the way he'd kissed her. And the way he'd pushed her away, refusing to see where that kiss might lead. Refusing even to try.

Bobby wasn't sure what to say. He felt like the worst kind of coward. Too scared even to try.

Even when her hand was on top of his, her fingers so cool against the heat of his skin. Even when he wished with all of his heart that she would leave her hand right there for a decade or two.

But Colleen took her hand away as she stood. He

watched as she placed the envelope with the pictures on the cluttered surface of a built-in desk in the corner of the room.

"You know, I've met most of the people who want to adopt these kids," she told him. "They're really wonderful. You look into their eyes, and you can see that they already love these children just from seeing their pictures, from reading their letters." Her voice wavered. "It just breaks my heart that those kids are in danger, that we can only *try* to help them. It kills me that there are no guarantees."

Bobby stood up. He didn't mean to. And as soon as he found himself on his feet, he forced himself to stop. To not move toward her, not take her into his arms. The last time he did that, he'd completely lost control.

But Colleen turned to face him. *She* came toward him. She reached for him, taking hold of both of his hands. "It's important to me that you know I'm not doing this purely to drive Wes crazy."

Her fingers were cool and strong and, again, he didn't want to let her go. *Help.* "I know."

But she didn't come any closer. She just smiled and squeezed his hands. "Good," she said as she released him. "So go. You're free. Escape. Lucky you—I need to hang with Ashley tonight. Guess I'll have to dance naked for you another night."

Her eyes sparkled as she laughed at him, at the pained look he couldn't keep off his face.

The door was right there. She'd given him permission to leave. He could have walked through it, walked out of her apartment, walked to a place where he—and she—were safe. Instead he didn't move. "Why do you keep doing that?"

She opted not to play dumb. She knew he was talking about her suggestive comments. "You're such an easy target and I want…"

"What?" He really wanted to know. Badly enough that

he almost touched her again. Almost. "You want what, Colleen?"

"You."

He'd known she was gutsy. And when she teased, she could be pretty outrageous. But he'd never expected her to say that.

She lowered her eyes as if she were suddenly shy. "I always have, you know."

She spoke barely loud enough for him to hear her, but he did. He heard. His ears were working perfectly. It was his lungs that were having trouble functioning.

"So now you know," she said quietly. When she looked up at him, her smile was rueful. "How's that for a powerful rebuttal to the 'I just want to be friends' speech?"

He couldn't respond. He didn't have any idea at all of what to say. She wanted him. She always had. He felt like laughing and crying. He felt like grabbing her, right there in the kitchen. He felt like running—as hard and as fast and as far as he possibly could.

"I figure either I'm right, and you didn't mean what you said this morning," she told him. "Or I'm wrong, and I'm a complete idiot who deserves humiliation and rejection twice in two days."

Bobby kept his mouth shut, wishing he *were* the kind of man who could just run for the door—and keep running when he hit the street. But he knew that he wasn't going to get out of there without saying *some*thing.

He just wasn't sure what that something should be. Tell the truth and admit he hadn't meant what he'd said? That was one hell of a bad idea. If he did that, she'd smile and move closer and closer and...

And he'd wake up in her bed.

And then Wes would kill him.

Bobby was starting to think he could maybe handle

death. It would be worth it for a chance at a night with Colleen.

What he would never be able to live with was the look of betrayal in his best friend's eyes. He clamped his mouth shut.

"I know I act as if it's otherwise," Colleen continued, turning away from him and fiddling with half a dozen organic apples that were on the kitchen counter. As she spoke, she arranged them into a pattern. Big, then little, then big. "But I haven't had too much experience. You know. With men, I mean. In fact, all I've had are a couple of really crummy short-term relationships. I've never been with someone who really wants me—I mean other than for the fact that I'm female and convenient." With the apples neatly arranged in two perfect rows, she turned to face him, to look him in the eye. "I know you say you don't—want me, that is. But I see something really different when I look into your eyes. And...Bobby, I just want to know what that's like—to be made love to the way you kissed me last night. It felt so right and..."

She took a deep breath. Smiled shakily. "So. You've been warned. Now you know. You also know that I'm not going to be talked out of going to Tulgeria. So if your admiral guy doesn't come through for you, you can tell my brother you did everything you could to keep me off that plane. And you can go back to California with a clear conscience. And I think you probably should go—if you really did mean what you said about just wanting to be friends. If you stay, though, you better put on your fireproof suit. Because starting tomorrow I'm turning up the heat."

"You really said that?" Ashley laughed. "What did he do?"

After her little speech, Bobby hadn't grabbed her and

kissed her. But then again, Colleen hadn't really thought he would.

"What did he *say?*" Ash persisted.

"Nothing," Colleen told her friend. "He looked a little pale—kind of like he was going to faint. So I told him we'd talk more tomorrow and I pushed him out the door."

Truth was, she hadn't wanted to hear what he might have to say in response to her painfully honest confession.

She'd pretty much been flashing hot and cold by then herself—alternately clapping herself on the back for her bravery and deriding herself for pure stupidity.

What if she *were* completely wrong? What if she were completely misinterpreting everything she'd seen in his eyes? What if he hadn't really been looking at her with barely concealed longing and desire? What if it had just been a bad case of indigestion?

"I had to try," Colleen told Ashley—and herself as well.

Ash was sitting cross-legged on her bed, hugging her beat-up, raggedy stuffed bear—the one she'd been given when she was three and had chicken pox. The one she still slept with despite the fact that she'd just turned twenty-four.

It was ironic. Colleen's friend had everything. Money. A beautiful face. A slim, perfect body. Weight that didn't fluctuate wildly given her moods. A 4.0 grade point average. Impeccable taste.

Of course, Colleen had something Ashley didn't have. And Colleen wouldn't have traded that one thing for Ashley's looks and body, even if her friend had thrown in all the gold in Ft. Knox, too.

Not a chance.

Because Colleen had parents who supported her, 100 percent. She knew, without a doubt, that no matter what she did, her mom and dad were behind her.

Unlike Mr. DeWitt, who criticized Ashley nonstop.

Colleen couldn't imagine what it had been like growing up in that house. She could picture Ash as a little girl, desperately trying to please her father and never quite succeeding.

"Ashley, what's this? A Father's Day gift? A ceramic bowl? You made it yourself on the wheel in pottery class? Oh, well, next time you'll do much better, won't you?"

It was true, Colleen's own parents weren't perfect. No one's parents were. But hers loved her unconditionally. She'd never doubted that.

"You ready to talk about what happened?" she asked Ashley now.

Her friend sighed. "I'm so stupid."

Colleen just waited.

"There was a new associate in my father's firm," Ash finally said. "Brad Hennesey." Tears filled her eyes, and she tried to laugh. "God, I'm such an idiot. I can't even say his name without…" She gestured to her face.

Colleen handed her a box of tissues and waited while Ashley blew her nose.

"He was so nice," Ash told her. "I mean, I didn't expect him *not* to be nice to me, because I'm the boss's daughter, but he seemed so genuine, and…"

"Oh, no," Colleen said. She was pretty sure she knew where this was going, and she prayed she was wrong.

"I did something really dumb," Ash admitted. "We started dating, and he was so…" She laughed but it was loaded with pain. "Yeah, he was completely perfect— smart and gorgeous with all those white teeth and that Land's End model body, and we loved the same books and movies, and… And I fell in love with him. God! How could I be so stupid?"

Colleen waited, praying that she was wrong.

"But then I found out that my father had hired him purposely. Brad was part of his plan to guarantee that I'd come home after law school and join the firm. He was going to be made partner instantly upon our engagement. I hear myself telling you this, and it sounds so ludicrous. Can you believe any of this?''

She could. She'd met Ashley's father. "Ah, Ash," Colleen said. "How did you find out?"

"Brad *told* me," Ashley said. "He confessed everything. He called me in the middle of the night and told me he had to see me. Right then. So he came over to the house and we went into the garden and... He was really upset and he told me he was in love with me. He said he'd fallen for me, and he told me that he had to come clean before it went any further, that he couldn't live with himself any longer.''

"But that's good," Colleen countered. "Isn't it? He was honest when it mattered the most.''

"Colleen, he accepted a position where the job description included tricking the boss's daughter into marrying him." Ashley was still aghast at the idea. "What kind of person would do that?''

"One who maybe saw your picture?" Colleen suggested.

Ashley stared at her as if she were in league with Satan.

"I'm not saying it's a good thing," she added quickly. "But how bad could the guy be if he really did fall in love with you?''

"Did he?" Ashley asked darkly. "Or is he just saying that he did? Is this confession just another lie?''

Oh, ick. Colleen hadn't thought of it that way. But Ash was right. If *she* were trying to con someone into marrying her, she'd pretend to be in love with them, confess everything and beg for forgiveness. That would save her butt in the event that the truth ever did surface after the wedding.

"He slept with me, Colleen," Ashley said miserably. "And my father was *paying* him.''

"Yeah," Colleen said, "I don't think your father was paying him to do that, though."

"It feels that way." Ashley was one of those women who still looked beautiful when she cried. "You know the really stupid thing?"

Colleen shook her head. "No."

"I didn't have the nerve to confront my father." Ashley's lip trembled. "I just ran away. I hid."

"But you're writing him a letter," Colleen pointed out. "That's a start."

"Clark keeps telling me I should take one of those assertiveness training courses. You know, the kind where you go out into the mountains with only a canteen of water and a hunting knife and come back after having killed a bear?"

Colleen laughed at the absurdity of that. "You'd take advice from a man with blue hair?"

Ash laughed, too. It was shaky, but it was laughter.

"You know what I think you should do?" Colleen said. "I think you should go back and have this raging, passionate affair with Brad. Flaunt it in your father's face. Make it really public. And then, next May, when you graduate from law school, you dump the creep and flip your father the bird. You pass the California bar exam, and take a job as a public defender in East L.A. and you do pro bono work for the community on the side just to *really* tick him off. That's what *I* would do."

"You could do that?" Ashley asked. "Really? Have that kind of a relationship with a man without falling even further in love? Without getting in too deep?"

Colleen thought about Bobby Taylor, about what would happen if she did succeed in talking her way into his bed. She thought about waking up beside him, smiling into his beautiful eyes as he bent to kiss her. She thought about driving him to the airport and watching his broad back and his long, easygoing stride as he headed into the terminal, as he walked away. From her. Without looking back.

She thought about the way that would make her heart die inside of her. Just a little bit.

Just enough to change her forever.

"No," she said quietly. "I guess I couldn't, either."

Chapter 8

"Wait," Bobby said. "Zoe, no, if he's taking a day off, don't…" Bother him. But Zoe Robinson had already put him on hold.

"Hey, Chief!" Admiral Jake Robinson sounded cheerful and relaxed. "What's up? Zo tells me you're calling from Boston?"

"Uh, yes, sir," Bobby said. "But, sir, this can wait until tomorrow, because—"

"How's the shoulder?" the admiral interrupted. Admirals were allowed to interrupt whenever they wanted.

"Much better, sir," Bobby lied. It was exactly like Admiral Robinson to have made certain he'd be informed about the injuries of anyone on the SEAL teams—and to remember what he'd been told.

"These things take time." It was also like Robinson to see through Bobby's lie. "Slow and steady, Taylor. Don't push it too hard."

"Aye, sir. Admiral, I had no idea that your secretary would patch me through here, to your home."

"Well, you called to talk to me, didn't you?"

"Yes, sir, but you're an *admiral,* sir, and—"

"Ah." Robinson laughed. "You wanted it to be harder to reach me, huh? Well, if you need me to, I'll call Dottie in my office and tell her to put you on hold for a half an hour."

Bobby had to laugh, too. "No, thank you. I'm just... surprised."

"I don't take everyone's call," Jake Robinson's voice was serious now. "In fact, Dottie's probably kissed off half a dozen captains, commanders and lieutenant commanders already this morning. But when I set up the Gray Group, Chief, I made a point to make myself available 24/7 to the men I call to go out on my missions. You work for me— you need me? You got me. You probably don't know it, but you were on a Gray Group mission when you were injured. That cycled your name to the top of the list."

"I wasn't told, but...I knew."

"So talk to me, Chief. What's going on?"

Bobby told him. "Sir, I've become aware of a situation in which a dozen U.S. citizens—mostly students from here in Boston—are about to walk into Tulgeria with a single, locally hired armed guard."

Robinson swore, loudly and pungently.

Bobby told the admiral about the earthquake relief organization. About the bus and the children in the orphanage. About the fact that these American Good Samaritans were not going to be talked out of making this trip.

"What's your connection to this group, Chief?" Robinson asked. "Girlfriend?"

"Negative, sir," Bobby said hastily. "No, it's Wes Skelly's sister. She's one of the volunteers who's going."

"What, did Skelly send you to Boston to talk her out of it?" Robinson laughed. "God, you're a good friend to him, Bobby."

"He's out of the country, Admiral, and I had the time. Besides, he'd do the same for me."

"Yeah, and I suspect *your* sister is a little easier to handle than this sister of Skelly's—what's her name?"

"Colleen, sir."

"Is Colleen Skelly as much like her brother as I'm imagining her to be, God help us all?"

Bobby laughed again. "Yes and no, sir. She's..." Wonderful. Beautiful. Amazingly sexy. Intelligent. *Perfect.* "She's special, sir. Actually, she reminds me of Zoe in a lot of ways. She's tough, but not really—it's just a screen she hides behind, if you know what I mean."

"Oh, yes. I do." The admiral laughed softly. "Oh, boy. So, I know it's none of my business, but does Wes know that you've got a thing for his sister?"

Bobby closed his eyes. Damn, he'd given himself away. There was no point in denying it. Not to Jake. The man may have been an admiral, but he was also Bobby's friend. "No, he doesn't."

"Hmm. Does *she* know?"

Good question. "Not really."

"Damn."

"I mean, she's incredible, Jake, and I think—no, I *know* she's looking for a fling. She's made that more than clear but I can't do it, and I'm..."

"Dying," Jake supplied the word. "Been there, done that. If she really is anything like Zoe, you don't stand a chance." He laughed. "Colleen Skelly, huh? With a name like that, I'm picturing a tiny redhead, kind of built like her brother—compact. Skinny. With a smart mouth and a temper."

"She's a redhead," Bobby said. "And you're right about the mouth and the temper, but she's tall. She might even be taller than Wes. And she's not skinny. She's..." Stacked. Built like a brick house. Lush. Voluptuous. All those descriptions felt either disrespectful or as if he were exchanging locker-room confidences. "Statuesque," he finally came up with.

"Taller than Wes, huh? That must tick him off."

"She takes after their father, and he's built more like their mother's side of the family. It ticks Colleen off, too. She's gorgeous, but she doesn't think so."

"Genetics. It's proof that Mother Nature exists," Jake said with a laugh. "She's got a strong sense of irony, doesn't she?"

"I need you to help me, sir." Bobby brought their conversation back to the point. "Colleen's determined to go to Tulgeria. This whole trip is an international incident waiting to happen. If this isn't something you want to get Alpha Squad or the Gray Group involved in, then I'm hoping you can give me—"

"It is," the admiral said. "Protection of U.S. citizens. In a case like this I like to think of it as preventative counterterrorism. The Tulgerian government will bitch and moan about it, but we'll get you in. We'll tell the local officials that we need two teams," he decided. "One'll accompany Colleen Skelly and her friends, the other'll go in covert. The timing is really good on this, Taylor. You're actually the one doing *me* the favor here."

Admiral Robinson didn't say it. He couldn't say it, but Bobby knew he was going to use this seemingly standard protection op as a chance to send in an additional highly covert and top-secret team on an entirely different mission. It was probably related to the ongoing investigation of those rumors that the Tulgerian government was mass slaughtering its own citizens.

God, what a world.

"Alpha Squad will be back from their current training op in three days, tops," Robinson continued. "I'll have them rerouted here to the East Coast—to Little Creek.

We'll both meet them there, Chief, you'll fill them in and work out a plan, then bring them back up to Boston to hash out the details with Colleen Skelly and her idealistic friends.''

The admiral wanted Bobby to be part of the op. ''I'm sorry, sir,'' he said. ''I may have misled you about the status of my shoulder. I still have limited movement and—''

''I'm thinking you're valuable because you've already established rapport with the civilians,'' Jake cut him off. ''But I'll let it be your choice, Bobby. If you don't want to go—''

''Oh, no sir, I *want* to go.'' It was a no-brainer. He wanted to be there, himself, to make sure Colleen stayed safe.

Yes, it would have been easier to toss the entire problem into Admiral Robinson's capable hands and retreat, swiftly and immediately, to California. But Wes would be back in three days. Bobby could handle keeping his distance from Colleen for three days.

Couldn't he?

''Good,'' Jake said. ''I'll get the ball rolling.''

''Thank you, sir.''

''Before you go, Chief, want some unsolicited advice?''

Bobby hesitated. ''I'm not sure, sir.''

The admiral laughed—a rich burst of genuine amusement. ''Wrong answer, Taylor. This is one of those times that you're supposed to 'Aye, aye, sir' me, simply because I'm an admiral and you're not.''

''Aye, aye, sir.''

''Trust your heart, Chief. You've got a good one, and when the time comes, well, I'm confident you'll know what to do.''

''Thank you, sir.''

''See you in a few days. Thanks again for the call.''

Bobby hung up the phone and lay back on his hotel room bed, staring up the ceiling.

When the time comes, you'll know what to do.

He already knew what he had to do.

He had to stay away from Colleen Skelly, who thought—God help them both—that she wanted him.

What did she know? She was ridiculously young. She had no clue how hard it was to sustain a relationship over long distances. She had no idea how difficult it was for *any*one to be involved with a SEAL, let alone someone ridiculously young. She was mistaking her desire for a physical relationship with a man she had a crush on, with her very real need for something more powerful and more permanent.

She said she wanted passion—well, he could give her that. He had no doubt. And maybe, if he were really lucky, she'd be so completely dazzled that she'd fall in love with him.

Yeah, right, *then* where would she be? In love with a man who spent most of his time out of the country with her brother—provided her brother would ever forgive him enough to speak to him again. But the key words there were *out of the country*. Colleen would get tired of *that* fast enough.

Eventually she'd be so tired of being second place in his life that she'd walk away.

And he wouldn't stop her.

But she'd want him to. And even though she was the one who left him, she'd end up hurt.

The last thing he wanted in the world was to leave her hurt.

Follow your heart. He would. Even though it meant killing this relationship before it even started. Even though it was the hardest thing he'd ever done.

* * *

Colleen slid the back door of the truck closed with a resounding bang.

"Okay," she said, as she attached a combination lock that was more to keep the door from bouncing open as they drove into Boston than to deter thieves. "Did someone lock my apartment?"

Kenneth looked blankly at Clark, and Clark looked blankly at Kenneth.

Colleen gave up on them and looked at Bobby, who nodded. "I took care of it," he said.

It was no surprise. He was dependable. Smart. Sexier than a man had the right to be at ten in the morning.

Their eyes met only briefly before he looked away—still it was enough to send a wave of heat through her. Shame. Embarrassment. Mortification. What exactly had she said to him last night? *I want you.* In broad daylight, she couldn't believe her audacity. What had she been thinking?

Still, he was here. He'd shown up bright and early this morning, hot cup of coffee in hand, to help lug all of the boxes of emergency supplies out of her living room and into the Relief Aid truck.

He'd said hardly anything to her. In fact, he'd only said, "Hi," and then got to work with Clark and Kenneth, hauling boxes down the entryway stairs and out to the truck. Bad shoulder or not, he could carry two at once without even breaking a sweat.

Colleen had spent the past ninety minutes analyzing that "Hi," as she'd built wall upon wall of boxes in the back of the truck. He'd sounded happy, hadn't he? Glad to see her? Well, if not glad to see her, he'd sounded neutral. Which was to say that at least he hadn't sounded *un*happy to see her. And that was a good thing.

Wasn't it?

Everything she'd said to him last night echoed in her head and made her stomach churn.

Any minute now they were going to be alone in the truck. Any minute now he was going to give her the friends speech, part two. Not that she'd ever been persistent and/or stupid enough before to have heard a part-two speech. But she had a good imagination. She knew what was coming. He would use the word *flattered* in reference to last night's no-holds-barred, bottom-line statement. He would focus on their differences in age, in background, in everything.

One major difference between them that she already knew was that she was an idiot.

Colleen climbed in behind the wheel and turned the key. Bobby got in beside her, picking her backpack up off the floor and placing it between them on the wide bench seat, like some kind of protective shield or definitive border.

She and her brother Ethan and her sister Peg, both who'd been closest to her in age among the seven Skelly children, had made similar boundaries in the far back seat of their father's Pontiac station wagon. Don't cross this line or else.

"Hey," Clark shouted over the roar of the diesel engine. "Can we bum a ride into Kenmore Square? You're going that way, right?"

"Sure," she said. "Squeeze in."

She felt Bobby tense. And then he moved. Quickly. He opened the passenger-side door, and would have leaped out to let the younger men sit in the middle—no doubt to keep from sitting pressed up against her—but Kenneth was already there, about to climb in.

As Colleen watched, Bobby braced himself and slid down the seat toward her.

She took her pack and set it on the floor, tucked between the seat and her door.

He moved as close as he possibly could without touching her. It was amazing, really, that he could be that close yet have absolutely no physical contact.

He smelled like baby shampoo and fresh laundry with a hint of the coffee that he seemed to drink each morning by the gallon. His hair was back in a ponytail again. She couldn't imagine him letting her braid it later today. She couldn't do it now, not the way they were sitting. And she knew that after Clark and Kenneth got out of the truck, Bobby wasn't going to let her get close enough to braid his hair ever again—not after what she'd said to him last night.

"Sorry," she said, her voice low. "I guess I must have embarrassed you to death last night."

"You scared me to death," he admitted, his voice pitched for her ears only. "Don't get me wrong, Colleen, I'm flattered. I really am. But this is one of those situations where what I want to do is completely different from what I should do. And should's got to win."

She looked up at him and found her face inches from his. A very small number of inches. Possibly two. Possibly fewer. The realization almost knocked what he'd just said out of her mind. Almost.

What he wanted *to do,* he'd said. True, he'd used the word *flattered* as she'd expected, but the rest of what he was saying was…

Colleen stared at that mouth, at those eyes, at the perfect chin and nose that were close enough for her to lean forward, if she wanted to, and kiss.

Oh, she wanted to.

And he'd just all but told her, beneath all those ridiculous *shoulds,* that he wanted her, too. She'd won. She'd *won!*

Look at me, she willed him, but he seemed intent upon reading the truck's odometer. *Kiss me.*

"I spoke to Admiral Robinson, who greenlighted U.S. military protection for your trip," he continued. "He wants me to remain in place as liaison with your group, and, well—" his gaze flicked in her direction "—I agreed. I'm here. I know what's going on. I have to stick around, even though I know you'd rather I go away.''

''Whoa, Bobby.'' She put her hand on his knee. ''I don't *want* you to go anywhere.''

He glanced at her briefly again as he gently took her hand and deposited it back into her own lap. ''The thing is…'' He fixed his gaze on a point outside the truck. ''I can't stay in the, uh—'' he closed his eyes briefly ''—the *capacity* in which you want me to stay.''

She laughed in disbelief. ''But that's crazy!''

He leaned forward to look out the passenger-side door, checking to see why Clark was taking so long to get in. Her roommate's brother was holding on to the door, blue head down, intent upon scraping something off the bottom of his shoe. ''The admiral told me that Wes'll be back in about three days,'' Bobby told her.

Three days. That meant they didn't have a lot of time to—

''Once he's back, it'll be easier for me to, you know, do the right thing. Until then…''

''Do the right thing?'' she repeated, loudly enough that Kenneth looked uncomfortable. ''How could this,'' she gestured between them, ''not be the *right thing* when everything about it feels so perfect?''

Bobby glanced back toward Kenneth and Clark before finally meeting and holding her gaze. ''Please, Colleen, I'm begging you—don't make this more difficult for me than it has to be,'' he said, still softly, and she knew, just like that, that she hadn't won. She'd lost. He wanted her, too, but he was begging her—*begging* her—not to push this attraction that hung between them too far.

He wanted her, but he didn't want her. Not really. Not enough to let what he was feeling take priority over all their differences and all his asinine personal rules.

Colleen felt like crying. Instead she forced a smile. ''Too

bad, Taylor, it would have been amazingly great,'' she told him.

His smile was forced, too. He closed his eyes, as if he couldn't bear looking at her, and shook his head slightly. ''I know,'' he said. ''Believe me, I know.''

When he opened his eyes, he looked at her, briefly meeting her gaze again. He was sitting close—close enough for her to see that his eyes truly were completely, remarkably brown. There were no other flecks of color, no imperfections, no inconsistencies.

But far more hypnotizing than the pure, bottomless color was the brief glimpse of frustration and longing he let her see. Either on purpose or accidentally, it didn't matter which.

It took her breath away.

''I need about three more inches of seat before I can close this door,'' Clark announced. He shifted left in a move reminiscent of a football player's offensive drive, making Kenneth yelp and ramming Bobby tightly against Colleen.

Completely against Colleen. His muscular thigh was wedged against her softer one. He had nowhere to put his shoulder or his arm, and even though he tried to angle himself, that only made it worse. Suddenly she was practically sitting in the man's lap.

''There,'' Clark added with satisfaction as he closed the truck door. ''I'm ready, dudes. Let's go.''

Just drive. Colleen knew the smartest thing to do was to just drive. If traffic was light, it would take about fifteen minutes to reach Kenmore Square. Then Clark and Kenneth would get out, and she and Bobby wouldn't have to touch each other ever again.

She could feel him steaming, radiating heat from the summer day, from the work he'd just done, and he shifted, trying to move away, but he only succeeded in making her aware that they both wore shorts, and that his bare skin was pressed against hers.

She was okay, she told herself. She'd be okay as long as she kept breathing.

Colleen reached forward to put the truck into drive. Raising her arm to hold the steering wheel gave Bobby a little more space—except now his arm was pressed against the side of her breast.

He tried desperately to move away, but there was nowhere for him to go.

"I can't lift my arm enough to put it on the back of the seat," he said in a choked-sounding voice. "I'm sorry."

Colleen couldn't help it. She started to laugh.

And then she did the only thing she could do, given the situation. She threw the truck into Park and turned and kissed him.

It was obviously the last thing he'd expected. She could taste his disbelief. For the briefest moment he tried to pull away, but then she felt him surrender.

And then he kissed her back as desperately and as hungrily as she kissed him.

It was a kiss at least as potent as the one they'd shared in the alley. Did he always kiss like this, with his mouth a strange mix of hard and soft, with a voracious thirst and a feverish intensity, as if she were in danger of having her very life force sucked from her? His hands were in her hair, around her back, holding her in place so that he could claim her more completely. And claim her he did.

Colleen had never been kissed quite so possessively in all her life.

But, oh, she liked it. Very much.

Quiet, easygoing Bobby Taylor kissed with a delirious abandon that was on the verge of out of control.

He pulled her toward him, closer, tugging as if he wanted her on his lap, straddling him. As if he wanted...

"You know, on second thought, Kenneth, we might get to Kenmore faster on the T."

Oh, my *God.*

Colleen pulled back the same instant that Bobby released her.

He was breathing hard and staring at her, with a wild look in his eyes she'd never seen before. Not on him, anyway, the King of Cool.

"This is how you help?" he asked incredulously.

"Yes," she said. She couldn't breathe, either, and having him look at her that way wasn't helping. "I mean, no. I mean—"

"Gee, I'm sorry," Kenneth said brightly. "We've got to be going. Clark, *move* it."

"Clark, don't go anywhere," Colleen ordered, opening the door. "Bobby's going to drive. I'm coming around to sit on the other side."

She got out of the truck's cab, holding onto the door for a second while she waited for the jelly in her legs to turn back to bone.

She could feel Bobby watching her as she crossed around the front of the truck. She saw Clark lean forward, across Kenneth, and say something to him.

"Are you sure, man?" Clark was saying to Bobby as she opened the door.

"Yes," Bobby said with a definiteness that made her want to cry. Clark had no doubt asked if Bobby wanted the two of them to make themselves scarce. But Bobby didn't want them to leave. He didn't want to be alone with Colleen until he absolutely had to.

Well, she'd really messed *that* up.

As Bobby put the truck in gear, she leaned forward and said, across Clark and Kenneth, "I wasn't trying to make it worse for you. That was supposed to be like, I don't know, I guess a...a kind of a kiss goodbye."

He looked at her and it was a look of such total incomprehension, she tried to explain.

"It seemed to me as if we'd just decided that our relationship wasn't going to move beyond the...the, I don't know, platonic, I guess, and I just wanted—" She swore silently—words she'd never say aloud, words she usually didn't even *think*. This wasn't coming out right at all. *Just say it.* What was he going to do? Laugh at her for being so pathetic? "I just wanted to kiss you one last time. Is that so awful?"

"Excuse me," Clark said. "But that was a *platonic* kiss?"

Bobby's hair had come out of his ponytail. She must've done that when she'd wrapped her arms around his neck and kissed him as if there were no tomorrow. As she watched, he tried to gather it up with his right hand—his good arm. He settled for hooking it behind his ears.

"Dude. If *that* was a *platonic* kiss," Clark started, "then I want to see one that's—" Kenneth clapped his hand over his mouth, muffling the rest of his words.

"I'm sorry," Colleen said.

Bobby glanced up from the road and over at her. The mixture of remorse, anger, and whatever those other mysterious emotions were that seemed to glisten in his dark eyes, was going to haunt her dreams. Probably for the rest of her life. "I am, too."

Chapter 9

There were protestors. On the sidewalk. In front of the AIDS Education Center. With signs saying NIMBY. Not In My Back Yard.

Bobby, following Colleen's directions, had taken a detour after letting Clark and Kenneth out near Kenmore Square. Colleen had something to drop at the center—some papers or a file having to do with the ongoing court battle with the neighborhood zoning board.

She'd been filling up the silence in the truck in typical Skelly fashion, by telling Bobby about how she'd gotten involved doing legal work for the center, through a student program at her law school.

Although she'd yet to pass the bar exam, there was such a shortage of lawyers willing to do pro bono work like this—to virtually work for free for desperately cash-poor nonprofit organizations—student volunteers were allowed to do a great deal of the work.

And Colleen had always been ready to step forward and volunteer.

Bobby could remember when she was thirteen—the year he'd first met her. She was just a little kid. A tomboy—with skinned knees and ragged cutoff jeans and badly cut red hair. She was a volunteer even back then, a member of some kind of local environmental club, always going out on neighborhood improvement hikes, which was just a fancy name for cleaning up roadside trash.

Once, he and Wes had had to drive her to the hospital to get stitches and a tetanus shot. During one of her tromps through a particularly nasty area, a rusty nail went right through the cheap soles of her sneakers and into her foot.

It had hurt like hell, and she'd cried—a lot like the way she'd cried the other night. Wiping her tears away fast, so that, with luck, he and Wes wouldn't see.

It had been a bad year for her. And for Wes, too. Bobby had come home with Wes earlier that year—for a funeral. Wes and Colleen's brother, Ethan, had been killed in a head-on with a tree, in a car driven by a classmate with a blood-alcohol level high enough to poison him.

God, that had hurt. Wes had been numb for months after. Colleen had written to Bobby, telling him she'd joined a grief counseling group connected to Mothers Against Drunk Drivers. She'd written to ask Bobby to find a similar support group for Wes, who had loved Ethan best out of all his brothers and sisters, and was hurt the worst by the loss.

Bobby had tried, but Wes didn't want any of it. He ferociously threw himself into training and eventually learned how to laugh again.

"Pull over," Colleen said now.

"There's no place to stop."

"Double park," she ordered him. "I'll get out—you can stay with the truck."

"No way," he said, harshly throwing one of Wes's favorite—although unimaginative and fairly offensive—adjectives between the two words.

She looked at him in wide-eyed surprise. He'd never used that word in front of her before. Ever.

Her look wasn't reproachful, just startled. Still, he felt like a dirtball.

"I beg your pardon," he said stiffly, still angry at her for kissing him after he'd begged her—*begged* her—not to, angry at himself, as well, for kissing her back, "but if you think I'm going to sit here and watch while you face down an angry mob—"

"It's not an angry mob," she countered. "I don't see John Morrison, although you better believe he's behind this."

He had to stop for the light, and she opened the door and slipped down from the cab.

"Colleen!" Disbelief and something else, something darker that lurched in his stomach and spread fingers of ice through his blood, made his voice crack. Several of those signs were made with two-by-fours. Swung as a weapon, they could break a person's skull.

She heard his yelp, he knew she had, but she only waved at him as she moved gracefully across the street.

Fear. That cold dark feeling sliding through his veins was fear.

He'd learned to master his own personal fear. Sky diving, swimming in shark-infested waters, working with explosives that, with one stupid mistake, could tear a man into hamburger. He'd taken hold of that fear and controlled it with the knowledge that he was as highly skilled as a human being could be. He could deal with anything that came along—anything, that is, that was in his control. As for those things outside of his control, he'd developed a zen-like deal with the powers that be. He'd live life to its fullest, and when it was his turn to go, when he no longer had any other options, well then, he'd go—no regrets, no remorse, no panic.

He wasn't, however, without panic when it came to watching Colleen head into danger.

There was a lull in the traffic, so he ran the light, pulling as close to the line of parked cars in front of the building as possible. Putting on his flashers, he left the truck sitting in the street as he ran as fast as he could to intercept Colleen before she reached the protestors

He stopped directly in front of her and made himself as big as possible—a wall that she couldn't get past.

"This," he said tightly, "is *the* last time you will *ever* disobey me."

"Excuse me," she said, her mouth open in outraged disbelief. "Did you just say...*disobey?*"

He'd pushed one of her buttons. He recognized that, but he was too angry, too upset to care. He was losing it, his voice getting louder. "In Tulgeria, you will not *move,* you will not lift a *finger* without my or Wes's permission. Do you understand?"

She laughed at him, right in his face. "Yeah, in your dreams."

"If you're going to act like a *child*—unable to control yourself—"

"What are you going to do?" she countered hotly. "Tie me up?"

"Yes, dammit, if I have to!" Bobby heard himself shouting. He was shouting at her. Bellowing. As loudly as he shouted in mock fury at the SEAL candidates going through BUD/S training back in Coronado. Except there was nothing mock about his fury now.

She wasn't in danger. Not now. He could see the protestors, and up close they were a far-less-dangerous-looking bunch than he'd imagined them to be. There were only eight of them, and six were women—two quite elderly.

But that was moot. She'd completely ignored his warning, and if she did that in Tulgeria, she could end up very dead very fast.

"Go on," she shouted back at him, standing like a boxer on the balls of her feet, as if she were ready to go a few rounds. "Tie me up. I dare you to try!" As if she honestly thought she could actually beat him in a physical fight.

As if she truly believed he would ever actually raise a hand against her or any other woman.

No, he'd never fight her. But there were other ways to win.

Bobby picked her up. He tossed her over his good shoulder, her stomach pressed against him, her head and arms dangling down his back. It was laughably easy to do, but once he got her there, she didn't stay still. She wriggled and kicked and howled and punched ineffectively at his butt and the backs of his legs. She was a big woman, and he wrenched his bad shoulder holding her in place, but it wasn't that that slowed him.

No, what made him falter was the fact that her T-shirt had gapped and he was holding her in place on his shoulder with his hand against the smooth bare skin of her back. He was holding her legs in place—keeping her from kicking him—with a hand against the silkiness of her upper thighs.

He was touching her in places he shouldn't be touching her. Places he'd been dying to touch her for years. But he didn't put her down. He just kept carrying her down the sidewalk, back toward the truck that was double parked in front of the center.

His hair was completely down, loose around his face, and she caught some of it with one of her flailing hands. Caught and yanked, hard enough to make his eyes tear.

"Ouch! God!" That was it. As soon as he got back to his room, he was shaving his head.

"Let! Me! Go!"

"You dared me," he reminded her, swearing again as she gave his hair another pull.

"I didn't think you were man enough to actually do it!"

Oh, ouch. That stung far worse than getting his hair pulled.

"Help!" she shrieked. "Someone *help!* Mrs. O'Hallaran!"

Mrs. who…?

"Excuse me, young man…"

Just like that, Bobby's path to the truck was blocked by the protestors.

One of the elderly women stood directly in front of him now, brandishing her sign as if it were a cross and he were a vampire. "What do you think you're doing?" she asked, narrowing her eyes at him from behind her thick glasses.

Take Back the Night, the sign said. Neighborhood Safety Council.

"He's being a jerk, Mrs. O'Hallaran," Colleen answered for him. "A complete idiotic, stupid, male-chauvinist *jerk.* Put me down, *jerk!*"

"I know this young lady from church," the elderly woman—Mrs. O'Hallaran—told him, her lips pursed in disapproval, "and I'm certain she doesn't deserve the indignity of your roughhousing, sir."

Colleen punched him in the back as she kneed him as hard as she could. She caught him in the stomach, but he knew she'd been aiming much lower. She'd wanted to bring him to his knees. "Put me *down!*"

"Colleen, do you want us to call the police?" one of the two men asked.

She knew these people. And they knew her—by name. From church, the old lady had said. Colleen had never even remotely been in danger.

Somehow that only served to make him even more mad.

She could have told him she knew them, instead of letting him think...

He put her down. She straightened her shirt, hastily pulling it back down over her exposed stomach, giving him a glimpse of her belly button, God help him.

She ran her fingers quickly through her hair, and as she did, she gave him a look and a smile that was just a little too smug, as if she'd won and he'd lost.

He forced himself to stop thinking about her belly button and glared at her. ''This is just some kind of game to you, isn't it?''

''No,'' she said, glaring back, ''this is my life. I'm a woman, not a child, and I don't need to ask *any*one's permission before I 'so much as lift my finger,' thank you very much.''

''So you just do whatever you want. You just walk around, doing whatever you want, *kissing* whoever you want, whenever you want—'' Bobby shut himself up. What the hell did that have to do with this?

Everything.

She'd scared him, yes, by not telling him why she was so confident the protestors didn't pose a threat, and that fear had morphed into anger. And he'd also been angry, sure, that she'd completely ignored his warning.

But, really, most of his anger came from that kiss she'd given him, less than an hour ago, in front of her apartment building.

That incredible kiss that had completely turned him upside down and inside out and...

And made him want far more than he could take.

Worse and worse, now that he'd blurted it out, she knew where his anger had come from, too.

''I'm sorry,'' she said quietly, reaching up to push his hair back from his face.

He stepped away from her, unable to bear the softness

of her touch, praying for a miracle, praying for Wes suddenly to appear. His personal guardian angel, walking down the sidewalk, toward them, with that unmistakable Skelly swagger.

Colleen had mercy on him, and didn't stand there, staring at him with chagrin and pity in her luminous blue-green eyes. God, she was beautiful.

And, God, he was so pathetic.

He'd actually shouted at her. When was the last time he'd raised his voice in genuine anger?

He couldn't remember.

She'd turned back to the protestors and was talking to them now. "Did John Morrison tell you to come down here with these signs?"

They looked at each other.

As Bobby watched, Colleen spoke to them, telling them about the center, reassuring them that it would be an improvement to the neighborhood. This wasn't an abortion clinic. They wouldn't be handing out copious handfuls of free needles or condoms. They would provide HIV testing and counseling. They would provide AIDS education classes and workshops.

She invited them inside, to introduce them to the staff and give them a tour of the facility, while Bobby stayed outside with the truck.

A parking spot opened up down the street, and as he was parallel parking the beast, the truck's phone rang. It was Rene, the coordinator from the Relief Aid office, wondering where they were. She had ten volunteers ready to unpack the truck. Should they wait or should she let them take an early lunch?

Bobby promised that Colleen would call her right back. He was a half a block away from the center when he saw the protestors take their signs and go home. Knowing Colleen, she'd talked half of them into volunteering at the center. The other half had probably donated money to the cause.

She came out and met him halfway. "I don't know why John Morrison is so determined to cause trouble. I guess I should be glad he only sent protestors this time, instead of throwing cinder blocks through the front windows again."

"Again?" Bobby walked her more swiftly toward the truck, wanting her safely inside the cab and out of this wretched neighborhood. "He did that before?"

"Twice," she told him. "Of course, he got neighborhood kids to do the dirty work, so we can't prove he was behind it. You know, I find it a little ironic that the man owns a bar. And his place is not some upscale hangout…it's a dive. People go there to get seriously tanked or to connect with one of the girls from the local 'escort service,' which is really just a euphemism for Hookers R Us. I'm sure Morrison gets a cut of whatever money exchanges hands in his back room, the sleaze, and *we're* a threat to the neighborhood…? What's he afraid of?"

"Where's his bar?" Bobby asked.

She gave him an address that meant nothing to him. But with a map he'd find it easily enough.

He handed her the keys. "Call Rene on the cell phone and tell her you're on your way."

She tried to swallow her surprise. "You're not coming?"

He shook his head, unable to meet her eyes for more than the briefest fraction of a second.

"Oh," she said.

It was the way she said it, as if trying to hide her disappointment that made him try to explain. "I need to take some time to…" What? Hide from her? Yes. Run away? Absolutely. Pray that he'd last another two and a half days until Wes arrived?

"Look, it's all right," she said. "You don't need to—"

"You're driving me crazy," he told her. "Every time I

turn around, I find myself kissing you. I can't seem to be able to stop."

"You're the only one of us who sees that as a bad thing."

"I'm scared to death to be alone with you," he admitted. "I don't trust myself to be able to keep the distance I need to keep."

She didn't step toward him. She didn't move. She didn't say anything. She just looked at him and let him see her wanting him. He had to take a step back to keep himself from taking a step forward, and then another step and another, and pulling her into his arms and...

"I've got to..." he said. "Go..."

He turned away. Turned back.

She still didn't say anything. She just waited. Standing there, wanting him.

It was the middle of the day, on the sidewalk of a busy city street. Did she really think he'd do something as crazy as kiss her?

Ah, God, he wanted to kiss her.

A goodbye kiss. Just one last time. He wanted to do it, to kiss her again, knowing this time that it would, indeed, be the last time.

He wanted—desperately—for her to kiss him the way she'd kissed him in the darkness of the backstreet off Harvard Square. So lightly. So sweetly. So perfectly.

Just one more time like that.

Yeah, like hell he could kiss her just one more time. If he so much as touched her again, they were both going to go up in flames.

"Get in the truck," he somehow managed to tell her. "Please."

For one awful moment he was certain she was going to reach for him. But then she turned and unlocked the door to the truck. "You know, we're going to have to talk about that 'obey' thing,'' she said. ''Because if you don't lighten up, I'm going to recommend that we don't accept your admiral's protection. We don't have to, you know.''

Oh, yes, they did. But Bobby kept his mouth shut. He didn't say another word as she climbed into the truck from the passenger's side, as she slid behind the wheel and started the big engine.

As he watched, she maneuvered the truck onto the street and, with a cloud of exhaust, drove away.

Two and a half more days.

How the hell was he going to survive?

Chapter 10

Colleen cleaned out her refrigerator.

She washed the bathroom floor and checked her e-mail.

She called the center's main office to find out the status of Andrea Barker, who'd been attacked just outside her home. There was no change, she was told. The woman was still in a coma.

By 9:00, Bobby still hadn't called.

By 9:15, Colleen had picked up the phone once or twice, but each time talked herself out of calling his hotel.

Finally, at 9:45, the apartment building front door buzzer rang.

Colleen leaned on the intercom. "Bobby?"

"Uh, no." The male voice that came back was one she didn't know. "Actually, I'm looking for Ashley DeWitt?"

"I'm sorry," Colleen said. "She's not here."

"Look, I drove up from New York. I know she was coming here and… Hold on a sec," the voice said.

There was a long silence, and then a knock directly on her apartment door.

Colleen looked out through the peephole. Brad. Had to be. He was tall and slender, with dark-blond hair and a yacht-club face. She opened the door with the chain still on and gave him a very pointedly raised eyebrow.

"Hi," he said, trying to smile. He looked awful. Like he hadn't slept in about a week. "Sorry, someone was coming out, so I came in."

"You mean, you sneaked in."

He gave up on the smile. "You must be Colleen, Ash's roommate. I'm Brad—the idiot who should be taken out and shot."

Colleen looked into his Paul-Newman-blue eyes and saw his pain. This was a man who was used to getting everything he wanted through his good looks and charisma. He was used to being Mr. Special, to winning, to being envied by half of the world and wanted by the other half.

But he'd blown it, big-time, with Ashley, and right now he hated himself.

She shut the door to remove the chain. When she opened it again, she stepped back to let him inside. He was wearing a dark business suit that was rumpled to the point of ruin— as if he'd had it on during that entire week he hadn't been sleeping.

He needed a shave, too.

"She's really not here," Colleen told him as he followed her into the living room. "She went to visit her aunt on Martha's Vineyard. Don't bother asking, because I don't know the details. Her aunt rents a different house each summer. I think it's in Edgartown this year, but I'm not sure."

"But she *was* here. God, I can smell her perfume." He sat down, heavily, on the sofa, and for one awful moment Colleen was certain that he was going to start to cry.

Somehow he managed not to. If this was an act, he deserved an Oscar.

"Do you know when she'll be back?" he asked.

Colleen shook her head. "No."

"Is this your place or hers?" He was looking around the living room, taking in the watercolors on the walls, the art prints, the batik-patterned curtains, the comfortable, secondhand furniture.

"Most of this stuff is mine," Colleen told him. "Although the curtains are Ashley's. She's a secret flower child, you know. Beneath those designer suits is a woman who's longing to wear tie-dyed T-shirts."

"Did she, uh, tell you what I did?" Brad asked.

"Yup."

He cleared his throat. "Do you think…" He had to start again. "Do you think she'll ever forgive me?"

"No," Colleen said.

Brad nodded. "Yeah," he said. "I don't think she will, either." He stood up. "The ferry to the Vineyard is out of Woods Hole, right?"

"Brad, she went there because she doesn't want to see you. What you did was unconscionable."

"So what do *you* recommend I do?" he asked her. "Give up?" His hands were shaking as if he'd had too much coffee on the drive up from New York. Or as if he were going into withdrawal without Ashley around.

Colleen shook her head. "No," she said. "Don't give up. Don't ever give up." She looked at the telephone—it still wasn't ringing. Bobby wasn't calling. That left only one alternative. She had to call him. Because *she* wasn't going to give up, either.

She followed Brad to the door.

"I quit my job," he told her. "You know, working for her father. If Ashley calls, will you tell her that?"

"If she calls," Colleen said, "I'll tell her you were here. And then, if she asks, I'll tell her what you said. But only if she asks."

"Fair enough."

"What should I tell her if she asks where you are?"

He started down the stairs. "Edgartown. Tell her I'm in Edgartown, too."

Bobby stared at the phone as it rang, knowing it was Colleen on the other end. Had to be. Who else would call him here? Maybe Wes, who had called earlier and left a message.

It rang again.

Bobby quickly did the math, figuring out the time difference.... No, it definitely wasn't Wes. Had to be Colleen.

A third time. Once more and the voice mail system would click on.

He reached for it as it began to ring that final time, silently cursing himself. "Taylor."

"Hi, it's me."

"Yeah," he said. "I figured."

"And yet you picked it up, anyway. How brave of you."

"What's happening?" he asked, trying to pretend that everything was fine, that he hadn't kissed her—again—and then spent the entire afternoon and evening wishing he was kissing her again.

"Nothing," Colleen said. "I was just wondering what you were up to all day."

"This and that." Mostly things he didn't want to tell her. That when he wasn't busy lusting after her, he'd been checking out John Morrison, for one. From what Bobby could tell from the locals, Morrison was mostly pathetic. Although, in his experience, pathetic men could be dangerous, too. Mostly to people they perceived to be weaker than they were. Like women. "Is your door locked?"

Colleen lowered her voice seductively. "Is yours?"

Oh, God. "This isn't a joke, Colleen," he said, working hard to keep his voice even. Calm. It wasn't easy. Inside he was ready to fly off the handle, to shout at her again. "A woman you work with was attacked—"

"Yes, my door is locked," she said. "But if someone really wants in, they can get in, since my windows are all open wide. And don't ask me to close and lock them, because it's hot tonight."

It was. Very hot. Even here in his air-conditioned hotel room.

Funny, but it had seemed nice and cool right up until a few minutes ago. When the phone rang.

He'd showered earlier in an attempt to chill out, but his hair, still down around his shoulders, was starting to stick to his neck again. As soon as he got off the phone with Colleen, he'd put it into a ponytail.

Shoot, maybe he'd take another shower. A nice, freezing-cold one this time.

"Colleen," he said. Despite his attempts to sound calm, there was a tightness to his voice. "Please don't tell me you sleep with your windows unlocked."

She laughed. "All right," she said. "I won't tell you."

Bobby heard himself make a strangled sound.

"You know, if you want me to be really, absolutely safe, you could come over," she told him. "Although, you've got air-conditioning over there, don't you? So you should really ask *me* to come to the hotel. I could take a cab and be there in five minutes."

He managed a word this time. "Colleen…"

"Okay," she said. "Right. Never mind. It's a terrible idea. Forget it. Just forget about the fact that I'm here, sitting on my bed, all alone, and that you're just a short mile away, sitting on yours, presumably also alone. Forget about the fact that kissing you is on my list of the five most wonderful things I've ever done in my life and—"

Oh, man.

"I can't do it," he said, giving up on not trying to sound

as desperate as he felt. "Dammit, even if you *weren't*
Wes's sister, I'm only here for a few more days. That's all
I could give you. I can't handle another long-distance re-
lationship right now. I can't do that to myself."

"I'll take the days," she said. "Day. Make it singular if
you want. Just once. Bobby——"

"I can't do that to you." But oh, sweet heaven, he
wanted to. He *could* be at her place in five minutes. Less.
One kiss, and he'd have her clothes off. Two, and… Oh,
man.

"I want to know what it's like." Her voice was husky,
intimate across the phone line, as if she were whispering
in his ear, her breath hot against him. "Just once. No
strings, Bobby. Come on…"

Yeah, no strings—except for the noose Wes would tie
around his neck when he found out.

Wes, who'd left a message for Bobby on his hotel voice
mail…

"Hey, Bobby! Word is Alpha Squad's heading back to
Little Creek in a few days to assist Admiral Robinson's
Gray Group in Tulgeria as part of some kind of civilian
protection gig. Did you set that up, man? Let me guess.
Leenie dug in her heels, so you called the Jakester. Brilliant
move, my friend. It would be perfect—if Spaceman wasn't
being such a total jerk out here on my end.

"He's making all this noise about finally getting to meet
Colleen. Remember that picture you had of her? It was a
few months ago. I don't know where you got it, but Spaceman saw it and wouldn't stop asking about her. Where does
she go to school? How old is she? Yada-yada-yada, on and
on about her hair, her eyes, her smile. Give me a break!
As if I'd ever let a SEAL within twenty-five feet of her—
not even an officer and alleged gentleman like Spaceman,
no way. Look, I'll call you when we get into Little Creek.
In the meantime, stick close to her, all right? Put the fear

of God or the U.S. Navy into any of those college jerks sniffing around her, trying to get too close. Thanks again for everything, Bobby. I hope your week hasn't been too miserable.''

Miserable wasn't even close. Bobby had left misery behind a long time ago.

"Maybe we should have phone sex," Colleen suggested.

"What?" Bobby dropped the receiver. He moved fast and caught it before it bounced twice. "No!"

She was laughing at him again. "Ah, come on. Where's your sense of adventure, Taylor? What are you wearing? Isn't that the way you're supposed to start?"

"Colleen—"

She lowered her voice. "Don't you want to know what I've got on?"

"No. I have to go now." Bobby closed his eyes and didn't hang up the phone. *Yes.* Oh, man.

"My nightgown," she told him, her voice even softer. Slightly breathy now. Deep and husky, her voice was unbelievable even when she wasn't trying to give him a heart attack. Right now, she was trying, and it was pure sex. "It's white. Cotton." She left long pauses between her words, as if giving him plenty of time to picture her. "Sleeveless. It's got buttons down the front, and the top one fell off a long time ago, leaving it a little…daring, shall we say? It's old—nice and soft and a little worn-out."

He knew that nightgown. He'd seen it hanging on the back of her bathroom door the last time he and Wes had visited. He'd touched it by mistake when he'd come out of the shower, thinking it was his towel. It wasn't. It *was* very soft to the touch.

Her body, beneath it, would be even softer.

"Want me to guess what you're wearing?" she asked.

Bobby couldn't speak.

"A towel," she said. "Just a towel. Because I bet you

just showered. You like to shower at night to cool down before you go to bed, right? If I touched you,'' her voice dropped another notch, ''your skin would be clean and cool and smooth.

''And your hair's down—it's probably still a little damp, too. If I were there, I'd brush it out for you. I'd kneel behind you on the bed and—''

''If you were here,'' Bobby said, interrupting her, his voice rough to his own ears, ''you wouldn't be brushing my hair.''

''What would I be doing?'' she shot back at him.

Images bombarded him. Colleen, flashing him her killer smile just before she lowered her head and took him into her mouth. Colleen, lying back on his bed, hair spread on his pillows, breasts peaked with desire, waiting for him, welcoming him as he came to her. Colleen, head back as she straddled him, as he filled her, hard and fast and deep and—

Reality intervened. Phone sex. Dear sweet heaven. What was she doing to him? Beneath the towel—yes, she was right about the towel he wore around his waist—he was completely aroused.

''What would you be doing? You'd be calling a cab to take you home,'' he told her.

''No, I wouldn't. I'd kiss you,'' she countered, ''and you'd pick me up and carry me to your bed.''

''No, I wouldn't,'' he lied. ''Colleen, I have…I really have to go now. Really.''

''Your towel would drop to the floor,'' she said, and he couldn't make himself hang up the phone, both dreading and dying to hear what she would say next. ''And after you put me down, you'd let me look at you.'' She drew in a breath, and it caught—a soft little gasp that made him ache from wanting her. ''I think you're the most beautiful man I've ever seen.''

He wasn't sure if he wanted to laugh or cry. "I think you're crazy." His voice cracked.

"No. Oh, your shoulders are so wide, and your chest and arms...mmmmm." She made a sound deep in her throat that was so sexy he was sure he was going to die.

Stop this. Now. Somehow he couldn't make his lips form the words.

"And the muscles in your stomach, leading down to..." She made another sound, a sigh, this time. "Do you know how incredibly good you look naked? There's...so *much* of you. I'm a little nervous, but you smile at me, and your eyes are so soft and beautiful, I know you'd never hurt me."

Bobby stood up. His sudden, jerky movement was reflected in the mirror above the dresser, on the other side of the dimly lit room. He looked ridiculous standing there, his towel tenting out in front of him.

He must've made some anguished noise, because she quieted him. "Shhh. It's okay."

But it wasn't. Nothing about this was okay. Still, he couldn't hang up. He couldn't make her stop.

He couldn't stand the sight of himself like that, standing there like some absurd, pathetic clown, and he took the towel off, flinging it across the room. Only now he stood there naked. Naked and aching for someone he couldn't have. Not really.

"After I look at you for a long time..." Her voice was musical. Seductive. He could have listened to her read a phone book and gotten turned on. This was driving him mad. "I unbutton my nightgown. I've got nothing on underneath, nothing at all, and you know it. But you don't rush me. You just sit back and watch. One button at a time.

"Finally, I'm done, but...I'm shy." She was silent for a moment, and when she spoke again, her voice was very small. "I'm afraid you won't...like me." She was serious. She honestly thought—

"Are you kidding? I love your body," Bobby told her. "I dream about you wearing that nightgown. I dream about—"

Oh, my God. What was he doing?

"Oh, tell me," she breathed. "Please, Bobby, tell me what you dream."

"What do you think I dream?" he asked harshly, angry at her, angry at himself, knowing he still wasn't man enough to hang up the phone and end this, even though he knew damn well that he should. "I dream exactly what you're describing right now. You in my bed." His voice caught on his words. "Ready for me."

"I am," she told him. "Ready for you. Completely. You're still watching, so I...I touch myself—where I'm dying for you to touch me."

She made a noise that outdid all of the other noises she'd been making, and Bobby nearly started to cry. Oh, man, he couldn't do this. This was Wes's sister on the other end of this phone. This was wrong.

He turned his back to the mirror, unable to look at his reflection.

"Please," she gasped, "oh, please, tell me what you dream when you dream about me."

Oh, *man.* "Where did you learn to do this?" He had to know.

"I didn't," she said breathlessly. "I'm making it up as I go along. You want to know what I dream about you?"

No. Yes. It didn't matter. She didn't wait for him to answer.

"My fantasy is that the doorbell rings, and you're there when I answer it. You don't say anything. You just come inside and lock the door behind you. You just look at me and I know. This is it. You want me.

"And then you kiss me, and it starts out so slowly, so delicately, but it builds and it grows and it takes over everything—the whole world gets lost in the shadow of this one amazing kiss. You touch me and I touch you, and I love touching you, but I can't get close enough, and somehow you know that, and you make my clothes disappear. And you still kiss me and kiss me, and you don't stop kissing me until I'm on my back on my bed, and you're—" her voice dropped to a whisper "—inside of me."

"That's what I dream," Bobby whispered, too, struggling to breathe. "I dream about being inside you." Hell. He was going to burn in hell for saying that aloud.

Her breath was coming in gasps, too. "I love those dreams," she told him. "It feels *so* good..."

"Yes..."

"Oh, please," she begged. "Tell me more...."

Tell her... When he closed his eyes, he could see Colleen beneath him, beside him, her body straining to meet his, her breasts filling his hands and his mouth, her hair a fragrant curtain around his face, her skin smooth as silk, her mouth soft and wet and delicious, her hips moving in rhythm with his....

But he could tell her none of that. He couldn't even begin to put it into words.

"I dream of touching you," he admitted hoarsely. "Kissing you. Everywhere." It was woefully inadequate, compared to what she'd just described.

But she sighed as if he'd given her the verbal equivalent of the Hope Diamond.

So he tried again, even though he knew he shouldn't. He stood there, listening to himself open his mouth and say things he shouldn't say to his best friend's sister.

"I dream of you on top of me." His voice sounded distant and husky, thick with desire and need. Sexy. Who would have thought he'd be any good at this? "So I can watch your face, Colleen.'' He dragged out her name, taking his time with it, loving the way it felt in his mouth, on his tongue. *Colleen.* ''So I can look into your eyes, your beautiful eyes. Oh, I love looking into your eyes, Colleen, while you...''

''Oh, yes,'' she gasped. ''Oh, Bobby, oh—''

Oh, *man.*

Chapter 11

Just after midnight the phone rang.

Colleen picked it up on the first ring, knowing it was Bobby, knowing that he wasn't calling for a replay of what they'd just done.

Pretended to do.

Sort of.

She didn't bother even to say hello. "Are you okay?"

He'd been so freaked out earlier that she'd made up an excuse to get off the phone, thinking he needed time alone to get his heart and lungs working again.

But now she was wondering if that hadn't been a mistake. Maybe what he'd really needed was to talk.

"I don't know," he answered her. "I'm trying to figure out which level of hell I'm going to be assigned to."

"He's able to make a joke," Colleen said. "Should I take that as a good sign?"

"I wasn't joking. Dammit, Colleen, I can't do that ever again. I can't. I shouldn't have even—"

"All right," she said. "Look, Guilt Man, let it go. I steamrolled over you. You didn't stand a chance. Besides, it's not as if it was real."

"No?" he said. "That's funny, because from this end, it sounded pretty authentic."

"Well, yeah," she said. "Sure. On a certain level it was. But the truth is, your participation was nice, but it wasn't necessary. All I ever really have to do is think about you. If you want to know the truth, this isn't the first time I've let my fantasies of you and me push me over the edge—"

"Oh, my God, don't tell me that!"

"Sorry." Colleen made herself stop talking. She was making this worse, telling him secrets that made her blush when she stopped to think about it. But his feelings of guilt were completely unwarranted.

"I've got to leave," he told her, his voice uncharacteristically unsteady. "I have to get out of here. I've decided—I'm going down to Little Creek early. I'll be back in a few days, with the rest of Alpha Squad."

With Wes.

One step forward, two steps back.

"I'd appreciate it if you didn't go into detail with my brother about—"

"I'm going to tell him that I didn't touch you. Much. But that I wanted to."

"Because it's not like I make a habit of doing that— phone sex, I mean. And since you obviously didn't like it, I'm not going to—"

"No," he interrupted her. "You know, if I'm Guilt Man, then you're Miss Low Self-Esteem. How could you even think I didn't like it? I loved it. Every excruciating minute. You are unbelievably hot, and you completely killed me. If you got one of those 900 numbers, you could make a fortune, but you damn well better not."

"You loved it, but you don't want to do it again?"

Bobby was silent on the other end of the line, and Colleen waited, heart in her throat.

"It's not enough," he finally said.

"Come over," she said, hearing her desire coat her voice. "Please. It's not too late to—"

"I can't."

"I don't understand why not. If you want me, and I want you, *why* can't we get together? Why does this have to be so hard?"

"If we were a pair of rabbits, sure," Bobby said. "It would be simple. But we're not, and it's not. This attraction between us…it's all mixed up with what I want, which is *not* to get involved with someone who lives three thousand miles away from me, and with what I want for you, which is for you to live happily ever after with a good man who loves you, and children if you want them, and a career that makes you jump out of bed with pleasure and excitement every single morning for the rest of your life. And if that's not complicated enough, there's also what I know *Wes* wants for you—which is more than just a man who loves you, but someone who will take care of you, too. Someone who's not in the Teams, someone who's not even in the Navy. Someone who can buy you presents and vacations and houses and cars without having to get a bank loan. Someone who'll *be* there, every morning, without fail."

"He also wants to make sure that I don't have any fun at all, the hypocrite. Making noise about how I have to wait until I'm married, when he's out there getting it on with any and every woman he can."

"He loves you," Bobby told her. "He's scared you'll end up pregnant and hating your life. Abandoned by some loser. Or worse—tied to some loser forever."

"As if I'd sleep with a loser."

Bobby laughed softly. "Yeah, well, I think I might fall into Wes's definition of a loser, so yes, you would."

"Ho," Colleen said. "Who's Mr. Low Self-Esteem now?"

"*Wes's* definition," he said again. "Not necessarily mine."

"Or mine," she countered. "It's definitely not mine."

"So, okay," he told her. "We toss the fact that I want to make love to you for about seventy-two hours straight into that mess of what you want and I want and Wes wants. Boom. What happens upon impact? You get lucky, I get lucky, which would probably be transcendental—no, not probably, *definitely*. So that's great...or is it? Because all I can see, besides the immediate gratification of us both getting off, is a boatload of pain.

"I risk getting too...I don't know, *attached* to someone who lives three thousand miles away from me.

"I risk my relationship with your brother....

"You risk your relationship with your brother....

"You risk losing any opportunities that might be out there of actually meeting someone special, because you're messing around with me."

Maybe you're the special one. Colleen didn't dare say it aloud. He obviously didn't think so.

"I've got a flight into Norfolk that leaves Logan just after 1500 hours," he said quietly. "I'm going into the Relief Aid office in the morning. I've got a meeting set up at 1100 hours to talk about the security we're going to be providing in Tulgeria—and what we expect from your group in terms of following the rules we set up. I figured you'd want to sit in on that."

"Yeah," Colleen said. "I'll be there." And how weird was *that* going to be—meeting his eyes for the first time since they'd...since she'd... She took a deep breath. "I'll borrow a truck, after, and give you a lift to the airport."

"That's okay. I'll take the T." He spoke quickly.

"What, are you afraid I'm going to jump you, right there in the truck, in the airport's short-term parking lot?"

"No," he said. He laughed, but it was grim instead of amused. "I'm afraid I'm going to jump you. From here on in, Colleen, we don't go anywhere alone."

"But—"

"I'm sorry. I don't trust myself around you."

"Bobby—"

"Good night, Colleen."

"Wait," she said, but he'd already hung up.

One step forward, two steps back.

Okay. Okay. She just had to figure out a way to get him alone. Before 1500—3:00 p.m.—tomorrow.

How hard could *that* be?

The Relief Aid office was hushed and quiet when Bobby came in at 1055. The radio—which usually played classic rock at full volume—was off. No one was packing boxes of canned goods and other donations. People stood, talking quietly in small groups.

Rene pushed past him, making a beeline for the ladies' room, head down. She was crying.

What the…?

Bobby looked around, more carefully this time, but Colleen was nowhere in sight.

He saw Susan Fitzgerald, the group's leading volunteer, sitting at the row of desks on the other side of the room. She was on the phone, and as he watched, she hung up. She just sat there, then, rubbing her forehead and her eyes behind her glasses.

"What's going on?" he asked.

"Another quake hit Tulgeria this morning," she told him. "About 2 a.m., our time. I'm not sure how it happened, whether it was from a fire caused by downed power lines or from the actual shock waves, but one of the local terrorist cells had an ammunitions stockpile, and it went up in a big way. The Tulgerian government thought they were under attack and launched a counteroffensive."

Oh, God. Bobby could tell from the look on Susan's face that the worst news was coming. He braced himself.

"St. Christof's—our orphanage—sustained a direct hit from some sort of missile," Susan told him. "We lost at least half of the kids."

Oh, Christ. "Does Colleen know?"

Susan nodded. "She was here when the news came in. But she went home. Her little girl—the one she'd been writing to—was on the list of children who were killed."

Analena. Oh, God. Bobby closed his eyes.

"She was very upset," Susan told him. "Understandably."

He straightened up and started for the door. He knew damn well that Colleen's apartment was the last place he should go, but it was the one place in the world where he absolutely needed to be right now. To hell with his rules.

To hell with everything.

"Bobby," Susan called after him. "She told me you're leaving for Virginia in a few hours. Try to talk her into coming back here when you go. She really shouldn't be alone."

Colleen let the doorbell ring the same way she'd let the phone ring.

She didn't want to talk to anyone, didn't want to see anyone, didn't want to have to try to explain how a little girl she'd never met could have owned such an enormous piece of her heart.

She didn't want to do anything but lie here, on her bed, in her room, with the shades pulled down, and cry over the injustice of a world in which orphanages were bombed during a war that really didn't exist.

Yet, at the same time, the last thing she wanted was to be alone. Back when she was a kid, when her world fell apart and she needed a shoulder to cry on, she'd gone to her brother Ethan. He was closest in age to her—the one Skelly kid who didn't have that infamous knee-jerk temper and that smart-mouthed impatience.

She'd loved him, and he'd died, too. What was it with her…that made the people she loved disappear? She stared up at her ceiling, at the cracks and chips that she'd memorized through too many sleepless nights. She should have learned by now just to stop loving, to stop taking chances. Yeah, like that would ever happen. Maybe she was stupid, but that was one lesson she refused to learn.

Every single day, she fell in love over and over. When she walked past a little girl with a new puppy. When a baby stared at her unblinkingly on the trolley and then smiled, a big, drooly, gummy grin. When she saw an elderly couple out for a stroll, still holding hands. She lost her heart to them all.

Still, just once, she wanted more than to be a witness to other people's happy endings. She wanted to be part of one.

She wanted Bobby.

She didn't care when the doorbell stopped ringing and the phone started up again, knowing it was probably Bobby, and crying even harder because she'd pushed too hard and now he was leaving, too.

Because he didn't want her love, not in any format. Not even quick and easy and free—the way she'd offered it.

She just lay on her bed, head aching and face numb from the hours she'd already cried, but unable to stop.

But then she wasn't alone anymore. She didn't know how he got in. Her door was locked. She hadn't even heard his footsteps on the floor.

It was as if Bobby had just suddenly materialized, next to her bed.

He didn't hesitate, he just lay down right next to her and drew her into his arms. He didn't say a word, he just held her close, cradling her with his entire body.

His shirt was soft against her cheek. He smelled like clean clothes and coffee. The trace of cigarette smoke that usually lingered on his shirt and even in his hair had finally been washed away.

But it was late. If he was going to get to Logan in time to catch his flight to Norfolk... "You have to leave soon," she told him, trying to be strong, wiping her face and lifting her head to look into his eyes.

For a man who could make one mean war face when he wanted to, he had the softest, most gentle eyes. "No." He shook his head slightly. "I don't."

Colleen couldn't help it. Fresh tears welled, and she shook from trying so hard not to cry.

"It's okay," he told her. "Go on and cry. I've got you, sweet. I'm here. I'll be here for as long as you need me."

She clung to him.

And he just held her and held her and held her.

As she fell asleep, still held tightly in his arms, his fingers running gently through her hair, her last thought was to wonder hazily what he was going to say when he found out that she could well need him forever.

Bobby woke up slowly. He knew even before he opened his eyes that, like Dorothy, he wasn't in Kansas anymore. Wherever he was, it wasn't his apartment on the base, and he most certainly wasn't alone.

It came to him in a flash. Massachusetts. Colleen Skelly.

She was lying against him, on top of him, beneath him, her leg thrown across his, his thigh pressed tight between her legs. Her head was on his shoulder, his arms beneath her and around her, the softness of her breasts against his chest, her hand tucked up alongside his neck.

They were both still fully dressed, but Bobby knew with an acceptance of his fate—it was actually quite calming and peaceful, all things considered—that after she awoke, they wouldn't keep their clothes on for long.

He'd had his chance for a clean escape, and he'd blown it. He was here, and there was no way in hell he was going to walk away now.

Wes was just going to have to kill him.

But, damn, it was going to be worth it. Bobby was going to die with a smile on his face.

His hand had slipped up underneath the edge of Colleen's T-shirt, and he took advantage of that, gliding his fingers across the smooth skin of her back, up all the way to the back strap of her bra, down to the waistband of her shorts. Up and back in an unending circle.

Man, he could lie here, just touching her lightly like this, for the rest of his life.

But Colleen stirred, and he waited, still caressing the softness of her skin, feeling her wake up and become as aware of him as he was of her.

She didn't move, didn't pull away from him.

And he didn't stop touching her.

"How long did I sleep?" she finally asked, her voice even huskier than usual.

"I don't know," he admitted. "I fell asleep, too." He glanced at the windows. The light was starting to weaken. "It's probably around 1900—seven o'clock."

"Thank you," she said. "For coming here."

"You want to talk about it?" Bobby asked. "About Analena?"

"No," she said. "Because when I say it out loud, it all sounds so stupid. I mean, what was I thinking? That I was going to bring her here, to live with me? I mean, come on—who was I kidding? I don't have room—look at this place. And I don't have money—I can barely pay my own bills. I couldn't live here without Ashley paying for half of everything. I had to sell my car to stay in law school. And that's *with* the school loans. And how am I supposed to take care of a kid while I'm going to school? I don't have time for an instant family—not now while I'm in law school. I don't have time for a husband, let alone a child. And yet…''

She shook her head. ''When I saw her pictures and read her letters… Oh, Bobby, she was so alive. I didn't even get a chance to know her, but I wanted to—God, I wanted to!''

''If you had met her, you would have fallen completely in love with her.'' He smiled. ''I know you pretty well. And she would've loved you, too. And you would have somehow made it work,'' he told her. ''It wouldn't have been easy, but there are some things you just have to do, you know? So you do it, and it all works out. I'm sorry you won't get that chance with Analena.''

She lifted her head to look at him. ''You don't think I'm being ridiculous?''

''I would never think of you as ridiculous,'' he told her quietly. ''Generous, yes. Warm. Giving. Loving, caring…''

Something shifted. There was a sudden something in her eyes that clued him in to the fact that, like him, she was suddenly acutely, intensely aware of every inch of him that was in contact with every inch of her.

''Sexy as hell,'' he whispered. ''But never ridiculous.''

Her gaze dropped to his mouth. He saw it coming. She was going to kiss him, and his fate would be sealed.

He met her halfway, wanting to take a proactive part in this, wanting to do more than simply be unable to resist the temptation.

Her lips were soft, her mouth almost unbearably sweet. It was a slow, languorous kiss—as if they both knew that from here on in, there was no turning back, no need to rush.

He kissed her again, longer this time, deeper—just in case she had any last, lingering doubts about what was going to happen next.

But before he could kiss her again, she pulled away. There were tears in her eyes.

"I didn't want it to happen this way," she said.

He tried to understand what she was telling him, tried to rein himself in. "Colleen, if you don't want me to stay—"

"No," she said. "I do want you to stay. I want you. Too much. See, I lay awake last night, figuring out ways to get you back here. I was going to make something up, try to trick you into coming here after the meeting and then…"

Comprehension dawned. She'd gotten what she'd wanted. He was here. But at what price? An earthquake and a war. A body count that included people she'd loved.

"No," he told her, not wanting her to believe that. "I would've shown up here sooner or later. Even if I'd gotten on that plane—and I'm not sure I would have been able to—I would've called you from Little Creek tonight. I wouldn't have been able to resist."

She wiped her eyes with the heel of her hands. "Really?"

"The things you do to me with just a telephone… Man, oh, man."

Tears still clung to her eyelashes, and her nose was slightly pink. But she was laughing.

As he held her gaze, he remembered the things she said to him last night and let her see that memory reflected in his eyes. She blushed slightly.

"I've really never done that before," she told him. "I mean, the phone part." She blushed again as she looked away, embarrassed by what she'd just again admitted.

He needed her to know what merely thinking about her—about that—did to him. He pulled her chin back so that she had to look into his eyes, as he answered her with just as much soul-baring honesty. "Maybe someday you'll let me watch."

Someday. The word hung between them. It implied that there was going to be more than just tonight.

"You don't do long-distance relationships," she reminded him.

"No," he corrected her. "I don't *want* to do it that way. I have in the past, and I've hated it. It's so hard to—"

"I don't want to be something that's hard," she told him. "I don't want to be an obligation that turns into something you dread dealing with."

He steeled himself, preparing to pull away from her, out of her arms. "Then maybe I should go, before—"

"Maybe we should just make love and not worry about tomorrow," she countered.

She kissed him, and it was dizzying. He kissed her back hungrily, possessively—all sense of laziness gone. He wanted her, now. He needed her.

Now.

Her hands were in his hair, freeing it completely from the ponytail that had already halfway fallen out. She kissed him even harder, angling her head to give him better access to her mouth—or maybe to give herself better access to *his* mouth.

Could she really do this?

Make love to him tonight and only tonight?

Her legs tightened around his thigh, and he stopped thinking. He kissed her again and again, loving the taste of her, the feel of her in his arms. He reached between them, sliding his hand up under her shirt to fill his hand with her breast.

She pulled back from him to tug at his T-shirt. She wanted it off, and it was easier simply to give up—temporarily—trying to kiss and touch as much of her as he possibly could, and take his shirt off himself. His shoulder was still stiff, and the only way he could get a T-shirt on or off was awkwardly. Painfully. One arm at a time.

Before he even got it off, she'd started on his shorts, her fingers cool against his stomach as she unfastened the button and then the zipper.

She had his shorts halfway down his legs by the time he tossed his shirt onto the floor.

He helped her, kicking his legs free, and then there he was. On her bed in only his briefs, while she was still fully clothed.

He reached for her, intending to rid her of her T-shirt and shorts as efficiently as she'd taken care of his, but she distracted him by kissing him. And then he distracted himself by touching her breasts beneath her shirt, by unfastening her bra and kissing her right through the cotton, by burying his face in the softness of her body.

It wasn't until he tried to push her shirt up over her breasts so that he could see her as well as touch and kiss, that he felt her tense.

And he remembered.

She was self-conscious about her body.

Probably because she wasn't stick thin like the alleged Hollywood ideal.

The hell with that—she was *his* ideal. She was curvaceous. Stacked. Voluptuous. She was perfection.

Man, if he were her, he would walk around in one of those little nonexistent tank tops that were so popular. She should wear one without a bra, and just watch all the men faint as she passed by.

Someday he'd get her one of those. She could wear it here, in the privacy of her room, if she didn't want to wear it in public. Man, he hadn't thought he could get any harder, any hotter, but just the thought of her wearing something like that, just because he liked it—just for him— heated him up another notch.

She would do it, too. After he made her realize that he truly worshiped her body, that he found her unbelievably beautiful and sexy, she would be just as adventurous about that as she was with everything else.

Phone sex. Sweet heaven.

Phone sex was all about words. About saying what he wanted, about saying how he felt.

He hadn't been very good at it—not like Colleen. Unlike her, words weren't his strong suit. But he had to do it again now. He had to use words to reassure her, to let her know just how beautiful he thought she was.

He could do it with body language, with his eyes, with his mouth and his hands. He could show her, by the way he made love to her, but even then, he knew she wouldn't completely believe him.

No, if he wanted to dissolve that edge of tension that tightened her shoulders, he had to do it with words.

Or did he? Maybe he could do a combination of both show *and* tell.

"I think you're spectacular," he told her. "You're incredible and gorgeous and..."

And he was doing this wrong. She wasn't buying any of it.

He touched her, reaching up beneath her shirt to caress her. He had the show part down. He wanted to taste her, and he realized with a flash that instead of trying to make up compliments filled with meaningless adjectives, he should just say what he wanted, say how he felt. He should just open his mouth and speak his very thoughts.

"I want to taste you right here," he told her as he touched her. "I want to feel you in my mouth."

He tugged her shirt up just a little, watching her face, ready to take it even more slowly if she wanted him to. But she didn't tense up, so he drew it up a little more, exposing the underside of her breast, so pale and soft and perfect.

And then he forgot to watch her eyes because there was her nipple, peeking out. He'd been holding his breath, he realized, and he let it out in a rush. "Oh, yeah."

She was already taut with desire, and he lowered his head to do just what he'd described. She made a sound that he liked, a sound that had nothing to do with being self-conscious and everything to do with pleasure.

He drew her shirt up then, up and over her head, and she sat up to help him.

And there she was.

As he pulled back to look at her, he opened his mouth and let his thoughts escape.

Unfortunately, his expression of sincere admiration was one of Wes's favorite, more colorful turns of phrase.

Fortunately, Colleen laughed. She looked at him, looked at the expression he knew was on his face, the pure pleasure he let shine from his eyes.

"You're so beautiful," he breathed. "I've died and gone to heaven."

"Gee," she said, "and I don't even have my pants off."

He grabbed her by the waist of her shorts, flipping her back onto the bed and, as she whooped in surprised laughter, he corrected that.

In five seconds flat she was naked and he was kissing her, touching, loving the feel of all that smooth, perfect skin against him. And when he pulled back to really look at her, there wasn't a bit of tension in the air.

But this talking thing was working so well, why stop?

"Do you know what you do to me?" he asked her as he touched, kissed, explored. He didn't give her time to answer. He just took one of her own exploring hands, and pressed it against him.

"You are *so* sexy, that happens to me every time I see you," he whispered, looking into her eyes to let her see the intense pleasure that shot through him at her touch. "Every time I *think* of you."

She was breathing hard, and he pulled her to him and kissed her again, reaching between them to help her rid him of his briefs.

Her fingers closed around him, and he would have told her how much he liked that, but words failed him, and all he could do was groan.

She seemed to understand and answered him in kind as he slipped his hand between her legs. She was so slick and soft and hot, he could feel himself teetering on the edge of his self-control. He needed a condom. *Now.*

But when he spoke, all he could manage to say was her name.

Again she understood. "Top drawer. Bedside table."

He lunged for it, found it. An unopened, cellophane-wrapped box. He both loved and hated the fact that the box was unopened. Growling with frustration, he tried to rip the damned thing in half.

Colleen took it from his hands and opened it quickly, laughing at the way he fumbled the little wrapped package, getting in the way, touching and kissing him as he tried to cover himself.

Slow down. She'd told him herself that she hadn't had much experience. He didn't want to be too rough, didn't want to hurt her or scare her or...

She pulled him back with her onto the bed in a move that Xena the Warrior Princess would have been in awe of. And she told him, in extremely precise language, exactly what she wanted.

How could he refuse?

Especially when she kissed him, when she lifted her hips and reached between them to find him and guide him and...

He entered her far less gently than he'd intended, but her moan was one of pure pleasure.

"Yes," she told him as he pushed himself even more deeply inside her. "Oh, Bobby, yes..."

He kissed her, touched her, stroked her, murmuring things that he couldn't believe were coming out of his mouth, things that he loved about her body, things he wanted to do to her, things she made him feel—things that made her laugh and gasp and murmur equally sexy things back to him, until he was damn near blind with passion and desire.

Gentle had long-gone right out the window. He was filling her, hard and fast, and she was right there with him, urging him on.

She told him when she began to climax—as if he wouldn't know from the sound of her voice. As if he couldn't feel her shatter around him. Still, he loved that she told him, and her breathless words helped push him over the edge.

And just like that he was flying, his release rocketing through him with so much power and force he had to shout her name, and even that wasn't enough.

He wanted to tell her how she made him feel, about the sheer, crystal perfection of the moment that seemed to surround him, shimmering and wonderful, filling his chest until it was hard to breathe, until he wanted to cry from its pure beauty.

But there were no words that could describe how he felt. To do it justice, he would have to invent a completely new vocabulary.

Bobby realized then that he was lying on top of her, crushing her, completely spent. His shoulder felt as if he'd just been shot all over again—funny, he hadn't felt even a twinge until now and—

Colleen was crying.

"Oh, my God," he said, shifting off her, pulling her so that she was in his arms. "Did I hurt you? Did I...?"

"No!" she said, kissing him. "No, it's just…that was so perfect, it doesn't seem fair. Why should I be so lucky to be able to share something so special with you?"

"I'm sorry," he said, kissing her hair, holding her close. He knew she was thinking about Analena.

"Will you stay with me?" she asked. "All night?"

"I'm right here," he said. "I'm not going anywhere."

"Thank you." Colleen closed her eyes, her head against his chest, her skin still damp from their lovemaking.

Bobby lay naked in Colleen's bed, holding her close, breathing in her sweet scent, desperately trying to fend off the harsh reality that was crashing down around him.

He'd just made love with Colleen Skelly.

No, he'd just had *sex* with Colleen Skelly. He'd just got it on with Wes's little sister. He'd put it to her. Nailed her. Scored. That was the way Wes was going to see it—not sweetly disguised with pretty words like *making love*.

Last night he'd had phone sex with Colleen. Tonight he'd done the real deal.

Just one night, she wanted. Just one time. Just to find out what it would be like.

Would she stick to that? Give him breakfast in the morning, shake his hand and thank him for the fun experience and send him on his way?

Bobby wasn't sure whether to hope so or hope not. He already wanted too much. He wanted— No, he couldn't even think it.

Maybe, if they only made love this once, Wes would understand that it was an attraction so powerful—more powerful than both of them—that couldn't be denied. Bobby tried that on for size, tried to picture Wes's calm acceptance and rational understanding and—

Nah.

Wes was going to kill him. No doubt about that.

Bobby smiled, though, as he ran his hand down Colleen's incredible body. She snuggled against him, turning so that they were spooned together, her back to his front. He tucked his good arm around her, filling his hand with the weight of her breasts.

Oh, man.

Yeah, Wes was going to kill him.

But before he did, Bobby would ask them to put four words on his tombstone: It Was Worth It.

Chapter 12

Colleen woke up alone in her bed.

It was barely even dawn, and her first thought was that she'd dreamed it. All of it. Everything that had happened yesterday and last night—it was all one giant combination nightmare and raging hot fantasy.

But Bobby's T-shirt and briefs were still on her floor. Unless he'd left her apartment wearing only his shorts, he hadn't gone far.

She could smell coffee brewing, and she climbed out of bed.

Muscles she didn't even know existed protested—further proof that last night hadn't been a dream. It was a good ache, combined with a warmth that seemed to spread through her as she remembered Bobby's whispered words as he'd... As they'd...

Who knew that such a taciturn man would be able to express himself so eloquently?

But even more eloquent than his words was the expressiveness of his face, the depth of emotion and expressions of sheer pleasure he didn't try to hide from her as they made love.

They'd made love.

The thought didn't fill her with laughter and song as she'd imagined it would.

Yes, it had been great. Making love to Bobby had been more wonderful than she'd ever dared to dream. More special and soul shattering than she'd imagined. But it didn't begin to make up for the deaths of all those children. Nothing could do that.

She found her robe and pulled it on, sitting back on the edge of the bed, gathering her strength.

She didn't want to leave her room. She wanted to hide here for the rest of the week.

But life went on, and there were things that needed to be done for the children who'd survived. And in order to get them done, there were truths that had to be faced.

There were going to be tears shed when she went into the Relief Aid office. She was also going to have to break the news to the church youth group that had helped raise money for the trip. Those kids had exchanged letters and pictures with the children in Tulgeria. Telling them of the tragedy wasn't going to be easy.

And then there was Bobby.

He had to be faced, too. She'd lied to him. Telling him that she'd be content with only one night. Well, maybe it hadn't been a lie. At the time, she'd talked herself into believing it was possible.

But right now all she felt was foolish. Deceitful. Pathetic. Desperate.

She wanted to make love to him again. And again. And again, and again.

Maybe he wanted her again, too. She'd read—extensively—that men liked sex. Morning, noon and night, according to some sources.

Well, it was morning, and she would never discover whether he was inclined to run away or to stay a little longer unless she stood up and walked out of this room.

She squared her shoulders and did just that. And after a quick pit stop in the bathroom—where she also made sure her hair wasn't making her look too much like the bride of Frankenstein—she went into the kitchen.

Bobby greeted her with a smile and an already-poured cup of coffee. "I hope I didn't wake you," he said, turning back to the stove where both oatmeal and eggs were cooking, "but I didn't have dinner last night, and I woke up pretty hungry."

As if on cue, her stomach growled.

He shot her another smile. "You, too, I guess."

God, he was gorgeous. He'd showered, and he was wearing only his cargo shorts, low on his hips. With his chest bare and his hair down loose around his shoulders, he looked as if he should be adorning the front of one of those romance novels where the kidnapped white girl finds powerful and lasting love with the exotically handsome Indian warrior.

The timer buzzed, and as Colleen watched, the Indian warrior look-alike in her kitchen used her pink-flowered oven mitts to pull something that looked remarkably like a coffee cake out of her oven.

It was. He'd baked a *coffee cake*. From scratch. He smiled at her again as he put it carefully on a cooling rack.

He'd set her kitchen table, too, poured her a glass of cranberry juice. She sat down as he served them both a generous helping of eggs and bowls of oatmeal.

It was delicious. All of it. She wasn't normally a fan of oatmeal, but somehow he'd made it light and flavorful instead of thick and gluey.

"What's on your schedule for today?" he asked, as if he normally sat across from her at breakfast and inquired about her day after a night of hot sex.

She had to think about it. "I have to drop a tuition check at the law school before noon. There's probably going to be some kind of memorial service for—"

She broke off abruptly.

"You okay?" he asked softly, concern in his eyes.

Colleen forced a smile. "Yeah," she told him. "Mostly. It's just…it'll take time." She took a deep breath. They'd been discussing her day. "I'll need to spend some time this afternoon spreading the word about the memorial service. And I should probably go into the Relief Aid office later, too. There's still a lot to do before we leave."

He stopped eating, his fork halfway to his mouth. "You're still planning on going…?" He didn't let her speak. He laughed and answered for her. "Of course you're still planning on going. What was I thinking?" He put down his fork. "Colleen, what do you want me to do? Do you want me to get down on my knees and beg you not to go?"

Before she could answer, he rubbed his forehead and swore. "I take that back," he continued. "I'm sorry. I shouldn't have said that. I'm a little…off balance today."

"Because…we made love last night?" she asked softly.

He looked at her, taking in her makeup-free face, her hair, the thin cotton of her robe that met with a deep vee between her breasts. "Yes," he admitted. "I'm a little nervous about what happens next."

She chose her words carefully. "What do you want to have happen next?"

Bobby shook his head. "I don't think what I want should particularly factor in. I don't even know what I want." He picked up his fork again. "So I'm just going to save my guilt for later and enjoy having breakfast with you—enjoy how beautiful you look in the morning.''

He did just that, eating his eggs and oatmeal as he gazed at her. What he really liked was looking at her breasts—she knew that after last night. But he never just ogled her. Somehow, he managed to look at her inoffensively, respectfully, looking into her eyes as well, looking at her as a whole person, instead of just a female body.

She looked back at him, trying to see him the same way. He was darkly handsome, with bold features that told of his Native American heritage. He was handsome and smart and reliable. He was honest and sincere and funny and kind. And impossibly buff with a body that was at least a two thousand on a scale from one to ten.

''Why aren't you married?'' she asked him. He was also ten years older than she was. It seemed impossible that some smart woman hadn't grabbed him up. Yet, here he was. Eating breakfast in her kitchen after spending the night in her bed. ''Both you and Wes,'' she added, to make the question seem a little less as if she were wondering how to sign up for the role of *wife*.

He paused only slightly as he ate his oatmeal. ''Marriage has never been part of my short-term plan. Wes's either. The responsibility of a wife and a family… It's pretty intense. We've both seen some of the guys really struggle with it.'' He smiled. ''It's also hard to get married when the women you fall in love with don't fall in love with you.'' He laughed softly. ''Harder still when they're married to someone else.''

Colleen's heart was in her throat. ''You're in love with someone who's married…?''

He glanced up at her, a flash of dark eyes. ''No, I was thinking of…a friend.'' He made his voice lighter, teasing. ''Hey, what kind of man do you think I am, anyway? If I could be in love with someone else while I messed around with you...?''

Relief made her giddy. ''Well, I'm in love with Mel Gibson and *I* messed around with you last night.''

He laughed, pushing his plate away from the edge of the table. He'd eaten both the pile of eggs and the mound of oatmeal and now he glanced over at the coffee cake, taking a sip of his cooling coffee.

''Is that really what we did last night?'' Colleen asked him. ''Messed around?'' She leaned forward and felt her robe gap farther open. Bobby's gaze flickered down, and the sudden heat in his eyes made her breathless. *He* may claim not to know what was going to happen next, but *she* did. And it didn't have anything to do with the coffee cake.

''Yeah,'' he said. ''I guess so. Isn't it?''

''I don't know,'' she said honestly. ''I don't have a lot of experience to compare it to. Can I ask you something?''

Bobby laughed again. ''Why do I get the feeling I should brace myself?''

''Maybe you better,'' she said. ''It's kind of a weird question, but it's something I need to know.''

''Oh, man. Okay.'' He put down his mug, held on to the table with both hands.

''Okay.'' Colleen cleared her throat. ''What I want to know is, are you really good in bed?''

Bobby laughed in genuine surprise. ''Wow, I guess not,'' he said. ''I mean, if you have to ask...''

''No,'' she said. ''Don't be dumb. Last night was incredible. We both know that. But what I want to know is if you're some kind of amazing superlover, capable of heating up even the most frigid of women—''

''Whoa,'' he said. ''Colleen, you are so completely the *farthest* thing from frigid that—''

''Yes,'' she said, ''that's what I thought, too, but...''

"But someone told you that you were," he guessed correctly. "Damn!"

"My college boyfriend," she admitted. "Dan. The jerk."

"I feel this overpowering urge to kill him. What did he tell you?"

"It wasn't so much what he said, but more what he implied. He was my first lover," she admitted. "I was crazy about him, but when we—I never managed to— You know. And he quit after the third try. He told me he thought we should just be friends."

"Oh, God." Bobby winced.

"I thought it had to be my fault—that there was something wrong with me." Colleen had never told all of this to anyone. Not even Ashley, who had heard a decidedly watered-down version of the story. "I spent a few years doing the nun thing. And then, about a year and a half ago..." She couldn't believe she was actually telling him this, her very deepest secrets. But she wanted to. She needed him to understand. "I bought this book, a kind of a self-help guide for sexually challenged women—I guess that's a PC term for frigid these days. And I discovered fairly early on that the problem probably wasn't entirely mine."

"So, you haven't—" Bobby was looking at her as if he were trying to see inside her head. "I mean, between last night and the jerk, you haven't...?"

"There's been no one else. Just me and the book," she told him, wishing she could read his mind, too. Was this freaking him out, or did he like the fact that he'd essentially been her first real lover? "Trying desperately to learn how to be normal."

"Yeah, I don't know," Bobby shook his head. "It's probably hopeless. Because I *am* somewhat legendary. And it's a real shame, but if you want to have any kind of satisfying sex life, you're just going to have to spend the rest of your life making love to me.''

Colleen stared at him.

"That was a joke," he said quickly. "I'm kidding. Colleen, last night I didn't do anything special. I mean, it was *all* special, but you were right there with me, the entire time. Except..."

"What?" She searched his face.

"Well, without having been there, it's hard to know for sure, but...my guess is that you were—I don't know—*tense* at the thought of getting naked, and the jerk was a little quick on the trigger. He probably didn't give you time to relax before it was all over. And in my book, that's more his fault than yours."

"He was always telling me he thought I should lose weight," Colleen remembered. "Not in so many words. More like, 'Gee, if you lost ten pounds you'd look great in that shirt.' And, 'Why don't you find out what kind of diet Cindy Crawford is on and try that? Maybe that'll work.' That kind of thing. And you're right, I hated taking off my clothes in front of him."

Bobby just shook his head as he looked at her. God, when he looked at her like that, he made her feel like the most beautiful, most desirable woman in the world.

"I liked taking off my clothes for you," she told him softly, and the heat in his eyes got even more intense.

"I'm glad," he whispered. "Because I liked it, too."

Time hung as she gazed into his eyes, as she lost herself in the warmth of his soul. He still wanted her. He wanted more, too.

But then he looked away, as if he were afraid of where that look was taking them.

Guilt, he'd said before, and she knew if she didn't act quickly, he was going to walk out of her apartment and never come back. At least not without a chaperone.

"Don't move," she told him. She pushed her chair back from the table and stood up. "Stay right there."

She was down the hall and in the bedroom in a flash, grabbing what she needed.

Bobby turned to look at her as she came back into the kitchen, still sitting where she'd commanded him to stay. He quickly looked away from her, and she realized that her robe had slipped open even farther—the deep vee now extending all the way down to her waist.

She didn't adjust it, didn't pull it closed. She just moved closer, so that she was standing beside him. Close enough that she was invading his personal space.

But she didn't touch him. Didn't even speak. She just waited for him to turn his head and look up at her.

He did just that. Looked at her. Looked away again. Swallowed hard. "Colleen, I think—"

Now was definitely not the time for thinking. She sat on his lap, straddling him, forcing him to look at her. Her robe was completely open now, the belt having slipped its loose knot.

He was breathing hard—and trying not to. "I thought we decided this was going to be a one-night thing. Just to get it out of our systems."

"Am I out of your system?" she asked, knowing full well that she wasn't.

"No, and if I'm not careful, you're going to get under my skin," he admitted. "Colleen, please don't do this to me. I spent the night convincing myself that as long as we didn't make love again, I'd be okay. And I know it's a long shot, but even your brother might understand that something like this could happen between us—once."

His words would have swayed her—if he hadn't touched her, his hands on her thighs, just lightly, as if he couldn't stop himself, couldn't resist.

She shrugged her robe off her shoulders, and it fell to

the floor behind her, and then there she was. Naked, in the middle of her kitchen, with daylight streaming in the windows, warming her skin, bathing her in golden sunshine.

Bobby's breath caught in his throat, and as he looked at her, she felt beautiful. She saw herself as if through his eyes, and she *was* beautiful.

It felt unbelievably good.

She shifted forward, pressing herself against him, feeling him, large and hard beneath his shorts. No doubt about it. He still desired her. He made a sound, low in his throat. And then he kissed her.

His passion took her breath away. It was as if he'd suddenly exploded, as if he needed to kiss her to stay alive, to touch as much of her as he possibly could or else he'd die. His hands were everywhere, his mouth everywhere else.

It was intoxicating, addicting—to be wanted so desperately. It was almost as good as being loved.

She reached between them and unfastened his shorts as she kissed him, taking him into her hand, pressing him against her, letting him know that she wanted him desperately, too.

She still held the condom she'd taken from her bedroom, although the little paper wrapper was tightly scrunched in her hand. She tore it open, and Bobby took it from her, covering himself and then—oh, yes!—he was inside of her.

He tried, but he couldn't keep from groaning aloud, from holding her close and burying his face in her breasts. She moved slowly, stroking him with her body, filling herself completely with him.

Making love to Bobby Taylor was just as amazing in the daylight as it had been last night.

She pulled back slightly to watch him as she moved on top of him, and he held her gaze, his eyes sparking with heat beneath heavy eyelids.

She couldn't get enough of him. She pressed against him,

wanting more, wanting forever, wanting him never to leave, wanting this moment never to end.

Wanting him to fall in love with her as completely as she'd fallen in love with him.

Oh, no, what had she done? She didn't love him. She couldn't love him.

She must've made some kind of noise of frustration and despair, because he stood up. He just lifted himself from the chair, with her in his arms, with his body still buried deeply inside her. Even deeper now that he was standing.

Colleen gasped, and then had to laugh as he carried her—effortlessly, as if she weighed nothing—across the room, her arms around his neck, her legs now locked around his waist. He didn't stop until he'd pressed her up against the wall by the refrigerator. The muscles in his chest and arms stood out, making him seem twice as big. Making her seem almost small.

Still… ''Don't hurt your shoulder,'' she told him.

''What shoulder?'' he asked hoarsely, and kissed her.

It was so impossibly macho, the way he held her, her back against the wall, the way he possessed her so completely with his mouth. His kiss was far from gentle, and that was so exciting, it was almost ridiculous. Still, there was no denying that she found it sexy beyond belief, to be pinned here, like this, as he kissed her so proprietarily.

She was expecting more roughness, expecting sex that was hard and fast and wild, but instead he began a long, lingering withdrawal, then an equally deliberate penetration that filled her maddeningly slowly.

It was sexier than she could have dreamed possible—this man holding her like this, taking his time to take her completely. On his terms.

He kissed her face, her throat, her neck as if he owned her.

And he did.

She felt her release begin before she was ready for it, before he'd even begun that slow, sensuous slide inside of her for the third heart-stopping time. She didn't want this to end, and she tried to stop herself, to hold him still for a moment, but she was powerless.

And she didn't mind.

Because she loved what he was doing. She loved his strength and his power, loved the fact that he was watching her with such intense desire in his eyes.

Loved that even though he was pretending to be in control, she knew that he wasn't. She owned him as absolutely as he owned her. More.

She held his gaze while she melted around him, while she flew apart from wave upon endless wave of pleasure.

He smiled, a fierce, proud, fairly obnoxious male grin. It would have made her roll her eyes a day or so ago, but today she found she loved it. She loved being pure female to his pure male. It didn't mean she was weaker. On the contrary. She was his perfect match, his opposite, his equal.

"I loved watching you do that last night," he murmured as he kissed her again. "And I love it even more this morning."

He was her first real lover in the physical sense of the word. And he was also the first man she'd ever known who liked who she was—not merely the promise of the person he could mold her into becoming.

"I want to do that to you again," he said. "Right now. Is that okay with you?"

Colleen just laughed.

He lifted her away from the wall and carried her down the hall to her bedroom, kicking the door shut behind them.

Chapter 13

Bobby was floating.

He was in that place halfway between sleep and consciousness, his face buried in Colleen's sweet-smelling hair, his body still cradled between the softness of her legs.

So much for willpower. So much for resolving not to make love to her again. So much for hoping that Wes would forgive him for one little, single transgression.

Ah, but how he'd loved making love to her again. And no red-blooded, heterosexual man could've resisted the temptation of Colleen Skelly, naked, on his lap.

And really, deep in his heart, he knew it didn't matter. Wes was going to go ape over the fact that Bobby had slept with Colleen. Realistically, how much worse could it be to have slept with her twice? What difference could it possibly make?

To Wes? None. Probably. Hopefully.

But the difference it made to Bobby was enormous.

As enormous as the difference between heaven and hell.

Speaking of heaven, he was still inside of her, he realized, forcing himself to return to earth. Falling asleep immediately after sex was not a smart move when using condoms as the sole method of birth control. Because condoms could leak.

He should have pulled out of her twenty minutes ago. And for that matter, he should also have been aware that he was still on top of her, crushing her.

But she hadn't protested. In fact, she still had her arms tightly wrapped around him.

He shifted his weight, pulling away from her and reaching between them to...

Uh-oh. "Uh, Colleen...?" Bobby sat up, suddenly fully, painfully, completely alert.

She stirred, stretched, sexy as hell, a distraction even now, when he should have been completely nondistractible.

"Don't leave yet, Bobby," she murmured, still half asleep. "Stay for a while, please?"

"Colleen, I think you better get up and take a shower." Condoms sometimes did something far worse than leak. "The condom broke."

She laughed as she opened her eyes. "Yeah, right." Her smile faded as she looked into his eyes. "Oh, no, you're not kidding are you?" She sat up.

Silently he shook his head.

Twenty minutes. She'd been lying on her back for at least twenty minutes after he'd unknowingly sent his sperm deep inside of her.

Was it possible she already was pregnant? How quickly could that happen?

Quickly. Instantly—if the timing was right. In a flash, a heartbeat.

In a burst of latex.

"Well," Colleen said, her eyes wide. "These past few days have certainly been full of first-time experiences for me, and this one's no exception. What do we do about this? Is a shower really going to help at this point?''

Count on Colleen not to have hysterics. Count on her to be upbeat and positive and proactive in trying to correct what could well be the biggest, most life-changing mistake either one of them had ever made.

"Probably not," he admitted. "Although…"

"I'll take one right now, if you want me to. I'm not sure where I am in my cycle. I've never really been regular." She was sitting there, unconcerned about her nakedness, looking to him for suggestions and options and his opinion, with complete and total trust.

That kind of trust was an incredible turn-on, and he felt his body respond. How could that be? The disbelief and cold fear that had surged through his veins at his discovery should have brought about an opposite physical response— more similar to the response one had from swimming in an icy lake.

And his mental reaction to a broken condom should have included not even *thinking* about having sex for the next three weeks without shaking with fear.

But there was Colleen, sitting next to him on her bed, all bare breasts and blue-green eyes and quiet, steadfast trust.

Right now she needed him to be honest about this. There was no quick fix. No miraculous solutions. "I think it's probably too late to do anything but pray."

She nodded. "That's what I figured."

"I'm sorry."

"It's not your fault," she said.

He shook his head. "It's not about fault—it's about responsibility, and I *am* responsible."

"Well, I am, too. You were coerced."

Bobby smiled, thinking of the way she'd sat on his lap, intending to seduce him, wondering if she had even the slightest clue that his last hope of resisting her had vanished the moment she'd appeared in the kitchen wearing only that robe.

"Yeah," he said, "as if that was really hard for you to do."

She smiled back at him, and his world shrank to a few square feet of her bed—to her eyes, her smile, her face and body.

"It was another one of those first-time endeavors for me," she told him. "I was proud of myself for not chickening out."

"You're a natural." His voice was husky. "But that's not what I meant. I meant it wasn't hard because when it comes to you, I'm a total pushover."

Just looking into her eyes like this made him want her again—badly enough that he wasn't able to keep it any kind of secret.

Colleen noticed and laughed softly. "Well now, *there's* an interesting, hedonistic approach to this problem." She crawled toward him, across the bed, her eyes gleaming and her smile filled with the very devil. "You know that old saying, when a door closes, somewhere a window opens? Well, how about, when a condom breaks, a window of opportunity opens?"

Bobby knew that wasn't necessarily true. He knew he should stop her, back away, stand up, do *any*thing but just sit there and wait for her to...

Too late.

Colleen sat up. "Oh, my God."

"Mmph," Bobby said, facedown on her bed.

It was 11:05. Fifty-five minutes to make it to her law school in the Fenway from Cambridge. Without a car, on the T. "Oh, my *God!*"

Bobby lifted his head. "What's the—"

She was already scrambling for the bathroom, climbing directly over him, inadvertently pushing his face back into the pillow.

"Mmmrph!"

"Sorry!"

Thanking the Lord—not for the first time today—that Ashley was still on the Vineyard, Colleen flew down the hallway stark naked and slapped on the bathroom light. One glance in the mirror and she knew she had to take a shower. Her hair was wild. And her face still held the satisfied look of a woman who'd kept her lover very busy all morning long.

She couldn't do anything about the face, but the hair she could fix with a fast shower.

She turned on the shower and climbed in before the water had a chance to heat up, singing a few operatic high notes in an attempt to counteract the cold.

"You all right?" Bobby had followed her in. Of course, she'd left the bathroom door wide open.

She peeked out from behind the shower curtain. He was as naked as she was, standing in front of the commode with that utterly masculine, wide-spread stance.

"I have to take a tuition check to my law school," she told him, quickly rinsing her hair, loving the fact that he was comfortable enough to be in the bathroom with her, feeling as if they'd crossed some kind of invisible, unspoken line. They were lovers now—not just two people who had given in to temptation and made love once. "The deadline's noon today, and like a total idiot, I pushed it off until the last minute." Literally.

"I'll come with you."

She turned off the water and pulled back the curtain, grabbing her towel and drying herself as she rushed back to her bedroom. "I can't wait for you," she called to him.

"I'm literally forty-five seconds from walking out the door."

She stepped into clean underwear and pulled her blue dress—easy and loose fitting, perfect for days she was running dangerously late—over her head, even though she was still damp. Feet into sandals.

"What do you know," Bobby said. "A woman who can go wheels-up in less than three minutes." He laughed. "I feel as if I should drop to my knees right now and propose."

Colleen was reaching for the tuition check, which she'd hidden for safety in her complete collection of Shakespeare, and she didn't freeze, didn't faint, didn't gasp and spin to face him, didn't let herself react at all. He was teasing. He didn't have a clue that his lightly spoken words had sent a rush of excitement and longing through her that was so powerful she'd nearly fallen over.

Oh, she was so stupid. She actually wanted…the impossible. As if he really would marry her. He'd told her just hours ago that staying single was part of his career plan.

She made herself smile as she turned around, as she stuffed the check and a book to read into her knapsack, as she checked to make sure she had money for the T, then zipped her bag closed.

"It's going to take me at least a few hours," she said, brushing out her wet hair as she headed back into the kitchen to grab an apple from the fridge. He followed her, followed her to the door, still naked and completely comfortable about that.

Colleen could picture him trailing her all the way out to the street. Wouldn't *that* give little old Mrs. Gibaldi who lived downstairs an eyeful?

She turned to face him. "I'd love it if you were still here when I got back. Wearing just that." She kissed him, lowered her voice, gave him a smile designed to let him read her very thoughts. "And if you think getting dressed in three minutes is fast, just wait and see how long it takes me to get *un*dressed."

He kissed her, pulling her into his arms, his hand coming up to cup her breast as if he couldn't not touch her.

Colleen felt herself start to dissolve into a puddle of heat. What would happen if she didn't get that check to the office on time?

She might have to pay a penalty. Or she'd get bumped from the admissions list. There were so many students wait-listed, the admissions office could afford to play hardball. Reluctantly, she pulled back from Bobby.

"I'll hurry," she told him.

"Good," he said, still touching her, looking at her as if she were the one standing naked in front of him, lowering his head to kiss her breast before he let her go. "I'll be here."

He wasn't in love with her. He was in lust.

And that was exactly what she'd wanted, she reminded herself as she ran down the stairs.

Except, now that she had it, it wasn't enough.

The phone was ringing as Bobby stepped out of Colleen's shower.

He grabbed a towel and wrapped it around himself as he went dripping into the kitchen. "'Lo?"

He heard the sound of an open phone line, as if someone were there but silent. Then, "Bobby?"

It was Wes. No, not just "It was Wes," but "Oh, God, it was Wes."

"Hey!" Bobby said, trying desperately to sound nor-mal—as opposed to sounding like a man who was standing nearly naked not two feet from the spot where mere hours earlier he'd pinned Wes's sister to the wall as they'd... As he'd...

"What are you doing at Colleen's place?" Wes sounded funny. Or maybe Bobby just imagined it. Guilt had a way of doing that—making everyone sound suspicious.

"Um…" Bobby said. He was going to have to tell Wes about what was going on between him and Colleen, but the last thing he wanted was to break the news over the telephone. Still, he wasn't going to lie. Not to Wes. Never to Wes.

Fortunately—as usual—Wes didn't particularly want his question answered. "You are one hard man to get hold of," he continued. "I called your hotel room last night—late—and you were either AWOL or otherwise occupied, you lucky son of a bitch."

"Well," Bobby said, "yeah." He wasn't sure if Wes particularly cared what he was agreeing to, but the truth was he'd been AWOL, otherwise occupied *and* a lucky son of a bitch. "Where are you?"

"Little Creek. You need to get your butt down here, bro, pronto. We've got a meeting with Admiral Robinson at 1900 hours. There's a flight out of Logan that leaves in just under two hours. If you scramble, you can make it, easy. There'll be a ticket there, waiting for you."

Scrambling meant leaving before Colleen got back. Bobby looked at the kitchen clock and swore. Best-case scenario didn't get her back here for another ninety minutes. That's if she had no holdups—if the T ran like a dream.

"I'm not sure I can make it," he told Wes.

"Sure you can. Tell Colleen to drive you to the airport."

"Oh," Bobby said. Now, here was a secret he could divulge with no pain. "No. She can't—she sold her car."

"What?"

"She's been doing all this charity work—pro bono legal stuff, you know? Along with her usual volunteer work,"

Bobby told Wes. "She sold the Mustang because she was having trouble making ends meet."

Wes swore loudly. "I can't believe she sold that car. I would've lent her money. Why didn't she ask me for money?"

"I offered to do the same. She didn't want it from either one of us."

"That's stupid. Let me talk to the stupid girl, will you?"

"Actually," Bobby told Wes, "it's not stupid at all." And she wasn't a girl. She was a woman. A gorgeous, vibrant, independent, sexy woman. "She wants to do this her way. By herself. And then when she graduates, and passes the bar exam, she'll know—*she* did this. Herself. I don't blame her, man."

"Yeah, yeah, right, just put her on the phone."

Bobby took a deep breath, praying that Wes wouldn't think it was weird—him being in Colleen's apartment when she wasn't home. "She's not here. She had to go over to the law school for something and—"

"Leave her a message then. Tell her to call me." Wes rattled off a phone number that Bobby dutifully wrote on a scrap of paper. But he then folded it up, intending to put it into his pocket as soon as he was wearing something that had a pocket. No way was he going to risk Colleen calling Wes back before he himself had a chance to speak to him.

"Put it in gear," Wes ordered. "You're needed for this meeting. If Colleen's going to be stupid and insist on going to Tulgeria, we need to do this right. If you get down here tonight, we'll get started planning this op a full twelve hours earlier than if we wait to have this meeting in the morning. I want those extra twelve hours. This is Colleen's safety—her *life*—we're talking about here."

"I'm there," Bobby said. "I'll be on that flight."

"Thank you. Hey, I missed you, man. How's the shoulder? You been taking it easy?"

Not exactly, considering that for the past twenty-four hours he'd been engaged in almost nonstop, highly gymnastic sex. With Wes's precious little sister. Oh, God.

"I'm feeling much better," Bobby told the man who was the best friend he'd ever had in his life. Not a lie—it was true. The shoulder was still stiff and sore, and he still couldn't reach over his head without pain, but he was, without a doubt, feeling exceptionally good this morning.

Physically.

Emotionally was an entirely different story. Guilt. Doubt. Anxiety.

"Hey," Bobby said. "Will you do me a favor and pick me up in Norfolk alone? There's something we need to talk about."

"Uh-oh," Wes said. "Sounds heavy. You all right? God—you didn't get some girl pregnant did you? I didn't even know you were seeing anyone since you and Kyra split."

"I didn't get anyone..." Bobby started to deny, but then cut himself off. Oh, Lord, it was possible that he had indeed gotten Colleen pregnant just this morning. The thought still made him weak in the knees. "Just meet my flight, okay?"

"Ho," Wes said. "No way can you make hints that something dire is going down and then not tell me what the—"

"I'll tell you later," Bobby said, and hung up the phone.

Chapter 14

When Colleen got home, Clark and Kenneth were sitting in her living room, playing cards.

"Hey," Clark said. "Where's your TV?"

"I don't have a TV," she told him. "What are you doing here? Is Ashley back?"

"Nah. Mr. Platonic called us," Clark answered. "He didn't want you coming home to an empty apartment."

"He had to go someplace called Little Creek," Kenneth volunteered. "He left a note on your bed. I didn't let Clark read it."

Bobby had gone to Little Creek. He'd finally run away, leaving the two stooges behind as baby-sitters.

"Thanks," she said. "I'm home now. You don't have to hang here."

"We don't mind," Clark said. "You actually have food in your kitchen and—"

"Please, I need you to go," Colleen told them. "I'm sorry." She had no idea what Bobby had written in that note that was in her bedroom. She couldn't deal with reading it while they were in her living room.

And she couldn't deal with not reading it another second longer.

"It's cool," Clark said. "I was betting we wouldn't get the warmest welcome, since you're one of those liberated, I-can-take-care-of-myself babes and—"

She heard the door close as Kenneth dragged Clark out.

Colleen took her backpack into her bedroom. Bobby had cleaned up the room. And made the bed, too. And left a note, right on her pillow.

"I got a call and had to run," it said in bold block letters—an attempt by someone with messy penmanship to write clearly. "Heading to Little Creek—to a meeting I can't miss. I'm sorry (more than I can say!) that I couldn't stick around to kiss you goodbye properly, but this is what it's like—being part of Alpha Squad. When I have to go, I go, whether I want to or not."

He'd then written something that he'd crossed out. Try as she might, Colleen couldn't see beneath the scribbled pen to the letters below. The first word looked as if it might be *maybe*. But she couldn't read the rest.

"Stay safe!" he wrote, both words underlined twice. "I'll call you from Little Creek." He'd signed it "Bobby." Not "Love, Bobby." Not "Passionately yours, Bobby." Just "Bobby."

Colleen lay back on her bed, trying not to overanalyze his note, wishing he hadn't had to go, trying not to wonder if he were ever coming back.

He'd come back if she were pregnant. Maybe she should wish she actually was. He'd insist that she marry him and...

The thought made her sit up, shocked at herself. What a terrible thing to wish for. She didn't want to be an obligation. A lifelong responsibility. A permanent mistake.

She wanted him to come back here because he liked

being with her. And yes, okay—because he liked making love to her. She wasn't going to pretend their relationship wasn't based mostly on sex. Great sex. Incredible sex.

She knew that he liked making love to her. And so she would see him again, Colleen told herself. And when he called from Little Creek—if he called—she'd make herself sound relaxed. As if she wasn't a bundle of anxiety. As if she had no doubt that he would be back in her bed in a matter of a day or two. And as if her world wouldn't end if he didn't come back.

The phone rang, and she rolled to the edge of her bed, lying on her stomach to look at the caller ID box, hoping… *Yes.* It was Bobby. Had to be. The area code and exchange was from Little Creek. She knew those numbers well—Wes had been stationed there when he'd first joined the Navy. Back before he'd even met Bobby Taylor.

Bobby must've just arrived, and he was calling her first thing. Maybe this wasn't just about sex for him….

Colleen picked up the phone, keeping her voice light, even though her heart was in her throat. "Too bad you had to leave. I spent the entire T ride imagining all the different ways we were going to make love again this afternoon."

The words that came out of the phone were deafening and colorful. The voice wasn't Bobby's. It was her brother's. "I don't know who you think I am, Colleen, but you better tell me who you thought you were talking to so that I can kill him."

"Wes," she said weakly. Oh, no!

"This is great. This is just great. Just what I want to hear coming out of the mouth of my little sister."

Her temper sparked. "Excuse me, I'm *not* little. I haven't been little for a long time. I'm twenty-three years old, thank you very much, and yes, you want to know the truth? I'm in a relationship that's intensely physical and *enormously* satisfying. I spent last night and most of the morning having wild sex.''

Wes shouted. "Oh, my *God!* Don't tell me that! I don't want to hear that!''

"If I were Sean or…or…'' She didn't want to say Ethan. Mentioning their dead brother was like stomping with both feet on one of Wes's more sensitive buttons. "Or *Frank* you'd be *happy* for me!''

"Frank's a *priest!*''

"You know what I mean," Colleen countered. "If I were one of the guys in Alpha Squad, and I told you I just got lucky, you'd be slapping me on the back and congratulating me. I don't see the difference—''

"The difference is you're a girl!''

"No," she said, tightly. "I'm a *woman*. Maybe that's the basis of your relationship problems, Wes. Maybe until you stop seeing women as *girls,* until you treat them as *equals*—''

"Yeah, thanks a million, Dr. Freud. Like you even have a half a clue about my *problems*.'' He swore.

"I know you're unhappy," she said softly. "And angry almost all the time. I think you've got some unresolved issues that you've really got to deal with before—''

He refused to follow her out of this argument and into a more personal, private discussion. "Damn straight I've got unresolved issues—and they're all about this jackass you've been letting take advantage of you. You probably think he loves you, right? Is that what he told you?''

"No," Colleen said, stung by his implications. "As a matter of fact he hasn't. He likes me, though. And he respects me—which is more than I can say about *you*.''

"What, is he some geeky lawyer?''

"That's not your business." Colleen closed her eyes. She couldn't let herself get mad and tell him it was Bobby. If Bobby wanted to tell him, fine. But her brother wasn't going to hear it first from her. No way. "Look, I have to go. You know, paint myself with body oil," she lied just to annoy him. "Get ready for tonight."

It got the response she'd expected, through gritted teeth. "Col*leen!*"

"I'm glad you're back safely."

"Wait," he said. "I'm calling for a reason."

"No kidding? A reason besides sibling harassment?"

"Yeah. I have to go pick up Bobby at the airport, but before I leave, I need info on your contacts in the Tulgerian government. Admiral Robinson is going to run a quick check on everyone involved." Wes paused. "Didn't you get my message to call me?" he asked. "When I spoke to Bobby just before noon, I told him to leave a message for you and—"

Silence.

Big, long silence.

Colleen could almost hear the wheels in Wes's head turning as he put two and two together.

Colleen had spent—in her own words—"most of the morning having wild sex" with her mysterious lover.

Her brother had spoken to Bobby earlier. In Colleen's apartment. Just before noon. As in the "just before noon" that occurred at the very end of a morning filled with wild sex.

"Tell me I'm wrong," Wes said very, very quietly— never a good sign. "Tell me it's not Bobby Taylor. Tell me my best friend didn't betray me."

Colleen couldn't keep quiet at that. "*Betray* you? Oh, my God, Wesley, that's absurd. What's between me and Bobby has nothing to do with you at all!"

"I'm right?" Wes lost it. "I *am* right! How could he *do* that, that son of a—I'm gonna kill him!"

Oh, *damn!* "Wes! Listen to me! It was *my* fault. I—"

But her brother had already hung up.

Oh, dear Lord, this was going to be bad. Wes was going to pick up Bobby from the airport and...

Colleen checked her caller-ID box and tried to call Wes back.

The flight to Norfolk was just long enough to set Bobby completely on edge. He'd had enough time to buy a book at the airport store, but he stared at the words on the page, unable to concentrate on the bestselling story.

What was he going to say to Wes?

"So, hey, nice to see you. Yeah, Cambridge was great. I liked it a lot—especially when I was having sex with your sister."

Oh, man.

Thinking about his impending conversation with Wes was making him feel edgy and unsettled.

Thinking about Colleen was making him crazy.

A glance at his watch told him that she had surely come back to her apartment by now.

If he hadn't left, she'd be naked, just as she'd promised, and he'd be buried deep inside of her and—

He shifted in his seat. Coach wasn't built for someone his size, and his knees were already pressed against the back of the seat in front of him. He was already uncomfortable as hell—thinking of Colleen wasn't going to help.

But as Bobby closed his eyes, he couldn't help but think of her.

It was probably good that he'd had to leave. If it had been left up to him, he never would have left. He would have just stayed there forever, in Colleen's bedroom, waiting for her to come and make love to him.

She had cast a spell over him, and he couldn't resist her. All she had to do was smile, and he was putty in her hands.

This way the spell was broken. Wasn't it? God, he hoped so. It would be just his luck to fall for another woman who didn't love him. Even better luck to fall for a woman who clearly only saw him as a sexual plaything. If he wasn't careful, his heart was going to get trashed.

Bobby tried to focus again on his book, tried to banish the image of Colleen, her eyes filled with laughter as she leaned forward to kiss him, as she pressed her body against him, as their legs tangled and...

Help.

He wanted her with every breath.

God, why couldn't he have felt this way about Kyra?

Because even back then, he was in love with Colleen.

Man, where had *that* thought come from? Love. God. This was already way too complicated without screwing it up by putting love into the picture.

In a matter of minutes Bobby was going to be hip deep in a conversation with Wes that he was dreading with every ounce of his being. And Wes was going to warn him away from Colleen. *Don't go near her anymore.* He could hear the words already.

If he were smart, he'd heed his friend.

If he weren't smart, if he kept thinking with his body instead of his brain, he was going to get in too deep. Before he even blinked, he would find himself in a long-distance relationship, God help him. And then it would be a year from now, and he'd be on the phone with Colleen again, having to tell her—again—that he wasn't going to make it out for the weekend, and she would tell him that was okay—again—but in truth, he'd know that she was trying not to cry.

He didn't want to make her cry—but that didn't mean he was in love with her.

And the fact that he wanted to be with her constantly, the fact that he missed her desperately even now, mere hours after having been in bed with her, well, that was just his body's healthy response to great sex. It was natural, having had some, to want more.

Bobby squeezed his eyes shut. Oh, God, he wanted more.

It wouldn't be too hard to talk Colleen into giving a bicoastal relationship a try. She was adventurous and she liked him. And, of course, he'd never had a long-distance relationship with someone who liked phone sex....

Bobby felt himself start to smile. Yeah, who was he kidding? Pretending he had any choice at all? Pretending that he wasn't going to spend every waking hour working on ways to get back to Cambridge to see Colleen. The truth was, unless she flat-out refused to see him again, he was going to be raking up the frequent flyer miles, big-time.

He was already in too deep.

And, jeez, if Colleen were pregnant...

Oh, hell. As the plane approached the runway for a landing, Bobby tried to imagine Wes's reaction to *that* news.

"Hey, man! Not only did I do the nasty with your sister more times than I can remember, but the condom broke and I probably knocked her up, ruining her dreams of finishing law school, condemning her to a life with a husband she doesn't particularly love, who isn't even around all that often, anyway. And how was your week?"

Bobby came off the plane the way he'd gotten on. With no luggage, wearing the same cargo shorts and shirt he'd worn over to Colleen's nearly a full twenty-four hours ago.

Not that he'd been wearing them for that entire time. On the contrary.

As he came out of the walkway that connected the plane to the terminal, he scanned the crowd, searching for Wes's familiar face.

And then, there he was. Wes Skelly. He was leaning against the wall, arms crossed in front of his chest, looking more like a biker than a chief in the elite U.S. Navy SEALs.

He was wearing baggy green cargo pants with lots of pockets and a white tank top that showed off his tan and revealed the barbwire tattoo on his upper arm. His hair was long and messy. The longer it got, the lighter it looked as it was bleached by the sun, as the reddish highlights were brought out.

Bobby and Wes had been virtually inseparable for nearly eleven years—even though they'd hated each other's guts at the outset of BUD/S training, when they'd been assigned together as swim buddies. That was something not many people knew. But Wes had earned Bobby's respect through the grueling training sessions—the same way Bobby earned Wes's. It took them a while, but once they recognized that they were made from the same unbreakable fabric, they'd started working together.

It was a case of one plus one equaling three. As a team, they were unstoppable. And so they became allies.

And when Wes's little brother Ethan had died, they'd taken their partnership a step forward and become friends. Real friends. Over the past decade that bond had strengthened to the point where it seemed indestructible.

But years of working with explosives had taught Bobby that indestructibility was a myth. There was no such thing.

And there was a very good chance that over the next few minutes, he was going to destroy ten years of friendship with just a few small words.

I slept with your sister.

"Hey," Wes said in greeting. "You look tired."

Bobby shrugged. "I'm okay. You?"

Wes pushed himself off the wall. "Please tell me you didn't check your luggage."

They started walking, following the stream of humanity away from the gate. "I didn't. I didn't bring it. There was no time to go back to the hotel. I just left it there."

"Bummer," Wes said. "Paying for a room when you don't even sleep there. That's pretty stupid."

"Yeah," Bobby agreed. *I slept with your sister.* How the hell was he supposed to say something like that? Just blurting it out seemed wrong, and yet there was no real graceful way to lead into a topic like that.

"How's Colleen?" Wes asked.

"She's—" Bobby hesitated. Beautiful. Heart-stoppingly sexy. Great in bed. Maybe carrying his baby. "Doing okay. Selling the car wasn't easy for her."

"Jeez, I can't believe she did that. Her Mustang… That's like selling a child."

"She got a good price. The buyer was a collector, and she was sure he'd take good care of it."

Wes pushed open a door that led toward the parking area. "Still…"

"Did Jake fill you in on the situation with this Tulgerian orphanage Colleen and her friends have been trying to move out of the war zone?" Bobby asked.

"Yeah, apparently the building was hit in some kind of skirmish a day or so ago. The place was pretty much destroyed, and the survivors were brought to a local hospital—but the place doesn't even have electricity or running water. We'll be going out there pretty much upon insertion in Tulgeria to move the kids back into the city."

"Good," Bobby said. "I'm glad the admiral's made that a priority. Wes, there's something you need to know…" The easy stuff first. "The little girl that Colleen was hoping to adopt was killed in that air strike."

Wes stared at him in the shadowy dimness of the parking garage. "Adopt?" he said, loud enough that his voice echoed. "She was going to *adopt* a kid? What, was she nuts? She's just a kid herself."

"No, she's not," Bobby said quietly. "She's a grown woman. And—" okay, here's where he had to say it "—I should know. I've…uh, been with her, Wes. Colleen. And me.''

Wes stopped walking. "Aw, come on, Bobby, you can do better than that. You've *been* with her? You could say *slept with,* but of course you didn't sleep much, did you, dirt wad? How about…" He used the crudest possible expression. "Yeah, that works. *That's* what you did, huh? You *son* of a…" He was shouting now.

Bobby stood there. Stunned. Wes had known. Somehow he'd already known. And Bobby had been too self-absorbed to realize it.

"I sent you there to take *care* of her," Wes continued. "And *this* is what you do? How could you do this to me?"

"It wasn't about you," Bobby tried to explain. "It was about me and— Wes, I've been crazy about her for years."

"Oh, this is fine," Wes had gone beyond full volume and into overload. "For *years,* and this is the first I hear of it? What, were you just waiting for a chance to get her alone, scumbag?" He shoved Bobby, both hands against his chest.

Bobby let himself get shoved. He could have planted himself and absorbed it, but he didn't. "No. Believe me I tried to stay away from her, but…I couldn't do it. As weird as it sounds, she got it into her head that she wanted me, and hell, you know how she gets. I didn't stand a chance."

Wes was in his face. "You're ten years older than she is, and you're trying to tell me that *she* seduced *you?*"

"It's not that simple. You've got to believe—" Bobby cut himself off. "Look, you're right. It *is* my fault. I'm more experienced. She offered, and God, I wanted her, and I didn't do the right thing. For *you.*"

"Ho, *that's* great!" Wes was pacing now, a tightly wound bundle of energy, ready to blow. "Meaning you did the right thing for Colleen, is that what you're saying? How right is it, Bobby, that she sits around and waits for you, that she'll have half a life, pretending to be okay, but really terrified, just waiting to get word that something's happened to you? And say you *don't* get your head blown off on some op. Say you do make it home. Retire from the teams in a few years. Then what? How right is it that she's the one who makes more money working as a lawyer? How's she supposed to have kids? Put 'em in day care? That's just great.''

Kids…day care… Bobby was shocked. "Wes, whoa, I'm not going to marry her.''

Wes stopped short, turning to stare with his mouth open, as if Bobby'd just announced his plan to detonate a nuclear warhead over New York City. "Then what the hell were you doing with her, dirt wad?''

Bobby shook his head, laughing slightly in disbelief. "Come on. She's twenty-three. She's just experimenting. She doesn't want to *marry* me.''

In hindsight, it was probably the laughter that did it.

Wes exploded. "You *son* of a bitch. You went into this with completely dishonorable intentions!'' He put his shoulder into a solid right jab, right in Bobby's face.

Bobby saw it coming. He didn't dodge it or block it. He just stood there, turning his head only slightly to deflect the force of the blow. It rocked him back on his heels, but he quickly regained his balance.

"Wes, don't do this.'' There were people around. Getting into and out of cars. It wouldn't be long until someone called a security team, who would call the police, who would haul their butts to jail.

Wes hit him again, harder this time, an ear-ringing blow, and again Bobby didn't defend himself.

"Fight back, you bastard,'' Wes snarled.

"No.''

"*Damn* it!'' Wes launched himself at Bobby, hitting him in the exact place that would knock him over, take him down onto his back on the concrete. After years of training together, Wes knew his weak spots well.

"Hey!" The shout echoed against the concrete ceilings and walls as Wes hit him with a flurry of punches. "Hey, Skelly, back off!"

The voice belonged to Lucky O'Donlon. An SUV pulled up with a screech of tires, and O'Donlon and Crash Hawken were suddenly there, in the airport parking garage, pulling Wes off him.

And the three newest members of Alpha Squad, Rio Rosetti, Mike Lee and Thomas King climbed out of the back, helping Bobby to his feet.

"You okay, Chief?" Rio asked, his Italian street-punk attitude completely overridden by wide-eyed concern. The kid had some kind of hero worship thing going for both Bobby and Wes. If this little altercation didn't cure him of it forever, Bobby didn't know what would.

He nodded at Rio. "Yeah." His nose was bleeding. By some miracle it wasn't broken. It should have been. Wes had hit him hard enough.

"Here, Chief." Mike handed him a handkerchief.

"Thanks."

Crash and Lucky were both holding on tightly to Wes, who was sputtering—and ready to go another round if they released him.

"You want to explain what this is all about?" Crash was the senior officer present. He rarely used his officer voice—he rarely spoke at all—but when he did, he was obeyed instantly. To put it mildly.

But Wes wouldn't have listened to the president of the United States at this moment, and Bobby didn't want to explain any of this to anyone. "No, sir," he said stiffly, politely. "With all due respect, sir…"

"We got a call from your sister, Skelly," Lucky O'Donlon said. "She was adamant we follow you down here to the airport. She said she had good reason to believe you were going to try to kick the hell out of Taylor, here, and she didn't want either of you guys to get arrested.''

''Did she say *why* I was going to kick the hell out of Taylor?'' Wes asked. ''Did she tell you what that *good reason* was?''

It was obvious she hadn't.

Bobby took a step toward Wes. ''What we were discussing is not public information. Show some respect to your sister.''

Wes laughed in his face, looked up at Crash and Lucky. ''You guys know what this *friend* of mine did?''

Bobby got large. ''This is between you and me, Skelly. So help me God, if you breathe a single word of—''

Wes breathed four words. He told them all, quite loudly, in the foulest possible language what Bobby had done with his sister. ''Apparently, she's doing some *experimenting* these days. All you have to do is go to Cambridge, Massachusetts, and look her up. Colleen Skelly. She's probably in the phone book. Anyone else want to give her a go?''

Wes Skelly was a dead man.

Bobby jumped on top of him with a roar. The hell with the fact that Wes was being held in place by Lucky and Crash. The hell with everything. No one had the right to talk about Colleen that way. *No* one.

He hit Wes in the face, harder than he'd ever hit him before, then he tackled him. It was enough to take them down to the concrete—Lucky and Crash with them.

He hit Wes again, wanting to make him bleed.

The other SEALs were on top of him then, grabbing his back and his arms, trying to pull him away, but they couldn't stop him. No one could stop him. Bobby yanked Wes up by the front of his shirt as he got to his feet, hauling him away from Lucky and Crash, with Rio, Mike and Thomas clinging to him like monkeys.

He pulled back his arm, ready to throw another brain-shaking punch when another voice, a new voice, rang out.

"Stop this. *Right. Now.*"

It was the senior chief.

Another truck had pulled up.

Bobby froze, and that was all the other SEALs needed. Lucky and Crash pulled Wes out of his grip and safely out of range, and then, God, Senior Chief Harvard Becker was there, standing in between him and Wes.

"Thank you for coming, Senior," Crash said quietly. He looked at Bobby. "I answered the phone when Colleen called. She didn't say as much, but I correctly guessed the cause of the, uh, tension between you and Skelly. I anticipated that the senior's presence would be helpful."

Wes's nose was broken, and as Bobby watched—not without some grim satisfaction—he leaned forward slightly, his face averted as he bled onto the concrete floor.

Lucky stepped closer to Harvard. He was speaking to him quietly, no doubt filling him in. Telling him that Bobby slept with Wes's sister.

God, this was so unfair to Colleen. She was going to Tulgeria with this very group of men. Who would all look at her differently, knowing that she and Bobby had...

Damn it, why couldn't Wes have agreed to talk this problem out...privately? Why had he turned this into a fist fight and, as a result, made Bobby's intimate relationship with Colleen public knowledge?

"So what do you want to do?" Harvard asked, hands on his hips as he looked from Bobby to Wes, his shaved head gleaming in the dim garage light. "You children want to move this somewhere so you can continue to beat the hell out of each other? Or you want to pretend to be grown-ups for a change and try working this out with a conversation?"

"Colleen doesn't sleep around," Bobby said, looking at Wes, willing him to meet his gaze. But Wes didn't look up, so he turned back to Harvard. "If he implies that again, Senior—or anything else even remotely disrespectful—I'll rip his head off." He used Wes's favorite adjective for emphasis.

Harvard nodded, his dark eyes narrowing slightly as he looked at Bobby. "Okay." He turned to Wes. "You hear that, Chief Skelly? Do you understand what this man is saying to you?"

"Yeah," Wes answered sullenly. "He'll rip my head off." He added his favorite adjective, too. "Let him try."

"No," Harvard said. "Those are the *words* he used, but the actual semantics—what he really means by saying those words—is that he cares a great deal for your sister. You fools are on the same side here. So what's it going to be? Talk or fight?"

"Talk," Bobby said.

"There's nothing to say," Wes countered. "Except from now on he better stay the hell away from her. If he so much as *talks* to her again, I'll rip *his* head off."

"Even if I wanted to do that," Bobby said quietly, "which I don't, I couldn't. I've got to talk to her again. There's more that you need to know, Skelly, but I'm not going to talk about it here in front of everyone."

Wes looked up, finally meeting Bobby's gaze, horror in his eyes. "Oh, my God," he said. "You got her pregnant."

"All right," Harvard commanded. "Let's take this someplace private. Taylor, in my truck. Rosetti, take Chief Skelly's keys, drive him to the base and escort him to my office. On the double."

"You're going to have to marry her."

Bobby sat back in his chair, his breath all but knocked out of him. "What? Wes, that's insane."

Wes Skelly sat across the table from him in the conference room on base that Harvard had appropriated and made into a temporary office. He was still furious. Bobby had never seen him stay so angry for such a long time.

It was possible Wes was going to be angry at Bobby forever.

He leaned forward now, glaring. "What's *insane* is for you to go all the way to Cambridge to *help* me and end up messing around with my sister. What's *insane* is that we're even having this conversation in the first place—that you couldn't keep your pants zipped. You got yourself into this situation. You play the game—you pay when you lose. And you lost big-time, buddy, when that condom broke."

"And I'm willing to take responsibility if necessary—"

"If necessary?" Wes laughed. "*Now* who's insane? You really think Colleen's going to marry you if she *has* to? No way. Not Colleen. She's too stubborn, too much of an idealist. No, you have to go back to Boston tomorrow morning. First thing. And make her think you *want* to marry her. Get her to say yes *now*—before she does one of those home tests. Otherwise, she's going to be knocked up and refusing to take your phone calls. And boy, won't *that* be fun."

Bobby shook his head. It was aching, and his face was throbbing where Wes's fists had connected with it—which was just about everywhere. He suspected Wes's nose hurt far worse; yet, both of their physical pain combined was nothing compared to the apprehension that was starting to churn in his stomach. Ask Colleen to marry him. God.

"She's not going to agree to marry me. She wanted a fling, not a lifetime commitment."

"Well, too bad for her," Wes countered.

"Wes, she deserves—" Bobby rubbed his forehead and just said it "—she deserves better than me."

"Damn straight she does," Wes agreed. "I wanted her to marry a lawyer or a doctor. I didn't want this for her—to be a Navy wife, like my mother." He swore. "I wanted her to hook up with someone rich, not some poor, dumb Navy chief who'll have to work double shifts to buy her a washer and dryer. Damn, if she's going to marry Navy, she should at least have been smart enough to pick an officer.''

This wasn't a surprise. Wes had voiced his wishes for Colleen often enough in the past. The surprise came from how bad Bobby felt hearing this. ''I wanted that for her, too,'' he told Wes quietly.

''Here's what you do,'' Wes told him. ''You go to Colleen's and you tell her we had a fight. You tell her that I wanted you to stay the hell away from her. You tell her that you told me that you wouldn't—that you want to marry her. And you tell her that I flat-out forbid it.'' He laughed, but there wasn't any humor in it. ''She'll agree to marry you then.''

''She's not going to ruin her life just to tick you off,'' Bobby argued.

''Wanna bet?'' Wes stood up. ''After the meeting I'll get you a seat on the next flight back to Boston.''

''Are you ever going to forgive me?'' Bobby asked.

''No.'' Wes didn't turn around as he went out the door.

Chapter 15

Colleen came home from the Tulgerian children's memorial service at St. Margaret's to find Ashley home and no new messages on the answering machine. Bobby had called last night, while she was at a Relief Aid meeting, so at least she knew he'd survived his altercation with her brother. Still, she was dying to speak to him.

Dying to be with him again.

"Any calls?" she called to Ashley, who was in her room.

"No."

"When did you get back?" Colleen asked, going to her roommate's bedroom door and finding her...*packing?*

"I'm not back," Ashley said, wiping her eyes and her nose with her sleeve. She had been crying but she forced an overly bright smile. "I'm only here temporarily and I'm not telling you where I'm going because you might tell someone."

Colleen sighed. "I guess Brad found you."

"I guess you would be the person who told him where I was...?"

"I'm sorry, but he seemed sincerely broken up over your disappearing act."

"You mean broken up over losing his chances to inherit my share of DeWitt and Klein," Ashley countered, savagely throwing clothes into the open suitcase on her bed. "How could you even *think* I'd consider getting back together with him? My father hired him to be my husband, and he went along with it! Some things are unforgivable."

"People change when they fall in love."

"Not *that* much." She emptied her entire drawer of underwear into the suitcase. "I figured out how to get my father off my back. I'm dropping out of law school."

What? Colleen took another step into the room. "Ashley—"

"I'm going to go to bartending school and get a job dancing in some exotic bar like the women in that video we rented before I left for New York."

Colleen laughed in surprise. She quickly stopped when Ashley shot her a dark look.

"You don't think I'd be any good at it?"

"No," Colleen protested. "No, I think you'd be great. It's just... Isn't it a little late in your childhood to start sporting the career equivalent of—" she thought of Clark. "—of blue hair?"

"It's never too late," Ashley said. "And my father deserves all the blue hair—symbolic or other—that he gets." She closed her suitcase, locked it. "Look, I'm going to send for the rest of my things. And I'll pay my share of the rent until you find a new roommate."

"I don't want a new roommate!" Colleen followed her into the living room. "You're my best friend. I can't believe you're so mad at me that you're leaving!"

Ashley set her suitcase down. "I'm not leaving because I'm mad at you," she said. "I'm not really mad at you at all. I just...I did a lot of thinking, and... Colleen, I have to get out of here. Boston's too close to my father in New York. And you know, maybe Clark's right. Maybe I should go to one of those survival training schools. Learn to swim with sharks. See if I can grow a backbone—although I suspect it's a little late for that.''

''You have a *great* backbone.''

''No, *you* have a great backbone. I'm really good at borrowing yours when I need it,'' Ashley countered. She pushed her hair back from her face, attempting to put several escaped tendrils neatly back into place. ''I have to do this, Colleen. I've got a cab waiting....''

Colleen hugged her friend. ''Call me,'' she said, pulling back to look into Ashley's face. Her friend's normally perfect complexion was sallow, and she had dark circles beneath her eyes. This Brad thing had truly damaged her. ''Whenever you get where you're going, when you've had a little more time to think about this—call me, Ash. You can always change your mind and come back. But if you don't—well, I'll come out to visit and cheer while you dance on the bar.''

Ashley smiled even though her eyes filled with tears. ''See, everything's okay with you. Why couldn't *you* be my father?''

Colleen had teared up, too, but she still had to laugh. ''Aside from the obvious biological problems, I'm not ready to be anyone's parent. I'm having a tough enough time right now keeping my own life straightened out.''

And yet, she could well be pregnant. Right now. Right this moment, a baby could be sparking to life inside her. In nine months she could be someone's mother. Someone very small who looked an awful lot like Bobby Taylor.

And somehow that thought wasn't quite so terrifying as she'd expected it to be.

She heard an echo of Bobby's deep voice, soft and rumbly, close to her ear. *There are some things you just have to do, you know? So you do it, and it all works out.*

If she were pregnant, despite what she'd just told Ashley, she would make it work out. Somehow.

She gave her friend one more hug. "You liked law school," she told Ashley. "Don't cut off your nose to spite your face."

"Maybe I'll go back some day—anonymously."

"That'll look good on your diploma—Anonymous DeWitt."

"The lawyer with blue hair." Ashley smiled back at Colleen, wiping her eyes again before dragging her suitcase to the door.

The door buzzer rang.

"That's probably the cab driver," Ashley said, "wondering if I sneaked out the back door."

Colleen pushed the button for the intercom. "She'll be right down."

"Actually, I was hoping to come up." The voice over the ancient speaker was crackly but unmistakable, and Colleen's heart leaped.

Bobby.

"I thought you were the cab driver," she told him, leaning close to the microphone.

"You're not going anywhere, are you?" Did he sound worried? She hoped so.

"No," she said. "The cab's Ashley's."

She buzzed him into the lobby as Ashley opened the apartment door. From the sound of his footsteps, he took the stairs two at a time, and then there he was. Carrying *flowers?*

He was. He had what looked like a garden in his arms— an outrageous mix of lilies and daisies and big, bold, crazy-looking flowers for which she didn't know the names. He thrust them toward her as he quickly took the suitcase from Ashley's hands. "Let me get that for you."

"No, you don't need to—" But he was already down the stairs. Ashley looked helplessly at Colleen. "See? No backbone."

"Call me," Colleen said, and then Ashley was gone.

Leaving Colleen face-to-face with the flowers that Bobby had brought. For *her*.

She had to smile. It was silly and sweet and a complete surprise. She left the door ajar and went into the kitchen to find a vase. She was filling it with water when Bobby returned.

He looked nice, as if he'd taken special care with his appearance. He was wearing Dockers instead of his usual jeans, a polo shirt with a collar in a muted shade of green. His hair was neatly braided. Someone had helped him with that.

"Sorry I didn't call you last night. The meeting didn't end until well after midnight. And then I was up early, catching a flight back here."

He was nervous. She could see it in his eyes, in the tension in his shoulders—but only because she knew him so very well. Anyone else would see a completely relaxed, easygoing man, standing in her kitchen, dwarfing the refrigerator.

"Thanks for the flowers," she said. "I love them."

He smiled. "Good. I didn't think you were the roses type, and they, well, they reminded me of you."

"What?" she said. "Big and flashy?"

His smile widened. "Yeah."

Colleen laughed as she turned to give him a disbelieving look. Their eyes met and held, and just like that the heat was back, full force.

"I missed you," she whispered.

"I missed you, too."

"Kinda hard for you to take off my clothes when you're way over there."

He yanked his gaze away, cleared his throat. "Yeah, well. Hmmm. I think we need to talk before…" He cleared his throat. "You want to go out, take a walk? Get some coffee?"

She put the flowers into the water. "You're afraid if we stay here, we won't be able to keep from getting naked."

"Yes," he said. "Yes, I am."

Colleen laughed, opening the refrigerator. "How about we take a glass of iced tea to the roof?"

"Am I going to get the urge to jump you there?"

"Absolutely," she said as she poured the tea. "But unless you're an exhibitionist, you won't. There's a taller building right behind this one. There are about three floors of apartments that have a bird's-eye view of this roof."

She gave him one of the glasses and a kiss.

His mouth was soft and warm and wonderful, his body so solid and strong, and she felt herself melt against him.

She looked up at him. "You sure you don't want to…?"

"Roof," he said. "Please?"

Colleen led the way, up the main staircase, through the exit door and out into the bright sunshine. A long-departed former tenant had built a sundeck, complete with large pots of dirt in which she and Ashley had planted flowers last May. It wasn't luxurious, but it was a far cry from the peeling tar paper on the neighboring buildings' roofs.

There was even a bench, placed strategically in the shade provided by the larger building next door.

Colleen sat down. Bobby sat, too—about as far away from her as he could manage.

"So I guess I should ask about my brother," she said. "Is he in intensive care?"

"No." Bobby looked down into his iced tea. "We *did* fight, though."

She knew. She could see the shadows of bruises on his face. "It must've been awful," she said quietly.

He turned to gaze at her, and her heart moved up into her throat. He had such a way of looking at her, as if he could see inside her head, inside her very heart and soul, as if he saw her completely, as a whole, unique, special person.

"Marry me."

Colleen nearly dropped her glass. *What?*

But she'd heard him correctly. He reached into his pocket and took out a jeweler's box. A *ring* box. He opened it and handed it to her—it was a diamond in a gorgeously simple setting, perfect for accenting the size of the stone. Which was enormous. It had to have cost him three months' pay.

She couldn't breathe. She couldn't speak. She couldn't move. Bobby Taylor wanted to marry her.

"Please," he said quietly. "I should have said, *please* marry me."

The sky was remarkably blue, and the air was fresh and sweet. On the street below, a woman shouted for someone named Lenny. A car horn honked. A bus roared past.

Bobby Taylor wanted to *marry* her.

And yes, *yes,* she wanted to marry him, too. *Marry* him! The thought was dizzying, terrifying, but it came with a burst of happiness that was so strong, she laughed aloud.

Colleen looked up at him then, into the almost palpable warmth of his eyes. He was waiting for her answer.

But she was waiting, too, she realized. This was where he would tell her that he loved her.

Except he didn't. He didn't say anything. He just sat there, watching her, slightly nervous, slightly...detached? As if he were waiting for her to say no.

Colleen looked hard into his eyes. He was sitting there, waiting, as if he expected her to turn him down.

As if he didn't really want her to marry him.

As if...

Her happiness fizzled, and she handed him the ring box. "Wes put you up to this, didn't he?" She saw the truth in his eyes. Oh, no, she was right. "Oh, Bobby."

"I'm not going to lie to you," he said quietly. "It *was* Wes's idea. But I wouldn't have asked if I didn't want to do it."

"Yeah," Colleen said, standing up and walking away so that her back was to him. She couldn't bear to let him see her disappointment. "Right. You look really enthusiastic. Grim is more like it. 'I'm here to be sentenced to life in prison, your honor.'"

"I'm scared. Can you blame me for that?" he countered. She heard the ice tinkling in his glass as he set it down, as he stood up and moved directly behind her. But he didn't touch her. He just stood there, impossible to ignore.

"This is a big step," he said quietly. "A major life decision for both of us. And I'm not sure marrying me is the right thing for *you* to do. I don't make a lot of money, Colleen, and my job takes me all over the world. Being a Navy wife sucks—I'm not sure I want to do that to you. I don't know if I could make you happy enough to ignore all the negatives of being married to me. And, yes, that scares me."

He took a deep breath. "But the fact is, you could be pregnant. With my child. That's not something I can ignore."

"I know," she whispered.

"If you *are* pregnant, you *will* marry me," he told her, his quiet voice leaving no room for argument. "Even if it's only just for a year or two, if that's how you want to play it."

Colleen nodded. "If I'm pregnant. But I'm probably not, so I'm not going to marry you." She shook her head. "I can't believe you would *marry* me, just because Wes told you to.'' She laughed, but her throat ached, and she knew she was dangerously close to crying. ''I can't decide if that makes you a really good friend or a total chump.''

She headed for the door to the stairs, praying she would make it into her apartment before her tears escaped. ''I should get back to work.''

God, she was a fool. If he'd been just a little more disingenuous, if he'd lied and told her he loved her, she would have given herself away. She would have thrown her arms around his neck and told him yes. Yes, she'd marry him, yes, she loved him, too.

She loved him so much…but there was no *too*.

''Colleen, wait.''

Oh, damn, he was chasing her down the stairs. He caught her at her apartment door as she fumbled her key in the lock, as her vision blurred from her tears.

She pushed open the door, and he followed. She tried to turn away, but it was too late.

''I'm so sorry,'' he said hoarsely, engulfing her in his arms. ''Please believe me—the last thing I wanted to do was upset you like this.''

He was so solid, so huge, and his arms gave her the illusion of safety. Of being home.

He swore softly. ''I didn't mean to make you cry, Colleen.''

She just held him tightly, wanting them both just to pretend this hadn't happened. He hadn't asked her to marry him, she hadn't discovered just how much she truly loved him. Yeah, that would be easy to forget. He could return the ring to the jeweler's, but she didn't have a clue what she was going to do with her heart.

She did, however, know exactly what to do with her body. Yes, she was going to take advantage of every second she had with this man.

She pushed the door closed behind them and, wrapping her arms around his neck, pulled his head down for a kiss.

He hesitated—for about one-tenth of a second. Then, with a groan, he kissed her, too.

And Colleen stopped crying.

How the hell had *this* happened?

As Bobby awoke, he knew exactly where he was before he even opened his eyes.

He could smell the sweet scent of Colleen, feel her softness nestled against him.

Her windows were open, and a soft breeze from this perfect summer day caressed his naked behind. Colleen caressed him, too. She was running her fingers lightly up and down the arm he'd draped around her after she'd succeeded in completely wearing him out. Had they made love twice or three times?

How *had* that happened—even once? It didn't quite line up with him asking to marry her, and her getting angry because she saw clear through him, saw it had been Wesley's idea in the first place.

Except she hadn't been so much angry as *hurt,* and...

He lifted his face from her pillow to find her watching him. She smiled. "Hi."

He wanted her again. Just from one smile. Except it wasn't so much his body that reacted this time. It was his *heart* that expanded. He wanted to wake up to her smile every day. He wanted...

"You need to go," she said to him. "I have to pack for Tulgeria, and you're distracting me."

"I'll help you."

"Yeah, right." She laughed and leaned forward to kiss him. "Ten minutes of your *help,* you'll have me back in bed."

"Seriously, Colleen, I know exactly what you need to

take. No bright colors, no white, either, otherwise you're setting yourself up as a potential sniper target. Think drabs—browns, greens, beiges. I also don't want you to bring anything clingy—wear loose overshirts, okay? Long sleeves, long skirts—and you know this already. Right.'' Bobby laughed, disgusted with himself. ''Sorry.''

She kissed him again. ''I love that you care.''

''I do,'' he said, holding her gaze, wishing there was some way to convey just how much.

But the door buzzer rang, and Colleen gently extracted herself from his arms. She slipped on her robe. Man, he loved that robe. He sat up. ''Maybe you should let me get the door.''

But she was already out of the room. ''I've got it.''

Whoever had buzzed had gotten past the building's security entrance and was now knocking directly on the door to Colleen's apartment.

Where *were* his shorts?

''Oh, my God,'' he heard Colleen say. ''What are *you* doing here?''

''What, I can't visit my own sister?'' Oh, damn! It was Wes. ''Sleeping in today, huh? Late night last night?''

''No,'' she said flatly. ''What do you want, Wes? I'm mad at you.''

''I'm looking for Taylor. But he better not be here, with you dressed like that.''

The hell with his shorts. Bobby grabbed his pants, pulling them on, tripping over his own feet in his haste and just barely keeping himself from doing a nosedive onto the floor. His recovery made an incriminating *thump*.

Wes swore—a steady stream of epithets that grew louder as he moved down the hall toward Colleen's bedroom.

Bobby was searching for his shirt among the sheets and blankets that spilled from the bed and onto the floor as Wes pushed the door open. He slowly straightened up, his hair wild around his shoulder, his feet bare and his shirt nowhere to be found.

Damn, there it was—over near Colleen's closet, near where he'd tossed his socks and shoes.

"Well, this is just beautiful," Wes said. His eyes were cold and hard—they were someone else's eyes. The Wes Skelly who'd been closer to him than a brother for years was gone. As Bobby watched, Wes turned to Colleen. "You're marrying this son of a bitch over my dead body."

Bobby knew Wes honestly thought that would make Colleen determined to marry him. "Wes—"

"You don't want me to marry him?" she asked innocently.

Wes crossed his arms. "Absolutely not."

"Okay," Colleen said blithely. "Sorry, Bobby, I can't marry you. Wes won't let me." She turned and went into the kitchen.

"What?" Wes followed, sputtering. "But you *have* to marry him. Especially now."

Bobby pulled on his shirt and grabbed his socks and shoes.

"I'm not marrying Bobby," Colleen repeated. "I don't *have* to marry Bobby. And there's nothing you can do to *make* me, thank you very much. I'm a grown woman, Wesley, who happens to be in a completely mutual, intimate relationship with a very attractive man. You either need to deal with that or get your negative opinions out of my apartment."

Wes was still sputtering. "But—"

She moved grandly from the kitchen to the door, opening it wide for him. "Leave."

Wes looked at Bobby. "No way am I leaving with him still here!"

"Then take him with you," Colleen said. "I have work to do." She pointed the way. "Go. Both of you."

Bobby moved, and Wes followed. But at the door Colleen stopped Bobby, kissed him. "Sorry about my brother the grouch. I had a lovely afternoon, thank you. I'll see you tonight."

If her intention was to infuriate her brother, she'd succeeded.

She closed the door behind them, with Bobby still holding his socks and shoes.

Wes gave him a scathing look. "What is *wrong* with you?"

How could he explain? He wasn't sure himself how it happened. Every time he turned around, he found himself in bed with Colleen. When it came to her, he—a man who'd set time-and-distance records for swimming underwater, a man who'd outlasted more physically fit SEAL candidates during BUD/S through sheer determination, a man who'd turned himself around from a huge man carrying quite a bit of extra weight into a solid, muscular monster—had no willpower.

Because being with her felt so right. It was *right.*

That thought came out of nowhere, blindsiding him, and he stood there for a moment just blinking at Wes.

"You were supposed to get her to marry you," Wes continued. "Instead you—"

"I tried. I was trying to—"

"That was *trying?*"

"If she's pregnant, she'll marry me. She agreed to that."

"Perfect," Wes said, "so naturally you feel inclined to keep trying to get her pregnant."

"Of course not. Wes, when I'm with her—"

"I don't want to hear it." Wes glared at him. "Just stay the hell away from her," he said, and clattered down the stairs. "And stay away from me, too."

Chapter 16

The early-afternoon meeting between Alpha Squad and the members of Relief Aid who were going to Tulgeria tomorrow had gone well.

Colleen had been afraid that some of the more left-wing group members would be opposed to protection from the U.S. military, but with the recent outbreak of violence in the dangerous country, there wasn't a single protest.

She'd sat quietly, listening to the information presented by the SEALs. Bobby and the squad's commander, Captain Joe Catalanotto, sat up on a desk in the front of the room, feet swinging, extremely casual, dressed down in shorts and T-shirts—just a coupla guys. Who also happened to be members of *the* most elite military force in the world.

Bobby did most of the talking—a smart move, since he'd been working alongside most of the Relief Aid volunteers for the past few days. They knew and trusted him.

He warned them of the dangers they'd be encountering and the precautions and methods the SEALs would be taking to protect them, in his usual straightforward, quiet manner. And everything he said was taken very seriously.

The SEALs would maintain a low profile, blending in with the volunteers. Only a few would be obvious guards and carry obvious weapons.

After the meeting they'd mingled over iced tea and lemonade. She'd met many of the SEALs her brother had mentioned in his letters and e-mails down through the years. Joe Cat, Blue, Lucky, Cowboy, Crash. Some of the nicknames were pretty funny.

Spaceman. His real name was Jim Slade, and he was tall and good-looking in an earthy way, with craggy features and the kind of blue eyes that were perpetually amused. He'd followed her around for a while and had even invited her back to the hotel, to have dinner with him later.

Bobby had overheard that, and Colleen had expected him to step forward, to make some kind of proprietary move. But he hadn't. He'd just met Colleen's eyes briefly, then gone back to the conversation he'd been having with Relief Aid leader, Susan Fitzgerald.

And Colleen was bemused—more with her own reaction. It was stupid really. If Bobby had gotten all macho and possessive on her, she would have been annoyed. But since he hadn't, she found herself wondering why not. Didn't he *feel* possessive toward her? And wasn't *that* a stupid thing to wonder? She didn't want to be any man's possession.

She'd spoken to Bobby only briefly before he'd left for another meeting with his team, held back at the hotel. She'd stayed behind and helped discuss plans for TV news coverage of tonight's bon voyage party.

That meeting was brief, and Colleen was on the T, heading toward Cambridge before four o'clock. She was inside the lobby of Bobby's hotel by 4:15.

She used the lobby phone to dial his room.

Bobby answered on the first ring, and she knew right away that she'd woken him up.

"Sorry," she said.

"No, I was just catching a nap. Are you, um... Where are you?"

"Downstairs. Can I come up?"

Silence. She heard the rustle of sheets as he sat up. "How about you give me a few minutes to get dressed? I'll meet you in the bar."

"How about I come up?"

"Colleen—"

"Room 712, right? I'll be there in a sec."

"Colleen..." She'd hung up.

Bobby dumped the phone's handset into the cradle and lay back in his bed.

What was the point in getting dressed? She was coming up here. In five minutes—ten tops—she'd have him out of his clothes.

He threw back the covers, anyway, got up and pulled on his pants and a T-shirt. If he was quick enough, he'd meet her in the hall, outside the elevators. He pulled on his sneakers, checked himself in the mirror to make sure his hair hadn't completely fallen out of its braid.

He opened the door, and Colleen was standing there, ready to knock.

"Hi," she said. "Good timing."

She swept past him, into the room.

No, it was bad timing. The last place they should be right now was here, alone in his hotel room. If Wes found out, he'd be furious.

Bobby had been shaken by what had happened this morning. He truly had not intended to take advantage of Colleen, but he honest-to-God could not stop himself from climbing into her bed and making love to her.

Even though she didn't want to marry him.

Was he turning into some kind of prude in his old age? So what if she didn't want to marry him. She wanted to do him, and that was what mattered.

Wasn't it?

"I have a favor to ask," she told him now.

God, she looked beautiful, in a blue-flowered sleeveless dress that flowed almost all the way to the floor. He'd been hyperaware of her all throughout the afternoon's meeting— aware of how easy it would be to get her out of that dress, with its single zipper down the back.

Bobby crossed the room and opened the curtains, letting in the bright late-afternoon sunshine. "Name it," he said.

"I know we don't officially need your protection until we enter Tulgeria," she told him, "but remember I told you about that bon voyage party? It's tonight at the VFW right down the street from St. Margaret's—the church where I had that car wash?"

Bobby nodded. "I know St. Margaret's." It was in that same crummy 'hood where the AIDS Center was creating a controversy among the locals.

Colleen put her backpack down and came to help as he attempted to make the bed. "We just found out that the local Fox affiliate is sending TV cameras tonight. That's great news—we could use all the public support we can get." Together they pulled up the bedspread. "But..."

"But the cameras are going to attract attention in the neighborhood." Bobby knew just where she was heading. "You're afraid John Morrison's going to show up. Crash your party."

She nodded. "It wouldn't surprise me one bit if he caused trouble, just to get the news camera pointed in his direction."

He took a deep breath. "There's something I should probably tell you. Don't be angry with me, but I checked up on John Morrison. I was worried about you, and I wanted to know how much of a wild card he was.''

''There's not much to find out,'' Colleen countered. ''I did the same thing right after he and I…met. He served in the army, did a tour in Vietnam. There's an ex-wife and a kid somewhere in New York. He inherited his bar from his father, who got it from *his* father. He's dating one of his waitresses—she shows up in the ER every now and then for some stitches. After I found *that* out, I started carrying one of those little spray cans of mace.''

''Good plan. He's got the potential to be violent,'' Bobby told her. ''Oh, I meant to tell you—I got a call right before I left the hotel. The woman who was attacked—Andrea Barker—she came out of her coma. Turns out it was her ex-husband who beat her up. He ignored a restraining order and…''

Colleen touched his arm. ''Andrea's out of her coma— that's great news.''

He stepped back slightly. ''So is the fact that it wasn't Morrison who put her into the hospital. That fits with what I found out about him—that he never leaves his neighborhood. He rarely leaves his bar. In fact, his drinking pals are all still talking about the trips he made to New York—one about a year ago, the other just a few months back. I also found out he used to be a member of St. Margaret's but he stopped going to church about a year ago. I played out a hunch and called his ex in New York, and sure enough, a year ago was when he found out his son was dying of AIDS.''

Colleen closed her eyes. ''Oh, no.''

''Yeah. John, Jr., died two months ago. He was living with Morrison's ex-wife in the Bronx. She's worried about John. According to her, he's angry and ashamed that even when his son was dying, he couldn't acknowledge the kid, couldn't bring himself to visit. God forbid anyone find out his son was gay, you know? And that's the thing, Colleen. No one up here knows anything. They don't even know that his kid is dead. He hasn't spoken to anyone about this. They still come into the bar and ask how Johnny's doing—if he's gotten that big break as an actor, if he's on Broadway yet.''

Oh, God. ''The poor man.''

''Regardless of that, this *poor man* is responsible for putting cinder blocks through the center's windows. If he gets near you tonight, his health will be at risk.''

''You'll be there?'' she asked.

''Absolutely. I'll bring some of the guys, too. Rio, Thomas and Mike. And Jim Slade. He'll definitely come. What time does it start?''

''Eight. The camera crew's due to arrive at 7:30.''

''We'll be there at seven.''

''Thank you.'' Colleen sat down on his bed. ''I liked meeting Rio, Thomas and Mike…Lee, right?'' She smiled. ''They really think the world of you. Make sure you tell them what you told me about John Morrison. If he shows up, let's try to treat him with compassion.''

''We'll get him out of there as quickly—and compassionately—as possible,'' he promised. ''I'm glad you had a chance to meet them—they're good men. All the guys in the squad are. Although some are definitely special. The senior chief—Harvard Becker. Did you meet him? I'd follow him into hell if he asked.''

''Big black man, shaved head, great smile?'' she asked.

''That's Harvard. Hey, whatdya think of Slade? Spaceman?'' Bobby tried to ask the question casually, as if he was just talking, as if her answer didn't matter to him. The stupid thing was, he wasn't sure if he wanted her to tell him that she liked the man or hated him.

Colleen was gazing at him. ''I thought he was nice. Why?''

"He's a lieutenant," Bobby told her. "An officer who's probably going to get out of the Teams pretty soon. He's having a tough time with his knees and… He's not sure what he's going to do. For a while he was thinking JAG—you know, going to law school, getting a degree, doing a stint in the regular Navy as a lawyer. I just thought you'd, um, you probably have a lot in common. You know, with you going to law school, too?"

Colleen shrugged. "Lawyers are boring."

"You're not. Slade's not, either."

She laughed. "Is there a reason you sound like you're trying to sell this guy to me?"

It was Bobby's turn to shrug. "He's a good man."

"You're a good man, too. A *very* good man."

She was gazing at him with that look in her eyes that made him crazy. And she smiled that smile that made his knees weak as she leaned back on her elbows. "So why are we talking about your friend? Why are we talking at all? Wouldn't you rather help me make Wes really mad—and spend the next half hour or so naked?"

Bobby was proud of himself. He didn't move toward her, didn't instantly strip off both his clothes and hers. "Colleen, I love being with you, you know that, but I don't want to be a pawn in this war you've got going with your brother."

She sat up, her smile instantly gone, wide-eyed. "Whoa—wait! Bobby, I was making a joke. I wasn't serious."

She wasn't serious. "That's part of the problem here," he told her quietly. "You and me, we're not serious, but Wes is. He doesn't want you messing around, not with a man that you don't have a serious shot at having a future with, you know? He thinks that's wrong and…" And Bobby was starting to think it was wrong, too.

It was one thing to have a casual sexual relationship with

a woman who was older, someone his age, who lived near the Navy base, who'd maybe been through a nasty divorce and had no intention of repeating that mistake in the near future.

But with Colleen there were expectations.

Although, God help him, it sure seemed as if all the expectations were *his*.

"Wes thinks what we've got going is wrong? Well, what's *wrong*," Colleen countered hotly as she got to her feet, "is strong-arming your best friend into proposing marriage to your sister. What if I'd said yes? Would you have married me just because Wes told you to?"

"No," he said. He would have married her because he wanted to. Because unlike Colleen, this relationship was more to him than great sex. He turned away from her. "Look, maybe you should go."

She moved in front of him, forced him to look at her. "And do what?" she said sharply. "Have an early dinner with Jim Slade?"

He didn't nod, didn't say yes, but somehow the answer was written on his face. Slade was the kind of man she should be with. How could she meet men like him if she was wasting her time with Bobby?

"Oh, my God," she said. "You were, weren't you? You were trying to set me up with your friend." Her voice caught as she struggled not to cry, and as she gazed at him, she suddenly looked and sounded impossibly young and so very uncertain. "Bobby, what's going on? Don't you want me anymore?"

Oh, damn, he was going to cry, too. He wanted her more than he could ever say. He wanted her with every breath, with every beat of his heart. "I want to do what's right for you, Colleen. I need to—"

She kissed him.

God help him, she kissed him, and he was lost.

Again.

In truth, it was no ordinary kiss. It was fire and hunger and need. It was passion and fury, with a whole lot of anger and hurt thrown in. It consumed him completely, until doing the right thing was no longer an option but an impossibility. Sure, he'd do the right thing—if the right thing meant sweeping her into his arms and carrying her to his bed. If the right thing meant nearly ripping her dress in his haste to get it off her, of pushing down his pants and covering himself and thrusting, hard, inside of her as she clung to him, as she begged him for more.

More.

He was ready to give her all he had to give—body, heart and soul, and he did, disguising it as near-mindless sex, hard and rough and fast.

She called out his name as she climaxed, shaking around him, and he joined her in a hot rush of pleasure so intense it was almost pain.

And then there he was again. Back from that place of insanity and passion, back to this extremely familiar real world that was filled with rumpled bedclothes and mind-numbing guilt.

He swore. "I'm sorry," he whispered as he rolled off her.

She sat up on the edge of the bed instead of snuggling against him, and he realized she was getting dressed. Bra, dress, sandals. Her panties had been torn—damn, he'd done that—and she threw them in the garbage.

She ran her fingers through her hair, picked up her pack. "I'm sorry that you're sorry," she said quietly, "but...I'm a fool—I still want to see you later tonight. Will you come to my place after the thing at the VFW?"

Bobby didn't answer right away, and she looked at him. "Please?"

"Yes," he whispered, and she let herself out the door.

*   *   *

The elevator door opened, and Colleen found herself face-to-face with Wes.

He was getting off on this floor, Bobby's floor, followed by the trio of young SEALs she was starting to think of as The Mod Squad. Pete, Link and Mike Lee.

Wes's expression was grim, and Colleen knew that she looked like a woman who'd just been with a man. She should have taken more time, should have gone into the bathroom and splashed water on her still-flushed face.

Except then she would have been in Bobby's room when Wes knocked on the door.

She went into the elevator, her head held high as her brother glared at her. "Don't worry," she told him. "You win. I'm not going to see him again after tonight."

They were leaving for Tulgeria in the morning. While they were there, she would be sharing a room with Susan and Rene, and Bobby would be in with one or two of the SEALs for the week. There would be no place to be alone, no time, either. Bobby would have no trouble avoiding her.

And after they got back to the States, he'd head for California with the rest of Alpha Squad.

He wasn't interested in a long-distance relationship.

She wasn't interested in one that created limitless amounts of anguish and guilt.

There was no way their relationship could work out. This was what he'd tried to tell her in his room. That was why he'd tried to spark her interest in his stupid friend.

What they'd shared—a few days of truly great sex—was almost over. It *was* over, and they both knew it in their hearts. It was just taking their bodies a little bit longer to catch up.

The elevator door closed, and Colleen put on her sunglasses, afraid of who else she'd run into on the way to the lobby, and unwilling to let them see her cry.

* * *

Bobby didn't answer the door.

He knew from the weight of the knock that it was Wes—the last person in the world he wanted to see.

No, Wes was the *second* to last person Bobby wanted to see right now. The first was Colleen. God forbid she see him and know that he'd been crying.

Man, he'd screwed this up, big-time. He should have stayed away from her. He should have taken the T to Logan and hopped the next flight to Australia. He should have hung up the phone that first night she'd called him. He should have—

"Open the damn door, Taylor. I know you're in there!"

Wes was the one person he should have been able to run to, the one person who could have helped him sort this out, to figure out what to do now that he'd completely messed it up by falling in love.

"I love her." Bobby said it aloud, to the door, knowing Wes couldn't hear him over the sound of his own knocking. "I'm in love with Colleen."

Still, it was a shock to speak the words, to admit these powerful feelings that he'd worked overtime to deny right from the very start.

Right from her nineteenth birthday, when he and Wes had taken Colleen and a group of her girlfriends from college to Busch Gardens. Bobby hadn't seen her in a few years, and suddenly there she was. All grown up. He'd gotten into an argument with her about some political issue, and she was so well-informed and so well-spoken, she'd convinced him that he was backing the wrong party. He'd fallen for her then—a girl-woman who wasn't afraid to tell a man that he was wrong.

Yeah, he'd loved her for years, but it wasn't until this past week, until they became lovers, that his love for her had deepened and grown into this complete, everlasting force. It was bigger than he was. It was all-consuming and powerful. He'd never felt anything like it in his entire life, and it scared the hell out of him.

"I can't say no to her," Bobby said to Wes, through the door. "She wants me to meet her tonight, and I'm going to be there, because, damn it, I can't stay away from her. It's tearing me up, because I know this isn't what you want for her. I know you wanted better. But if she came to me and told me she loved me, too, and that she wanted to marry me, I'd do it. Tonight. I'd take her to Vegas before she changed her mind. Yeah, I'd do it, even though I know what a mistake it would be for her.

"But she doesn't want to marry me." Bobby wiped his face, his eyes. "She only wants to sleep with me. I don't have to worry about her waking up seven years from now and hating her life. I only have to worry about spending the rest of *my* life wanting someone I can't have."

Bobby sat on the edge of the hotel room bed, right where Colleen had sat just a short time ago.

"God, I want her in my life," he said aloud. "What am I going to do, Wes?"

No one answered.

Wes had stopped knocking on the door. He was gone.

And Bobby was alone.

As the TV news cameras arrived, Colleen glanced at her watch. It was about 7:20.

Bobby and his friends were already there, already in place—Thomas and Jim Slade seemingly casually hanging out on the sidewalk in front of the church parking lot, Rio and Mike up near the truck that held the camera.

Bobby was sticking close to her in the crowd.

"There's a good chance if Morrison's going to try anything, he's going to target you," he explained. He was dressed in jeans and a white button-down shirt with a jacket over it, despite the heat.

"Are you wearing a jacket because you've got on a gun under there?" She had to ask.

He laughed. "I'm wearing a jacket because I'm here posing as a member of Relief Aid, and I wanted to look nice."

Oh. "You do," she said. "You look very nice."

"So do you." His gaze skimmed appreciatively down her denim skirt, taking in the yellow daisies that adorned her blouse. "You always do."

Time hung for a moment, as she fell into the bottomless depths of his eyes. But then he looked away.

"I'm sorry," Colleen said. "About this afternoon."

"No." He glanced at her. "I was the one who was—"

"No," she said. "You weren't."

His eyes were apologetic. "I can't come over tonight. I'm sorry, but…"

She nodded. Had to ask. "Are you sure?"

"No." He met her gaze again, smiled ruefully. "I mean, five minutes ago, yeah, I was sure. But here you are and…" He shook his head.

"Well, if you change your mind, I'll be home." Colleen tried to sound casual, tried to sound as if sharing this one last night with him didn't mean so much to her. She cleared her throat. "I should probably go inside pretty soon. If John Morrison were coming, he'd probably be here by now."

Famous last words.

"Hey! Hey, hippie chick! Nice party you're throwing here. What are we celebrating? The fact that you're going away and won't be around to annoy us for a whole week?"

It was John Morrison, and he was drunk, holding a bottle wrapped in a paper bag.

As Bobby stepped in front of her, he seemed to expand, and Colleen realized that a baseball bat was dangling from Morrison's other hand.

"How about we let those cameras cover some real news?" Morrison asked loudly—loudly enough for heads to turn in his direction.

Loudly enough for the other SEALs to move toward them. But the crowd was thick, and they were having trouble getting through the crush. As were the police officers who'd been assigned to keep traffic moving.

"I'm going down the street," Morrison continued, "just a block or so over, to that AIDS Center they're building down there. I'm going to break the windows in protest. We don't want it in our neighborhood. We don't want *you* in our neighborhood."

He pointed at Colleen with the baseball bat, swinging it up toward her, and just like that, it was over.

She barely saw Bobby move. Yet somehow he'd taken the bat away from Morrison and had the man down on the ground before she even blinked.

The other SEALs made the scene a few seconds before the police.

Bobby lifted Morrison to his feet, handed the man to Spaceman. "Take him inside. There are some empty rooms upstairs." He turned to Rio. "Find Father Timothy. Tell him it has to do with that matter I discussed with him earlier this week." He looked at Colleen. "You okay?"

She watched as Spaceman hustled Morrison inside. "Yeah. I don't think he was going to hurt me."

"What's going on here?" the police officer—a big, ruddy-cheeked beat cop named Danny O'Sullivan—planted himself in front of them.

Bobby touched her arm and lowered his voice. "You want to press charges? Lifting the bat like that could be considered assault. At the least, we could get him for drunk and disorderly."

She met his gaze. "No." Not if Father Timothy was getting involved. Bobby had talked to Timothy earlier in the week, he'd said.

Be compassionate, she'd told him, just that afternoon. Obviously, he hadn't needed the reminder.

"Just a little outburst from a friend who had too much to drink," Bobby told O'Sullivan. He squeezed Colleen's arm. "You want to take it from here? I want to go inside to talk to Morrison."

She nodded, and he pulled Thomas King over. "Don't let Colleen out of your sight."

"Aye, aye, Chief."

The crowd parted for Bobby as Colleen turned back to the cop. "Really, Dan," she said. "Everything's fine. We'll see John gets home safely."

O'Sullivan looked at the bat that Mike Lee had picked up through narrowed eyes. "What, did Johnny want to get a game going or something?"

"Or something," Colleen agreed.

"Sometimes it does a body more harm than good to be protected by friends," O'Sullivan said.

"He's had a recent tragedy in his family," she told him. "He doesn't need a night in jail, Dan. He needs to talk to his parish priest."

O'Sullivan smiled as he shook his head. "I wish I were twenty-something and still believed I could save the world, one poor loser at a time. Good luck on your trip to Tulgeria." He nodded to Thomas, who was still standing beside her.

She glanced at Thomas, too. "Let's go inside."

Bobby was in an upstairs storage room, talking to John Morrison about Vietnam. He was much too young to have been there, but he must've been something of a historian, because he knew the names of the rivers and the towns and the battles in which Morrison had fought.

John Morrison was drunk, but not as drunk as Colleen had first thought. His speech was slightly slurred, but he was following the conversation easily.

As she listened, lingering with Thomas King just outside the door, the two men talked about Admiral Jake Robinson, who'd also served in 'Nam. Morrison knew of the man and was impressed that Bobby thought of him as a friend. They talked about Bobby's career in the SEAL units. They talked about Morrison's bar, and his father who'd served in a tank division in World War II—who had died just two years ago after a long struggle with cancer. They talked about elderly parents, about loss, about death.

And suddenly they were talking about Wes.

"My best friend is still jammed up from his little brother's death," Bobby told Morrison. "It happened ten years ago, and he still won't talk about it. It's like he pretends the kid never existed." He paused. "Kind of like what you're doing with John Jr."

Silence.

"I'm sorry for your loss," she heard Bobby say quietly. "But you've got to find a way to vent your anger besides taking out the windows at the AIDS Center. Someone's going to end up hurt, and that will make my friend Colleen Skelly—and you know who she is—unhappy. And if you make Colleen unhappy, if you hurt someone, if you hurt *her,* then I'm going to have to come back here and hurt *you.* This is not a threat, John, it's a promise."

His friend. She was his *friend* Colleen—not his lover, not his girlfriend.

And Colleen knew the truth. He'd told her right from the start—he wanted to be friends. And that's all they were, all they ever would be. Friends who had hot sex.

Despite his promise to hurt John Morrison, Bobby was, without a doubt, the kindest, most sensitive man she'd ever met. He was too kind to tell her again that he didn't love her, that he would never love her.

The sex they had was great, but he was the kind of man who would want more in a relationship than great sex.

She could hear Father Timothy coming, puffing his way

up the stairs to talk to John Morrison, to try to set him on a path that would lead him out of the darkness into which he'd fallen.

The cynic in her knew that a talk with his priest probably wouldn't change anything. Morrison needed serious help. Chances were when he sobered up he'd be embarrassed and angry that the secret about his son's death had slipped out. Maybe he'd be angry enough to burn down the center.

Or maybe he'd go to grief counseling. She could almost hear Bobby's gentle voice telling her that maybe John Morrison would find peace and stop hating the world—and hating himself.

Father Timothy had almost reached the landing.

Colleen stepped closer to Thomas King, lowered her voice. "I need you to do me a favor and give Bobby a message for me."

Thomas nodded, his face serious to the point of grimness. That was his default expression. He was very black, very serious, very intense. He now turned that intensity directly upon her.

"Please tell him that I thought he probably shouldn't come to my place tonight." Good Lord, could she sound any more equivocal? "Tell him I'm sorry, but I don't want him to come over."

An expression outside of his serious and grim repertoire—one of disbelief—flashed across Thomas King's face and he suddenly looked his actual, rather tender age. "Maybe that's something you should tell Chief Taylor yourself."

"Please," she said. "Just give him the message."

Father Timothy had cleared the top of the stairs, and she went down, as swiftly as she could, before she changed her mind.

Chapter 17

They'd won.

Well, they weren't going to be able to bring the orphans back to the United States at the end of the week, but no one had really expected that. The Tulgerian government *had* given the Relief Aid volunteers permission to move the children to a location near the American Embassy. Paid for, of course, with American dollars.

The other good news was that the government was making it possible for American citizens to travel to the capital city, Tulibek, to petition to adopt. The older children in particular would be allowed to leave, for exorbitant adoption fees.

It *was* a victory—although it was a bittersweet one for Colleen. She was sitting, looking out the window, her forehead against the glass, as the bus moved steadily north, into the even more dangerous war zone.

Bobby watched her, well aware of what she was thinking. In a matter of minutes they would arrive at the hospital where the children had been taken after the orphanage had been destroyed. As they went inside, Analena wouldn't be among the children who rushed to greet her.

Yes, it was a bittersweet victory for Colleen.

It was a city bus—this vehicle they were in. Some of the hard plastic seats faced forward, some faced the center of the bus. There was space for people to stand, bars and straps to hold on to.

Colleen was facing forward, and the seat next to her was empty. He sat down beside her, wishing for the privacy that came with seats that had high backs. He lowered his voice instead. "You okay?"

She wiped her eyes, forced a smile. "I'm great."

Yeah, sure she was. He wanted to hold her hand, but he didn't dare touch her. "The past few days have been crazy, huh?"

She gave him another smile. "Yeah, I've been glad many times over that you and Alpha Squad are here."

God, he'd missed her. When Thomas King had given him her message—don't come over—he'd known that it was over between them. Right up until then he'd harbored hope. Maybe if he went to her and told her that he loved her... Maybe if he begged, she'd agree to keep seeing him. And maybe someday she'd fall in love with him, too.

"You and Wes are on friendlier terms again," she noted. "I mean, at least you seem to be talking."

Bobby nodded, even though that was far from the truth. The final insult in this whole messed-up situation was the damage he'd done to his decade of friendship with Wes. It seemed irreparable.

Wes was talking to him, sure—but it was only an exchange of information. They weren't sharing their thoughts, not the way they used to. When he looked at Wes, he could no longer read the man's mind.

How much of that was his own fault, his own sense of guilt? He didn't know.

"Life goes on, huh?" Colleen said. "Despite all the disappointments and tragedies. There's always good news happening somewhere." She gestured to the bus, to the four other Relief Aid volunteers who sat quietly talking in the back of the bus. "This is good news—the fact that we're going to bring those children back to a safer location. And, oh, here's some good news for you—I'm not pregnant. I got my period this morning. So you can stop worrying about Wes coming after you with a shotgun, huh?"

She wasn't pregnant.

Colleen tried to smile, but just managed to look…almost wistful? "You know, it's stupid, but I imagined if I was, you know, pregnant, the baby would be a boy who would look just like you."

She was kidding, wasn't she? Bobby tried to make a joke. "Poor kid."

"Lucky kid." She *wasn't* kidding. The look she was giving him was fierce. "You're the most beautiful man I've ever known, Bobby. Both inside and out."

He didn't know what to say. He didn't know what to think.

And Colleen went back to looking out the window. "Funny, isn't it, how one person's good news can be someone else's disappointment?"

"You're disappointed? About…" He had to search for the words. "You wanted to have a baby? But, Colleen, you said—"

"Not just any baby." When she looked at him, the tears were back in her eyes. "I wanted Analena. And I wanted *your* baby. I'd make a terrible mother, wouldn't I? I'm already playing favorites."

"Colleen. I'm…" Speechless.

"I had this stupid fantasy going," she said in a very

small voice, almost as if she were talking to herself, not to him, ''that I'd be pregnant, and you'd have to marry me. And then, after we were married, I'd somehow make you love me, too. But real life doesn't work that way. People who have to get married usually end up resenting each other, and I'd hate it if you ever resented me.''

Make you. Love me. Too. Bobby wasn't sure, but he thought it was possible he was having a heart attack. His chest was tight and his brain felt numb. ''Colleen, are you telling me—''

''Heads up, Taylor. We're getting close,'' Senior Chief Harvard Becker's voice cut through. ''I need your eyes and ears with me right now.''

Damn.

Colleen had turned her attention back to the drab scenery flashing past, outside the window.

Bobby stood up, shouldering his weapon, using every ounce of training he'd ever had to get his head back in place, to focus on the mission.

Rio Rosetti was nearby, and he caught Bobby's eye. ''You okay, Chief? Your shoulder all right?''

His shoulder? ''I'm fine,'' he said shortly. Dammit, he needed to talk to Wes. Just because Colleen loved him— and she only *maybe* loved him, he didn't know it for sure— didn't mean that gave him the right to go and ruin her life by marrying her. Did it?

''Okay, listen up,'' Captain Joe Catalanotto said for the benefit of the Relief Aid volunteers, the bus driver and the Tulgerian guard who was leading them down the unmarked roads to the hospital.

All of the SEALs knew precisely how this was going to go down. Swiftly and efficiently.

''We sent a small team in early, to do surveillance,'' Joe Cat continued. ''One of those men will meet us on the road about a mile from the hospital, tell us if there's anyth unusual to watch out for. If it's all clear, we'll pull up right outside the hospital doors, but everyone will stay in their seats. Another team will go in to check the place out, join forces with the rest of the surveillance team. Only when they secure entrances and give the all-clear do any of you get off this bus. Is that understood?''

A murmur of voices. Yes, sir.

"At that point," Joe Cat said even though they'd already gone over it dozens of times, "you'll move from the bus to the building as quickly as possible. Once inside, you will stay close. You do not wander off under any circumstances."

"You all right?"

Bobby turned to see Wes right behind him.

"The bus driver will stay in the vehicle," Joe Cat continued. "The plan is to return to the bus with the children and nuns as quickly—"

"Your head's not here," Wes said quietly. "Come on, Bobby. Now's not the time to screw around."

"I'm in love with your sister."

"Ah, jeez, perfect timing," Wes muttered.

"I think she loves me, too."

"No kidding, genius. You're just figuring that out now?"

"If she'll have me, I'm going to marry her." Damn it, he was as good as any doctor or lawyer out there. He'd figure out a way to make money, to buy her the things she deserved. When she was with him, he could do *any*thing. "I'm sorry, Wes."

"What are you crazy? You're *sorry?*" Wes stared at him. "You're apologizing for something I'd sell my left nut to have. If it were me in love with your sister, Bobby, you better believe I would have told you to flip off days ago." He shook his head in disgust.

"But you said…"

"Marry her," Wes said. "All right? Just don't do it right this second if you don't flipping mind. We're all a little busy, making sure these tourists stay alive—in case you haven't noticed?"

These tourists—including Colleen.

"I'll forgive you for damn near anything," Wes continued, "but if you get Colleen killed, I swear to God, you're a dead man."

Colleen. Killed.

Wham.

Just like that, Bobby's head was together. He was back and ready—200 percent ready—for this op, for keeping Colleen and the others safe.

"Yeah, that's more like it," Wes said, glancing up at him as he checked his weapon. "You're all here now."

Bobby leaned over to look out the windows, to scan the desolate countryside. "I love you, man. Do you really forgive me?"

"If you hug me," Wes said, "I'll kill you."

There was nothing out the window. Just rocks and dust. "I missed you, Wesley."

"Yeah," Wes said, heading toward the front of the bus. "I'm going to miss you, too."

Something was wrong.

Colleen shifted in her seat, trying to see the men having a discussion at the front of the bus.

They'd stopped, supposedly to pick up one of the SEALs who'd been sent ahead on surveillance.

But instead of picking him up and driving the last mile to the hospital at the outskirts of the small town, they'd all but parked here at the side of the road.

The SEAL had come onto the bus—it looked like the man who was nicknamed Lucky, allegedly from his past exploits with women. Yeah, that perfect nose was unmistakable despite the layers of dust and camouflage grease-paint. He was talking to the captain and the SEAL who, according to Wes, had actually gone to Harvard University—the senior chief who was almost as tall as Bobby. The other men were listening intently.

Susan came forward a few seats to sit behind Colleen. "Do you know what's going on?" she whispered.

Colleen shook her head. Whatever they were saying, their voices were too low. Please, God, don't let there be trouble.

"All right," the captain finally said. "We have a situation at the hospital. For a place that's supposedly staffed by a single doctor and four nuns, we've got twelve men inside, wearing surgical scrubs and long white coats—the better to hide their Uzis.

"We've ID'd them as members of two particularly nasty local terrorist cells. We're actually surprised they haven't blown each other to pieces by now—but apparently their goal of taking out a bus-load of hated Americans is more than enough to overcome their natural distaste for each other."

Colleen flashed hot and then cold. Terrorists. In the hospital with the nuns and the children. "Oh, my God," she breathed.

Behind her, she heard Rene start to cry. Susan moved back to sit with her.

Captain Catalanotto held up his hand. "We're going in there," he told them. "Covertly—that means secretly, without them knowing we're there. Lieutenant O'Donlon's report indicates these are amateur soldiers we're up against. We can take them out quickly. And we will.

"We're leaving Lieutenant Slade and Chiefs Taylor and Skelly here with you on the bus. They are in command, if there's an emergency, you will do as they say. I considered sending the bus back into Tulibek…"

He held up his hand again as there was a murmur of voices. It was amazing, really, how effective that was.

"But I made a command decision. I think you'll be safer right here until we secure the hospital. Once we have possession of that building, the bus will approach, but you will *not* leave the vehicle. We'll be going over the hospital inch by inch, making sure the terrorists didn't leave any booby traps or other nasty surprises. Our priority will be to check the children and get them out of there and onto the bus.

"Are there any questions?"

Susan Fitzgerald, head of Relief Aid, stood up. "Yes, sir. You've just basically told us that you and your men are going to sneak into a building where there are twelve terrorists with twelve machine guns waiting for you. I'm just curious, sir. Does your wife know about the danger you're going to be in this afternoon?"

For a moment there was complete silence on the bus. No one moved, no one breathed.

But then Captain Catalanotto exchanged a look with his executive officer, Lieutenant Commander McCoy. They both wore wedding rings. In fact, many of the men in Alpha Squad were married.

Colleen looked up and found Bobby watching her. As she met his eyes, he smiled very slightly. Ruefully. His mouth moved as he spoke to her silently from across the bus. "This is what we do. This is what it's like."

"Yeah, Dr. Fitzgerald," Captain Catalanotto finally said. "My wife knows. And God bless her for staying with me, anyway."

"I don't care," Colleen mouthed back, but Bobby had already looked away.

Colleen sat on the bus in silence.

Wes and Jim Slade both paced. Bobby stood, across the aisle from her. He was still, but he was on the balls of his feet—as if he were ready to leap into action at the slightest provocation.

Colleen tried not to look at him. God forbid she distract him. Still, he was standing close, as if he wanted to be near her, too.

"How much longer?" Susan Fitzgerald finally asked.

"We don't know, ma'am," Wes answered from the back of the bus. He touched his radio headset. "They'll open a channel we can receive at this distance only after they've got the place secure. Not until then."

"Will we hear gunshots?" one of the men, Kurt Freidrichson, asked.

"No, sir," Wes told him. "Because there'll be no weapons discharged. Alpha Squad will take them down without a struggle. I can guarantee that as much as I can guarantee anything in this world."

"This isn't the time for conversation," Bobby said quietly.

And once again there was silence.

"Jackpot," Wes said, into his radio headset. "Affirmative, sir. We copy that." He made an adjustment to his lip microphone. "We've been given the order to move toward the hospital. The building has been secured with no casualties."

"Oh, thank God," Colleen breathed. It was over. They were all safe—children, nuns, SEALs.

"Let's move it out," Spaceman—Jim Slade—said to the bus driver.

"No!" Wes shouted from the back of the bus. "Bobby!"

Colleen barely looked up, she barely had time to think, let alone react.

But the Tulgerian guard, the man who'd been hired by the bus driver to guide them to the hospital, had pulled a gun out of nowhere. He was sitting three rows up and across the aisle. She was the closest to him.

The closest target.

But Colleen got only a glimpse of the bottomless dark hole of the gun's barrel before Bobby was on top of her, covering her, pushing her down.

The noise was tremendous. A gunshot. Was that really what it sounded like? It was deafening. Terrifying.

A second one, and then a third. But Colleen couldn't see. She could only hear. Screaming. Was that her voice? Wes, cursing a blue storm. Spaceman. Shouting. For a helo. Man down.

Man down? Oh, God.

"Bobby?"

"Are we clear?" That was Bobby's voice. Colleen could feel it rumbling in his chest.

But then she felt something else. Something wet and warm and...

"We're clear." Wes. "Jeezus!"

"Are you all right?" Bobby pulled back, off her and, thank God, she *was*. But she was covered with blood.

His blood.

"Oh, my God," Colleen said, starting to shake. "Don't die. Don't you dare die on me!"

Bobby had been shot. Right now, right this minute, he was bleeding his life away onto the floor of the bus.

"Of all the *stupid* things you've done," she said, "stepping in front of a loaded gun again—again—has to take the cake."

"I'm okay," he said. He touched her face, forced her to look into his eyes. They were still brown, still calm, still Bobby's eyes. "Breathe," he ordered her. "Stay with me, Colleen. Because I'm okay."

She breathed because he wanted her to breathe, but she couldn't keep her tears from spilling over. "You're bleeding." Maybe he didn't know.

He didn't. He looked down, looked amazed. "Oh, man."

Wes was there, helping him into the seat next to Colleen, already working to try to stop the flow. "God *damn,* you've got a lot of blood. Bobby, I can't get this to stop."

Bobby squeezed Colleen's hand. "You should get out of here." His voice was tight. "Because you know, it didn't hurt at first—probably from adrenaline, but God, oh my God, now it does, and you don't need to be here to see this. I don't want you here, Colleen. Please."

"I love you," she said, "and if you think I'm going anywhere right now—besides with you to a hospital—then you don't know me very well."

"He wants to marry you," Wes told her.

"Oh, wonderful timing," Bobby said, gritting his teeth. "Like this is the most romantic moment of my life."

"Yeah?" Colleen said, trying to help Wes by keeping Bobby still, by holding him tightly. "Well, too bad, because I'm marrying you whether you ask me or not."

"She said that she loved you," Wes countered.

"Don't die," Colleen begged him. She looked at her brother. "Don't you dare let him die!"

"How could I die?" Bobby asked. "I'm surrounded by Skellys. Death couldn't get a word in edgewise."

Wes shouted toward the driver. "Can we move this bus a little faster? I need a hospital corpsman and I need him *now!*"

Chapter 18

Bobby woke up in a U.S. Military hospital.

Someone was sitting beside his bed, holding his hand, and it took him a few fuzzy seconds to focus on...

Wes.

He squeezed his best friend's fingers because his throat was too dry to speak.

"Hey." Wes was on his feet almost immediately. "Welcome back."

He grabbed a cup, aimed the straw for Bobby's mouth. Hadn't they just done this a few months ago?

"The news is good," Wes told him. "You're going to be okay. No permanent damage."

"Colleen?" Bobby managed to say.

"She's here." Wes gave him another sip of water. "She went to get some coffee. Do you remember getting moved out of ICU?"

Bobby shook his head. He remembered...

Colleen. Tears in her beautiful eyes. *I love you....*

Had she really said that? Please, God, let it be true.

"You had us scared for a while there, but when they moved you into this room, you surfaced for a while. I was pretty sure you were zoned out on painkillers, but Colleen got a lot of mileage out of hearing your voice. She slept after that—first time in more than seventy-two hours. She really loves you, man."

Bobby looked into his best friend's eyes. He didn't say anything. He didn't have to. Wes always did enough talking for both of them.

"And you know, I love you, too," Wes told him. "And you know how I mean that, so no making any stupid jokes. I'm glad Colleen's not here right now, because I need to tell you that I know I was wrong. She doesn't need a doctor or a lawyer. That's garbage. She doesn't need an officer. She doesn't need money. Of all the women in the world, Colleen doesn't give a damn about money.

"What she needs, bro, is a man who loves her more than life itself. She needs you."

I love her. Bobby didn't have to say the words aloud. He knew Wes knew.

"The really stupid thing is," Wes continued, "that I probably knew that right from the start. You and Colleen. I mean, she was made for you, man. And you're going to make her really happy. She's been crazy about you forever.

"See, my big problem is that I'm scared," Wes admitted. "When I found out that you and she had—" He shook his head. "I knew right at that moment that you were going to marry her, and that things would never be the same. Because you'd be one of the guys who'd found what they were looking for, and I'd still be here, on the outside. Searching.

"You know, on that training op that you missed because of your shoulder, because you were in Cambridge—it was just me and a bunch of mostly married men. After the op, we had a night to kill before our flight back, and everyone went to bed early. Even Spaceman—he had to ice his knees, he's really hurting these days. Thomas King—he's worse than some of the married guys. He just goes and locks himself in his room. And Mike Lee's got a girl somewhere. So that leaves Rio Rosetti. Can you picture me and Rosetti, out on the town?''

Actually, Bobby could.

''Yeah, well, believe me, it sucked. He went home with some sweet young tourist that he should've stayed far away from, and I'm thinking about how that's me ten years ago, and how I'm looking for something different now. Something *you* managed to find.

''Scared and jealous—it's not a good combination. I hope someday you'll forgive me for the things I said.''

''You know I already do,'' Bobby whispered.

''So marry her,'' Wes said. ''If you don't, I'll beat you senseless.''

''Oh, this is just perfect.'' Colleen. ''Threatening to beat up the man who just saved your sister's life.'' She swept into the room, and everything was heightened. It was suddenly brighter, suddenly sharper, clearer. She smelled great. She looked gorgeous.

''I'm just telling him to marry you,'' Wes said.

Bobby used every ounce of available energy to lift his hand and point to Wes and then to the door. ''Privacy,'' he whispered.

''Attaboy,'' Wes said, as he went out the door.

Colleen sat beside him. Took his hand. Her fingers were cool and strong.

''Colleen—''

''Shhh. We have plenty of time. You don't need to—''

It was such an effort to speak. ''I want...now...''

''Bobby Taylor, will you marry me?'' she asked. ''Will

you help me find a law school near San Diego, so I can transfer and be with you for the rest of my life?''

Bobby smiled. It was much easier to let a Skelly do the talking. "Yes."

"I love you," she said. "And I know you love me."

"Yes."

She kissed him, her mouth so sweet and cool against his.

"When you're feeling better, do you want to..." She leaned forward and whispered into his ear.

Absolutely. Every day, for the rest of their lives. "Yes," Bobby whispered, knowing from her beautiful smile that she knew damn well what he was thinking, glad that Wes wasn't the only Skelly who could read his mind.

Epilogue

"What time does the movie start?" Bobby asked as he cleared the Chinese food containers off the kitchen table.

"Seven thirty-five. We have to leave in ten minutes." Colleen was going through the mail, opening today's responses to the wedding invitations. She looked tired—she'd been getting up early to meet with the administrators of a local San Diego women's shelter who were in the process of buying a big old house. She was handling tomorrow morning's closing—pro bono, of course.

"Are you sure you want to go?" he asked.

She looked up. Smiled. "Yes. Absolutely. You've wanted to see this movie for weeks. If we don't go tonight…"

"We'll go another night," he told her. They were getting married. They had a lifetime to see movies together. The thought still made him a little dizzy. She loved him….

"No," she said. "I definitely want to go tonight."

Aside from her legal work, there were a million things

to do, what with finding a new apartment big enough for the two of them and all the wedding plans.

They were getting married in four weeks, in Colleen's mother's hometown in Oklahoma. It was where the Skellys had settled after her dad had retired from the Navy. Colleen had only lived there her last few years of high school, but her grandparents and a whole pack of cousins were there. Besides, softhearted Colleen knew how important it was to her mother to see her daughter married in the same church in which she'd taken her own wedding vows.

But it made planning this wedding a real juggling act.

And no way was Bobby willingly going to let Colleen head back to Oklahoma for the next four weeks. No, he'd gotten real used to having her around, real fast. They were just going to have to get good at juggling.

She frowned down at the reply card she'd just opened. "Spaceman's not coming to the wedding?"

"No, he told me he's going in for surgery on his knees."

"Oh, rats!"

Bobby tried to sound casual. "Is it really that big a deal?"

Colleen looked up at him. "Are you jealous?"

"No."

"You are." She laughed as she stood up and came toward him. "What, do you think I want him there so I can change my mind at the last minute and marry him instead of you?" She wrapped her arms around his neck as she twinkled her eyes at him.

Something tightened in his chest and he pulled her more tightly to him. "Just try it."

"I was going to try to set him up with Ashley."

Ashley? And Jim Slade? Bobby didn't laugh. At least not aloud.

"Ashley DeWitt," Colleen said. "My roommate from Boston?"

"I know who she is. And…I don't think so, Colleen." He tried to be tactful. "She's not exactly his type. You know, icy blonde?"

"Ash is very warm."

"Yeah, well…"

She narrowed her eyes at him. "Her warmth has nothing to do with it. What you really mean is that she's too skinny. She's not stacked enough for Spaceman, is that what you're trying to say?"

"Yes. Don't you hate him now? Thank God he's not coming to the wedding."

She laughed and his chest got even tighter. He wanted to kiss her, but that would mean that he'd have to stop looking at her, and he loved looking at her.

"Didn't he have that friend who started that camp—you know, mock SEAL training for corporate executives?" she asked. "Kind of an Outward Bound program for business geeks? Someone—Rio, I think—was telling me about it."

"Yeah," Bobby said, settling on sliding his hand up beneath the edge of her T-shirt and running his fingers across the smooth skin of her back. "Randy Something—former SEAL from Team Two. Down in Florida. He's doing really well—he's constantly understaffed."

"Ashley wants to do something like that," Colleen told him. "Can you find out Randy's phone number so I can give it to her?"

Ashley DeWitt, in her designer suits, would last about ten minutes in the kind of program Randy ran. But Bobby kept his mouth shut because, who knows? Maybe he was wrong. Maybe she'd kick butt.

"Sure," he said. "I'll call Spaceman first thing tomorrow."

Colleen touched his face. "Thank you," she said. And he knew she wasn't talking about his promise to call Spaceman. She'd read his mind, and was thanking him for not discounting Ashley. "I love you so much."

And that feeling in his chest got tighter than ever.

"I love you, too," he told her. He'd started telling her that whenever he got this feeling. Not that it necessarily made his chest any less tight, but it made her eyes soften, made her smile, made her kiss him.

She kissed him now, and he closed his eyes as he kissed her back, losing himself in her sweetness, pulling her closer, igniting the fire he knew he'd feel for her until the end of time.

"We'll be late for the movie," she whispered, but then whooped as he swung her up into his arms and carried her down the hall to the bedroom.

"What movie?" Bobby asked, and kicked the bedroom door closed.

* * * * *

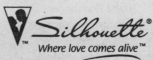

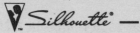

Babies are en route in a trio of brand-new stories of love found on the way to the delivery date!

Labor of Love

Featuring

USA Today bestselling author
Sharon Sala

Award-winning author
Marie Ferrarella

And reader favorite
Leanne Banks

On sale this July at your favorite retail outlet!

Only from
Silhouette Books

Silhouette®
Where love comes alive™

Feel like a star with Silhouette.

We will fly you and a guest to New York City for an exciting weekend stay at a glamorous 5-star hotel. Experience a refreshing day at one of New York's trendiest spas and have your photo taken by a professional. Plus, receive $1,000 U.S. spending money!

Flowers...long walks...dinner for two... how does Silhouette Books make romance come alive for you?

Send us a script, with 500 words or less, along with visuals (only drawings, magazine cutouts or photographs or combination thereof). Show us how Silhouette Makes Your Love Come Alive. Be creative and have fun. No purchase necessary. All entries must be clearly marked with your name, address and telephone number. All entries will become property of Silhouette and are not returnable. **Contest closes September 28, 2001.**

Please send your entry to: **Silhouette Makes You a Star!**

In U.S.A.	In Canada
P.O. Box 9069	P.O. Box 637
Buffalo, NY, 14269-9069	Fort Erie, ON, L2A 5X3

Look for contest details on the next page, by visiting www.eHarlequin.com or request a copy by sending a self-addressed envelope to the applicable address above. Contest open to Canadian and U.S. residents who are 18 or over. Void where prohibited.

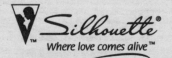

Where love comes alive™

Our lucky winner's photo will appear in a Silhouette ad. Join the fun!

HARLEQUIN "SILHOUETTE MAKES YOU A STAR!" CONTEST 1308
OFFICIAL RULES
NO PURCHASE NECESSARY TO ENTER

1. To enter, follow directions published in the offer to which you are responding. Contest begins June 1, 2001, and ends on September 28, 2001. Entries must be postmarked by September 28, 2001, and received by October 5, 2001. Enter by hand-printing (or typing) on an 8 ½" x 11" piece of paper your name, address (including zip code), contest number/name and attaching a script containing 500 words or less, along with drawings, photographs or magazine cutouts, or combinations thereof (i.e., collage) on no larger than 9" x 12" piece of paper, describing how the Silhouette books make romance come alive for you. Mail via first-class mail to: Harlequin "Silhouette Makes You a Star!" Contest 1308, (in the U.S.) P.O. Box 9069, Buffalo, NY 14269-9069, (in Canada) P.O. Box 637, Fort Erie, Ontario, Canada L2A 5X3. Limit one entry per person, household or organization.

2. Contests will be judged by a panel of members of the Harlequin editorial, marketing and public relations staff. Fifty percent of criteria will be judged against script and fifty percent will be judged against drawing, photographs and/or magazine cutouts. Judging criteria will be based on the following:

   - Sincerity—25%
   - Originality and Creativity—50%
   - Emotionally Compelling—25%

   In the event of a tie, duplicate prizes will be awarded. Decisions of the judges are final.

3. All entries become the property of Torstar Corp. and may be used for future promotional purposes. Entries will not be returned. No responsibility is assumed for lost, late, illegible, incomplete, inaccurate, nondelivered or misdirected mail.

4. Contest open only to residents of the U.S. (except Puerto Rico) and Canada who are 18 years of age or older, and is void wherever prohibited by law; all applicable laws and regulations apply. Any litigation within the Province of Quebec respecting the conduct or organization of a publicity contest may be submitted to the Régie des alcools, des courses et des jeux for a ruling. Any litigation respecting the awarding of a prize may be submitted to the Régie des alcools, des courses et des jeux only for the purpose of helping the parties reach a settlement. Employees and immediate family members of Torstar Corp. and D. L. Blair, Inc., their affiliates, subsidiaries and all other agencies, entities and persons connected with the use, marketing or conduct of this contest are not eligible to enter. Taxes on prizes are the sole responsibility of the winner. Acceptance of any prize offered constitutes permission to use winner's name, photograph or other likeness for the purposes of advertising, trade and promotion on behalf of Torstar Corp., its affiliates and subsidiaries without further compensation to the winner, unless prohibited by law.

5. Winner will be determined no later than November 30, 2001, and will be notified by mail. Winner will be required to sign and return an Affidavit of Eligibility/Release of Liability/Publicity Release form within 15 days after winner notification. Noncompliance within that time period may result in disqualification and an alternative winner may be selected. All travelers must execute a Release of Liability prior to ticketing and must possess required travel documents (e.g., passport, photo ID) where applicable. Trip must be booked by December 31, 2001, and completed within one year of notification. No substitution of prize permitted by winner. Torstar Corp. and D. L. Blair, Inc., their parents, affiliates and subsidiaries are not responsible for errors in printing of contest, entries and/or game pieces. In the event of printing or other errors that may result in unintended prize values or duplication of prizes, all affected game pieces or entries shall be null and void. **Purchase or acceptance of a product offer does not improve your chances of winning.**

6. Prizes: (1) Grand Prize—A 2-night/3-day trip for two (2) to New York City, including round-trip coach air transportation nearest winner's home and hotel accommodations (double occupancy) at The Plaza Hotel, a glamorous afternoon makeover at a trendy New York spa, $1,000 in U.S. spending money and an opportunity to have a professional photo taken and appear in a Silhouette advertisement (approximate retail value: $7,000). (10) Ten Runner-Up Prizes of gift packages (retail value $50 ea.). Prizes consist of only those items listed as part of the prize. Limit one prize per person. Prize is valued in U.S. currency.

7. For the name of the winner (available after December 31, 2001) send a self-addressed, stamped envelope to: Harlequin "Silhouette Makes You a Star!" Contest 1197 Winners, P.O. Box 4200 Blair, NE 68009-4200 or you may access the www.eHarlequin.com Web site through February 28, 2002.

Contest sponsored by Torstar Corp., P.O Box 9042, Buffalo, NY 14269-9042.

SRMYAS2

How To Marry A Monarch

Wanted: One Prince

But Princess Sophie Vlastos of Carpathia knew how unlikely she was to find him in her home kingdom. So she reinvented herself—as Lisa Stone. Nanny extraordinaire. In Detroit. Detroit?

Now, instead of reporting to the queen, her boss was Steven Koleski. Plumber. Part-time photographer. Guardian of five beautiful children.

And handsome as any prince she'd ever seen...

Plain-Jane Princess.
The first book in Karen Templeton's new miniseries, *How To Marry a Monarch.* Coming in August 2001, only from Silhouette Intimate Moments.

And coming in December 2001, look for *Honky-Tonk Cinderella,* Prince Alek's story, only from Silhouette Intimate Moments.

Available at your favorite retail outlet.

Silhouette®
Where love comes alive™